SHADOWS

SHADOWS

KIM PRITEKEL

SAPPHIRE BOOKS

SALINAS, CALIFORNIA

This and other Sapphire Books titles can be found at
www.sapphirebooks.com

Kim Pritekel Books

Standalones
1049 Club
After Shadow
Blinded
Connection
Control – with Alex Ross
Damaged
Shadow Box
Swann Song
The Gift
The Plan
Wild – with Alex Ross
Zero Ward
Unmasked Desire
Unbroken

Dance with Me Series
Curtain Call
Encore Performance

The Traveler Series
The Traveler: The Hunted
The Traveler: The Huner

The Wynter Series
Finding Faith
Taking Liberty
Justice Won
Keeping Hope
Showing Mercy
Having Honor

The Destiny Series
She Who Would be King
Daughter of Ankou
Doors
She Who Dreams
Shadows

Dedication

For Mom - a woman who has gone through so much but came out of the shadows swinging every time.

Prologue

Part I
Sursha — 1385

Roishin still wasn't feeling one hundred percent herself, but in the two days since, it was getting better. Her voice was still a bit scratchy from the damage he'd done to her throat, and it was hard to take a deep breath after taking a sword through the gullet.

But, Dr. Leah had said to give it a week or two and she should be fully back to normal. She was the same doctor treating Elsie, though of course the white doctor's coat and stethoscope had to go when she was in Sursha.

Enori had tried to get her to put it off for another day, but Roishin felt she needed to do this. She needed to talk to Fallon and tell her what had happened. Plus, work would need to be done in the kingdom for messaging. The Surshan public had a right to know their prince was dead.

Her stride a bit slower than usual, she headed to the king's chambers, where she knew Fallon would be this time of day. Cateline hadn't yet returned from Spain, though word had been sent that she needed to return. Roishin would happily just go get her, but unfortunately, in the earthbound, it wasn't so simple.

The chamber doors were closed, so Roishin raised a fist and used the special, obnoxious knock that belonged solely to her. She waited, bouncing lightly on the balls of her feet. Her smile was instant when she heard hurried footfalls to the door before it was yanked open. An extremely relieved-looking Fallon stood on the other side.

"Oh, thank the gods," she gushed, grabbing Roishin to her.

Roishin winced as the intensity of that hug made her whole body hurt, but she returned it as best she could. Finally, she was released, and the king looked her over. A deep furrow of worry gathered between her eyes.

"Are you all right?" Fallon asked softly.

Roishin nodded. "Aye. I'll heal."

Nodding, Fallon stepped back into the room, Roishin following until they took their seats in the solar area of the massive king's chambers. It was an area off by itself where the king could hold important meetings with advisors or other leaders and dignitaries. There were two fireplaces in the space, one in the bedchamber proper and a smaller one, which was lit, in the solar.

Roishin took a seat as Fallon poured her a cup of wine, handing it to her. "Thank you, Daidí."

Pouring herself one as well, Fallon set the wine jug down and joined her daughter in the matching chair near the fireplace. In that moment, Fallon had to hold the concern of a parent alongside the concern of a king. Roishin truly had no idea how she balanced both, but it was impressive. Roishin wasn't entirely sure she could juggle with such grace and dignity.

"Tell me what happened," Fallon said.

"I found him," Roishin said, taking a sip of the sweet wine, which automatically began to spread a loving, warm blanket throughout her insides. This was nice, as they currently needed a little bit of love. "He was in London, bunked up with some woman."

Fallon said nothing, simply stared into the flames as she sipped from the goblet. Roishin swore she'd aged about ten years since Elsie had been attacked a week before. She let out a heavy sigh, knowing she needed to continue. She wasn't sure how much exactly Fallon wanted to know. Garratt had turned himself into an enemy of the State, but he was still a son.

"I took him out of the city so no one else would get hurt."

Fallon nodded, taking another sip. Clearing her throat after she swallowed, she asked quietly, "Did he suffer?"

Oh, how to answer that. Roishin looked down at her hands, which cradled the goblet that held her wine. "We both got in our hits," was all she said.

After a long moment, Fallon said, "So, it's over, then? Garratt is…" She cleared her throat again, the last word tinged with emotion.

"Aye, Daidí," Roishin said. "Garratt is dead."

Her attention was garnered by a soft gasp. Looking over toward the open door, she saw Elsie standing there, Isla by her side, helping to stabilize her. Instantly smiling to see the princess upright, Roishin pushed up from her seat and set down her goblet before hurrying over to her.

"He's gone?" Elsie whispered, hope in her eyes.

Nodding, Roishin caught the woman, who nearly collapsed in her arms. "It's okay," she murmured, holding her tightly against her. "It's okay."

She held her as Elsie cried tears of relief. It was the most horrible position to be in, Roishin thought. Garratt's death would open a wound for some while helping to heal one for others. She resented the bastard for putting any of them in this situation.

Looking over the top of a blond head, she met Isla's gaze. The concern was clear in her lovely brown eyes.

Finally, Elsie began to calm, and Roishin pulled out of the embrace just enough to look into her face. In that moment, seeing the damage that he'd done, she was absolutely thrilled that she'd gotten justice for her. Some of the more superficial wounds had healed while others were still ugly and stark.

But the wound that struck Roishin the most—and the one she worried would never fully heal—was visible in the sapphire eyes that looked back at her, bloodshot and surrounded by the black and blue of bruises. Roishin looked from her to Isla.

"Want to join us, ladies?" she asked. "Sit down and have some wine?" At Elsie's nod, Roishin turned to Fallon, who was headed their way. "Can you help her, Daidí? I want to talk to Isla for a moment."

Fallon offered her arm for Elsie to take and Roishin turned to look at the dressmaker, who looked nervously back at her. Giving her a kind smile, she waved for her to follow as Roishin headed toward the family chamber just down the hall.

To her surprise, part of the large space had been turned back into a sleeping chamber, as that had been its original purpose. A bed had been brought in, clearly where Elsie had been set up—no doubt to keep her close to the king and queen and for them to be there for her, but also so Elsie could feel safe.

Roishin headed to the two chairs that sat before the fireplace, Isla joining her. She smiled and reached over to briefly squeeze one of Isla's hands. "No need to fear me, Isla."

The other woman nodded and blew out a very slow breath. "Aye."

"How is she?" Roishin asked. "And, be honest."

Isla nodded. She clasped her hands in her lap before she spoke. "She's healing physically, milady."

Roishin eyed her playfully. "'Milady' is my mother.

I'm just Roishin."

Isla gave her a shy smile. "Aye. Roishin. The physician who has come to see her every day says she is healing well. She doesn't believe there's any permanent damage, but she has horrible night terrors." She nodded toward the bed. "I've been staying in here with her because she doesn't want to be alone." She tucked in her bottom lip beneath her teeth for a moment before adding, "I know she misses Mariota something fierce."

"The baby misses her, too. Very much."

Isla looked at her, confused. "You've seen the baby?"

Oh boy. Roishin wasn't sure what to say on that one. She ran a hand through her hair, wincing as she hit a bit of a tender spot on her head from the fight with Garratt. "I have, yes."

Isla eyed her, something going through those large, doe eyes, though Roishin couldn't tell quite what it was. The dressmaker said nothing, but there were clear questions there.

Swallowing, she added, "She's staying with Enori and I." Never expecting anything like this to happen, Elsie would have gotten their daughter back long before any questions could have arisen. So now, she wasn't entirely sure what to say, how to explain any of this. It was clear Elsie trusted Isla, but to what degree?

"All Elsie would say was that Mariota was safe," Isla said slowly.

Roishin nodded. "And, she is."

Isla looked at her, *really* looked at her, taking in every feature, every detail. "Mariota has your eyes," she finally said. "Such an unusual color of green, so dark. Are you her aunt or something? A cousin, perhaps?" Her voice trailed off, but Roishin heard her whisper to herself, "What am I missing?"

Roishin just sat there, allowing the other woman to really look at her, almost hoping she'd figure it out, but how could she? What they'd done—created a baby together—was not anything the average person would even consider. In that way, they were largely safe. But for those who were close to the princess, it created a bit of a dilemma.

There was no way Roishin would speak for Elsie. She could skip off back to Duras where things of every color happened every day, but not in Elsie and Isla's world. Elsie would have to live with the consequences.

"Well," Isla said at length, looking away. "I have no doubt there is much I don't understand, but I'm glad to know Elsie will be all right." She looked back to Roishin. "Safe."

Nodding, Roishin said, "She will. And so much of that is due to you. None of us will forget your dedication to her, Isla."

A small smile graced her lovely face as Isla looked down at her hands again. So much was in that expression, as much as she was clearly trying to hide it. "Of course, Roishin."

The two women stood and headed back to Fallon and Elsie. The two were speaking quietly by the fire, Fallon explaining what had happened, as she knew it, with Garratt. Elsie glanced over at the two women walking in, and she met Roishin's eyes. Roishin saw it plain as day—the immensity of her gratitude for what Roishin had done.

Giving her a little smile, Roishin nodded in acceptance. When she reached the two seated women, Elsie held her hand out to her, which Roishin took.

"I'd like to speak with you," Elsie said softly.

"Of course."

The two ended up in the private dining room for the family downstairs where Millie had nearly crushed Roishin with hugs and kisses. She also plied them both with her famous bread and honey butter. It had been by pure luck that the cook had been at Caisleán Thiar that night, the night of the attack. She'd traveled in with Fallon and her entourage to help cook for the big gala they had. She was to head out the following day.

Roishin would forever be grateful for that bit of luck, as there was nobody better to be there during that. Millie was tough as nails, and the staff of both castles knew her well and knew not to cross her. None had said a word of what they'd witnessed.

So now, Roishin buttered a piece of bread, her mouth watering in anticipation. She spared a glance to the woman sitting to her left. She sensed Elsie was trying to gather her thoughts, so she quietly waited her out. Finally, the princess spoke.

"I'm not entirely sure how to feel about the fact that you had to execute your own brother on my behalf, Roishin." She met Roishin's gaze. "I don't know how to handle that."

Roishin was quiet for a moment, trying to think how she wanted to respond. Finally, she said, "I told you that what I do from Duras takes me all over the world to different places. The reason for that, Elsie, is that Enori and I and many, many others head out to right wrongs. Such as Isabeau. I did that innately, but something like that would have been a mission we would take on, someone sent to prevent the event, save her, whatever the case would be. Does that make sense?"

Elsie nodded sagely. "Aye."

"Well, the reason Enori came to see if you were

okay that night was because she'd gotten her next target, the person for her next mission. It was Garratt." Her gaze bored into Elsie's to make sure she was hearing her. "And, the mission was for him to be assassinated."

Eyes open wide, a hand covered Elsie's mouth. "Because of what he did?"

Roishin shook her head. "He hadn't done that yet when the orders went out. He would have gone on to raise an army to attack Sursha. Thousands would have died, all for one man's hurt feelings."

"My gods…"

Roishin nodded in agreement. "But the reason *I* carried out the mission rather than Enori was because *I* wanted justice for you, and *I* wanted to mete it out."

Tears in her eyes, Elsie's hand left her mouth and covered Roishin's hand. "Thank you."

Roishin kissed her fingers and nodded. "You have a little girl who is getting awfully anxious about not seeing her mamaí," she said, sensing a change in subject was in order as she could see that Elsie was still struggling mightily with the whole thing.

"I miss her so much," Elsie whispered, eyes again beginning to well with tears. "I think I can handle pumping more—"

"No," Roishin said, waving her off. "We have a neighbor who is nursing her son who has been amazing." She met her gaze. "She needs you. I can bring her to you to see you, Elsie, but I'm pretty sure she won't want to leave you."

Elsie nodded. "All right. I think I can take care of her. Isla is close by if there's anything I can't do." She blew out a long breath. "I miss her so much it hurts, Roishin."

"Trust me," Roishin said with a soft smile. "I get it. Which…speaking of Isla. She asked me some pointed questions today. You need to tell her something, Elsie."

"I know. I hate lying to her. I really do. She knows how close Mariota and I are so has been baffled that she's not around here somewhere, even if a servant or even Fallon was taking care of her until I was on my feet. I honestly was just able to get up and around somewhat yesterday for the first time."

"Can you trust her?" Roishin asked, taking a bite from her buttered bread, nearly moaning obscenely at the flavors. She'd be taking some home to Enori for sure.

"I can trust her, absolutely." Elsie gave her a shy smile. "I just have no idea how to go about explaining all this to her."

"I think we may have to show her," Roishin murmured around the food in her mouth. "We can take her through the door or something."

Elsie nibbled on her own piece of bread, seemingly in thought. Finally, she nodded. "She has absolutely no reference point for anything like this." Her smile was soft, much like the one Roishin had seen on Isla's face while talking to her in the family chamber, Elsie the source.

"Can she handle this?" Roishin asked gently. "If she's going to be in your life…" Elsie met her gaze, clearly understanding what Roishin was insinuating. "This is part of your life, too. Not just because of me, but we don't even yet know who Mariota will end up being." She smirked. "She may make me look like nothing more than a parlor trick."

Elsie groaned. "Don't even say that." She was quiet for a moment, picking another small piece of the bread off with her fingers. She chewed on it before swallowing it down with a bit of wine. "I took your advice."

Roishin glanced over at her as she chewed her own bite. "Which?"

"I kissed her," Elsie said quietly, looking down at her cup of wine, which her fingers lightly played with.

Admittedly, a carousel of feelings and emotions went through Roishin at that little admittance, but she mostly felt happiness for a woman who so very much deserved to be loved in the way she needed to be.

Throwing out any other thought than that, she raised her eyebrows. "And? Has it been while you've been here?"

Elsie shook her head. "Oh, no. Isla has been wonderful, Roishin." She met her gaze. "She's taken care of me twenty-four-seven. She's been anticipatory of my every need, and just…*here.*" She smiled again, her gaze falling back to her own fingers.

It was hard for Roishin not to take that as a jab, even though she knew it wasn't at all meant to be one. She'd forever hold guilt over how everything had happened, despite it happening as it needed to.

"Just a solid force," Elsie continued, pulling Roishin out of her morose thoughts. "And no, it was not long before the attack happened, actually. A week, maybe."

"Did she respond?" Roishin thought she knew the answer to that, based on the smile she'd seen on Isla's lips earlier.

"She did." Elsie chuckled, amusement in her expression. "Poor thing. I think all of this has been a bit confusing for her."

"Are you going to move back into Caisleán Thiar?"

"Aye," Elsie said. "I'll be honest, I don't look forward to going back there. But, I have a duty. Our daughter is now the heir apparent. I have a legacy to build for her." Her beautiful sapphire eyes grew hard. "I will not let that bastard destroy that *or* me. He tried, Roishin. But if for no other reason than to spite him, I'll go back."

Roishin's smile was full. "I'd expect nothing less from

you, Elsie. And, without him there, with you legitimately a widow and the mother of the future queen, you have a lot of room to make things as you want them." She eyed the other woman. "And, with whom."

Part II

A re you sure?" Fallon asked the woman who sat across from her at the large, ornate desk the king used for business.

Elsie nodded, hands tucked into her lap as the only outward sign of the nervousness that was inside her. "I am. I cannot hide here forever, Fallon." She sent her a pleading look to understand, as she could see the concern and doubt in her eyes. "I need to show my people that I'm stronger than this whole situation. Plus," she added with a small smile. "I miss my baby something terrible. Yes, she's with her other mother, but she's been uprooted for more than a week."

Fallon studied her for a long time before, with a nod and look that was nothing but affection and respect, she acquiesced. "I'll send word to make sure your bedchamber is in perfect condition." She eyed her. "You know, tomorrow I'll be making the announcement of Garratt's death. And the attack. You're still all right with that?'

Elsie nodded. "Aye."

They'd spoken with Livia about this: should it be revealed to the people what happened, should it not? They ultimately decided it was best for Elsie's reputation now, as the regent heir apparent until Mariota was of age, to have public opinion on her side. Garratt was gone, and though no details would be given about the manner of—nor the person behind—his death, it would be announced.

Elsie may hate the son of a bitch, but Garratt had been the son of the hurting woman who sat before her.

She had deep sympathy for the king and queen, as well as Laigen, who was Garratt's true blood sibling. She was heading back with Cateline and Isabeau, and Laigen's own newborn son, Lorenzo, as they spoke.

"Fallon," she said softly, unable to look into those tortured eyes. "I am so sorry all this happened." She shook her head as she took a deep, steadying breath. She was so tired of crying, yet she felt it was all she did. "If it weren't for me—"

"No!" Fallon was up and over to her in two seconds. She knelt beside Elsie's chair and looked up at her. "Don't you dare take on Garratt's failings as your own, Elsie. *He* did this, nobody else." She smiled, reaching up and lightly cupping Elsie's cheek, the bruises slowly healing. "Certainly not you." She took Elsie's hand and left an affectionate kiss to her fingers. "All right?"

Elsie nodded. "I'm trying to believe that, Fallon. I truly am." She gave her a small smile. "Perhaps someday."

Fallon nodded before pushing to her feet. "So, you mentioned something about Isla and the door Roishin created." She perched on the edge of her desk, looking down at the seated woman. "Are you planning to share that with her?"

Elsie was quiet for a moment, not entirely sure how to proceed. She'd never spoken with Fallon about her relationship with Roishin as she had with Cateline. No doubt Fallon knew the basics, if not all of it, but she wasn't sure what to say in regard to what seemed to be building with Isla. How could she talk about that when Fallon's son, Elsie's *husband*, had just been killed?

Clearing her throat, Elsie began. "Isla has become a very close friend and confidante." She met Fallon's eyes, wanting to be as open with her as she felt she could. "She's also been a wonderful advisor, along with Livia, regarding my work with changing the rights for women here in Sursha."

All of these things were true, but she could see Fallon was watching her carefully, head slightly cocked to the side as she seemed to be calculating what Elsie was telling her, perhaps reconciling it with what she already knew or suspected. She knew the king was very smart and very observant, and she didn't want to lie. She just wasn't sure how honest she could be.

Looking down at her hands for a moment, Elsie finally said, "She's a bit of a companion to me." Her voice was quiet. She thought of all the nights Isla had joined her for supper, had spent time with her and Mariota, all outside of any duties she carried within the castle. Simply two women who enjoyed each other's company spending time together. Then, of course, the kiss they'd shared.

"And," Fallon said gently. "You trust Isla with all of this?" she asked, indicating the open door Roishin had created between the two castles, which perpetually shimmered behind a dressing screen in the bedchamber she shared with her wife.

Letting out a quiet breath, Elsie nodded. "I know I can trust her with it, I'm just not entirely sure how she'll react." She met Fallon's gaze again. "Roishin said Isla asked her some questions regarding Mariota's parentage. She's raised them to me as well."

Crossing her arms over her chest, Fallon sat back a bit. "I know you're aware of this, but in the matter of what Garratt did, public opinion will be on your side," she assured. "However, if it ever came out that Mariota was not his child…" She snapped her fingers. "That opinion will change like the wind."

They'd discussed the situation before the conception, all understanding what it meant. Even so, they also all knew it was something that had to be done. Elsie knew Mariota was an extremely well-loved child by her parents and her grandparents, but Fallon spoke true.

Chewing on her lip, Elsie considered. She gave Fallon a sheepish look. "Perhaps we can just begin with the doors."

Fallon's grin showed the young, dashing, and beautiful warrior she'd been when Cateline had first met her, no doubt. Elsie could certainly see how she'd so utterly swept the young princess off her feet. It seemed to Elsie that she continued to do so after nearly twenty years together. She yearned for that.

❧ ❧ ❧ ❧

Later that night, Elsie eased herself up onto the bed. Her body was still so sore from what had happened, and she felt tired often as her body used so much energy to heal itself. She glanced over to see Isla stepping out of the garderobe and over to the bed, also in her sleep gown. Her hair was loosed and brushed to a chestnut shine. Though the strands were brown, the auburn undertones were easily seen in the firelight.

She thought Isla was so beautiful. Certainly she was physically, but there was something about her that went so far beyond that. It was the gentleness in her way, her kindness, her compassion, her silly sense of humor. She smiled at that thought. It was the way Isla handled everything that came at her with a steady mind and thoughtful approach.

Her caring for Elsie over the past week after such a horrible situation had been no different. Elsie truly had no words to express her gratitude, as words just didn't seem adequate. Isla had literally put her entire life on hold to ensure the healing, safety, and comfort of her friend. Now, as she watched the other woman approach the bed, Elsie was struck all over again at her beauty of heart.

"What?" Isla asked, looking at her as she climbed into her side of the bed. She froze as she sat up. "Do you want me to move to the couch? You seem better—"

"No." Elsie reached over and stilled her readied retreat with a hand to Isla's arm. "No, I don't want you to go anywhere." She gave her a sweet smile, allowing her hand to fall away so the dressmaker could get settled. "In fact, I don't know how I'll get used to sleeping alone again once we get back home."

Elsie nearly burst into laughter at the absolutely adorable look that crossed Isla's face. It was a combination of shy and excited at the same time. No idea how she managed that one, Elsie thought. She turned to her left side to face the other woman, who lay on her back, a foot of space between them.

"Isla?" When the other woman glanced over at her, she continued. "I just want you to know how incredibly grateful I am for you this week." She held her gaze for a long moment. "I honestly don't know that I could have gotten through this without you. I mean that."

Isla turned to her right side, mirroring the princess's position. "You know," Isla began softly. "When I was married to Martin, after he'd finished   with me, angry at gods only knew what, I'd just lay there, all in broken pieces. I'd send out a prayer to whoever could hear me, 'Make it end. Don't know if I can handle another.'" She smiled, though it was sad. "Yet, I did."

"You are so strong," Elsie whispered. "I don't think I could handle this again."

Isla shrugged the shoulder that wasn't pressed to the mattress. "When you have little choice, Elsie, you'd be surprised at just what you can handle." She reached across the short distance between them and took one of Elsie's hands in her own. "There was no way I was going to allow you to go through this alone."

Elsie entwined their fingers. She felt so close to Isla in that moment, like they were in a little bubble that nobody else in all the world could penetrate. Perhaps it was the quiet in the large castle. Perhaps it was only the glow of firelight around them. Perhaps it was just because it was Isla.

"When Enori woke me that night," Isla continued, her voice soft. "I was so startled." She smiled. "For one, how did she get into my room? I always lock the door. Anyway, I was so scared for you. I had the most horrible feeling in my gut."

Elsie studied her for a long time, something hitting her that she'd never thought about before now. "That had to have been so hard for you, Isla. I'm so sorry. It had to have brought back so many awful, awful memories."

Isla studied Elsie's face, taking in the healing cuts and bruising. Her gaze settled on the black eye. Tears welled in her brown eyes, so much seeming to go through them. "Sorry," she whispered, turning to her back and then her other side.

Elsie scooted over to her, spooning up loosely behind her. She held her, resting her cheek on Isla's shoulder. "I'm sorry," she whispered. "So sorry."

Isla took several deep breaths, seeming to try and calm herself. Finally, she covered the hand at her belly with her own. "Can I tell you something?"

"Of course you can."

"I've never been held before," Isla said shyly. "Not since I was a lass back in Scotland."

Elsie smiled, absolutely understanding that. She

scooted her body even closer, her front fully pressed to Isla's back and thighs tucked up under Isla's bent legs. "I guess I'll just have to hold you, then."

⁂

Isla chewed on her bottom lip nervously as she looked around then back to Elsie. "Um," she said. "Will the king get angry we're in here?"

Elsie smiled and shook her head. "No. Fallon is fully aware we're in here." She led them over to the dressing screen tucked in the corner of the bedchamber portion of the huge space. She studied the other woman for a minute, trying to figure out how to go about what she had to say. Isla's expression was open and curious. "You said something last night that caught my ear. You said Enori managed to get into your room, which you keep locked."

Isla nodded. "I must have forgotten that night…" Her words trailed off as Elsie slowly shook her head, never taking her eyes off her. "Um…"

"As you know, Enori is the High Priestess in the Order of Ankou," Elsie began. At Isla's nod, she continued. "There's much more to that than meets the eye, Isla. Roishin is also part of that Order."

Isla swallowed and nodded. "I noticed they wear the same cloak, both have short hair."

"Exactly. They both have…special gifts, I guess you'd say. Things that you and I could never even consider." She smiled at the look on Isla's face, a mixture of *What?* and *Tell me more!* "I assure you that you locked your room that night," she said. "Though I have no idea what Enori did to get in, you did lock your door."

She reached out and took Isla's hand, pulling her behind the dressing screen with her. She walked over to the door, which to her was so obvious now, as she'd seen them for so long they had become commonplace to her, but she understood that wasn't the case for Isla.

"Roishin has a very special gift," she explained. Still holding Isla's hand, she gently tugged her behind her "Follow me."

Isla looked at her like she was out of her mind but had enough trust in her to do as asked. They stepped through the door…

…and into the darkness of the secret passageway. She heard a loud gasp, and Isla was holding on to her, clearly shocked and frightened.

"Where are we?" Isla whispered.

"You'll see."

Elsie got them moving—essentially as one, as Isla was nearly wrapped around her while still standing— to the door that entered into Elsie's bedchamber. She listened, as it wouldn't do to stroll in there while servants were working. Hearing nothing, she pulled the door open and pushed the tapestry aside. She turned to see Isla's eyes were as big as dinner plates as realization dawned on her where they were.

She relaxed her hold—a bit—as she took it in. The room had been cleaned, freshened, and all that had been broken removed or fixed. She looked at Elsie, her lips moving but no sound coming out.

Elsie smiled, gently caressing a pale cheek with her fingertips in understanding. "Fallon and Cateline come visit their granddaughter almost daily this way."

"How… How is this possible?"

Elsie shrugged as she began to wander the room. She had such horribly mixed feelings being back there, but she knew she needed to get past it. "I honestly don't know.

Somehow, Roishin cuts a path through space and time."

Finally, Isla released her completely. The look of fear was slowly turning to that of wonder. "You know," she said, slowly shaking her head. "Somehow, this makes sense. I mean, I had no idea such a thing could be done, but both Roishin and Enori made me so nervous."

"Why?"

"I don't know." She gave Elsie a small smile. "Both just kind of have this way about them, an air, I suppose. Makes them seem like they don't belong here." She shrugged. "Does that make sense?"

Elsie nodded. "Very much so. I used to work for the family, Isla," she explained. "They took me in when I was fourteen, after my mam died." She couldn't stop her smile. "I was assigned to Roishin, who was ten at the time."

Isla's eyes grew large in surprise. "Really?"

Elsie nodded, hugging herself. "Oh, that one…" She chuckled. "Precocious doesn't begin to describe her."

Isla was watching her carefully as she told her story.

"But even then, and for the nearly three years I was her personal servant, she had that same way about her." She met the dressmaker's gaze. "She just didn't belong here somehow."

"The two of you…" Isla hedged. "Were close?"

Elsie wondered what Isla had seen on her face or heard in her voice to ask that. She wanted to be honest with her, even as she had to be careful. "Aye. We were very close." She met her gaze. "For a time."

Isla also hugged herself, almost as though she were closing herself off, walls going up. Nodding, she looked around the room as if she wasn't quite sure what to say. Elsie walked over to her, feeling the need to explain. She suspected that Isla was attracted to women, or at least her, but also that she was unsure what to make of the whole thing.

"Isla," she said softly, a hand to her shoulder as she turned her to face her. "Roishin was my first love. We both were, for each other. We do remain very close, but she's with Enori now, where she belongs." Elsie gave her an understanding smile, as the jealousy was obvious in those brown eyes even if she didn't think Isla was aware it was showing. "We haven't been together since just before I married Garratt."

Isla studied her eyes for a long time, Elsie not entirely sure what she was looking for. Perhaps to make sure she was telling the truth? Understanding? "You…*loved* her?" she finally asked. "You were physical?"

Elsie nodded. "Aye. We were each other's first." She gave her a soft smile of understanding as she took Isla's hand, unsure what the dressmaker would do. Would she pull away? She didn't. "Talk to me. What are you thinking?"

Isla looked down at the floor for a moment, as if trying to gather her thoughts. Finally, she met Elsie's patient gaze again.

"I thought it was just me." She gave her a shy smile. "Since I was a little girl, I would look at other girls or the women in our village and was so awed by them. Even if Martin hadn't been a monster, I would never have been attracted to him. I just didn't understand why." A small laugh escaped her lips, sounding relieved. "I thought there was something wrong with me." She shrugged. "That's why I've stayed alone, even after he died."

Elsie shook her head. "No, nothing wrong with you." She smiled. "And, I wondered the same thing about myself." They shared a look of mutual understanding. "Until I came here." She indicated the castle around them. Granted, she wasn't about to tell her about Fallon and Cateline, as Isla seemed none the wiser about Fallon's true identity, and it wasn't her place to tell her.

Isla looked down again, that full bottom lip tucked beneath her top teeth nervously before she said. "I thought that…that you kissing me, touching me…" She shrugged. "Wanting to spend time with me. That it was just because you were lonely, Garratt gone all the time."

Elsie used two fingers to urge Isla's head up. Shaking her head, she cupped Isla's cheek and brought their lips together. The kiss was soft, a bit more substantial than their first, but Elsie kept it measured and short. They couldn't chance getting caught, but she wanted Isla to understand and to truly know that she wasn't being used. And, she wanted her to know that, yes, she felt it, too.

Part III

"Are you excited?" Roishin asked in that voice that instantly excited her seven-month-old daughter. "Are you?" She laughed at the little squeal she got in response. Roishin began to bounce the little one on her hip as she walked, giving the bestest-ever horsey ride to a giggling little buckaroo.

They stopped at the kitchen, where Enori was cutting up fruit for her dinner. She turned, and instantly her smile was wide. Mariota babbled, arms and legs kicking in excitement to see who had essentially become her third mother. Setting the knife down, Enori took her from Roishin.

"Hello, my little princess," she said, leaving noisy kisses all over a giggling Mariota's face. The raspberry she left on her neck garnered an all-out belly laugh. Enori and Roishin laughed at that one. "I am going to miss this little one," she said, hugging the infant to her.

Roishin nodded and let out a heavy sigh. "Me, too."

"So sorry I cannot go with you, love," Enori said, meeting Roishin's gaze. "I have no idea what Ankou needs to talk to me about, but he was insistent."

"Not your fault, baby." Roishin leaned over and stole a kiss before she accepted the wiggling bundle back in her arms. "I love you."

"And I love you." Enori brushed back some of the soft blond hair on Mariota's head. "And I love you, my sweet little one." She smiled at the babbled response she got. She met Roishin's amused gaze. "She loves me, too."

"Oh, she said that, did she?"

"She did," Enori said with a nod.

Roishin chuckled. "All right, sexy." She slapped Enori playfully on her gorgeous behind, earning a quirked eyebrow in response. "I'll see you later."

Roishin grabbed the bag all of Mariota's belongings had been stowed into, including a new toy Ankou had given them for her and which he asked stay with her in both households. She hitched the strap onto her shoulder and, doing her level best to keep her emotions in place, she created a door directly to the king's residence, where everyone was to meet.

The air in front of her began to shimmer, Mariota squealing at it, her green eyes wide. Roishin grinned. "How old will you be when you start this, huh?" she asked, stepping through the door…

…and into a back hallway that she knew wasn't often used. Sure enough, it was empty. She was on the second floor so made her way up to the fourth floor to the king and queen's chambers. As she strode down the hallway past the queen's chambers that had been turned into a family chamber, she heard Fallon and Elsie talking in the king's chamber.

Slowing, she decided to give Elsie a little surprise. She began making weird faces at Mariota and making the stupid noises that she knew would get her giggling uncontrollably. One thing about their daughter—she had the most laid-back temperament and was so easy to make laugh. She grinned when immediately the discussion stopped. Elsie wheeled around the corner to the hallway.

She was in tears as she hurried over to them. Little Mariota was about to vibrate out of Roishin's arms in high-pitched, squealing excitement. "My baby!" Elsie gushed.

Despite her excited state, the two women carefully did the baby swap, but as soon as she was safely in Elsie's arms, she held her tightly to her, tears streaming down her face. She closed her eyes as she moved in a small circle, just seeming to absorb the feel and smell of her daughter. Leaving several kisses, she finally opened her eyes and looked at Roishin and mouthed the words *thank you.*

Roishin smiled and nodded. She looked past the two to see Fallon heading their way. She could tell that she was biting at the bit to get her sugar from Mariota as well. Instead, she walked to her own daughter, giving Roishin a hug and once-over.

"You're looking better," Fallon said, indicating the bruises and such on Roishin's face that had largely healed. Roishin was tempted to show her the nasty bruise on her gut where she'd been run through but figured this wasn't the time to compare owies.

"Has Mamaí arrived yet?" she asked instead.

"Any time, now," Fallon responded.

As if on cue, a loud burst of excitement exploded down below on the first floor. Four stories up, echoes of the loud voices ping-ponged off the stone walls and floor until they reached them. The two met eyes before grinning.

"You stay here," Fallon said. "I'll go grab them and bring them up."

Left alone with Elsie and their daughter, Roishin watched the two continue their reunion. It was beyond heartwarming. Though Mariota was a pretty hearty and good-natured baby, the absence of Elsie had clearly begun to take its toll.

Elsie met her gaze. "She looks so good, Roishin. Thank you, and Enori, from the bottom of my heart."

"You don't need to thank us, Elsie," Roishin said

softly, lightly running her hand down the back of the baby's head. "I love this kid with everything in me, and honestly, so does Enori."

Elsie studied her, looking over her face. "You're healing."

Roishin grinned and nodded. "One good thing about being the daughter of Ankou…super-fast healing powers." They shared a smile before they both looked to the stairs. Loud, excited voices were headed up.

"Aye," Elsie said. "Well, tell Ankou I could use some of those, too."

Roishin's stomach was flipping, both in excitement and happiness to see her mother and sisters, but also in nervousness of having to face Laigen in her grief over Garratt's death. She, Fallon, Elsie, Millie, and Isla had spoken extensively the night before about what needed to become the message.

Fallon would handle the country, Millie the servants at the king's residence, while Isla would help get the message into the bloodstream of Caisleán Thiar. All stories would match, and Roishin would fill in where she needed to in helping the narrative. They worried that Laigen would be a challenge, as well as any men loyal to Garratt in the military.

This was going to be a very tight line to walk, but it had to be done. Roishin's smile was instant when a wild Isabeau launched herself at her, Roishin just barely kneeling in time to catch her. She hugged the girl tightly to her, overjoyed to see her, and it was obviously returned.

"How's my big girl?" Roishin asked once the stranglehold of a hug ended. The grinning little one dropped her smile as soon as she looked into Roishin's face.

"He hurt you," she said softly. Gentle fingers came

up and lightly traced a fading bruise. The concern in the deep blue eyes did not belong to a six-and-a-half-year-old.

Roishin took her hand and lightly kissed her little palm. "I'm okay, sweetie." She gave her another tight squeeze before pushing to her feet. Next came Cateline. The look on the beautiful face nearly brought Roishin to tears.

The relief in the expressive gray-blue eyes was palpable. She took Roishin in a tight embrace, her hand cupping the back of her dark head. Nothing was said for long moments as Cateline simply held her. Roishin felt so much righted in that moment, as she was so afraid of what her mother would think of her.

After all, one child had effectively been pitted against the other due to Garratt's present actions and those he would have perpetrated against the kingdom in the not too distant future.

"I'm sorry, Mamaí," she finally whispered into the hug. "So sorry."

Cateline left a kiss on the side of her head. "No," she responded softly. "*I'm* sorry, my love." She left another kiss before pulling out of the hug and looking into Roishin's eyes. The queen's were red-rimmed, clearly tears shed, but they also held the love of a mother dedicated to her children—*all* of them—her wife, and her country. "We will get through this."

Roishin nodded, swallowing hard to not allow her emotion to come forth. Another kiss left to her forehead and Cateline moved on to Elsie, Fallon having taken Mariota and squatting so Isabeau could say hello to her "favorite sister." The tenderness with which Cateline gathered Elsie in her arms, murmuring soft words of motherly love and comfort in her ear, had Elsie crying and Roishin's own emotions on the verge.

The tap on her shoulder got Roishin's attention. She turned and found herself with an armful of crying Laigen. For the majority of her life, Laigen had been Roishin's only sister, and the two couldn't be more different if they tried. One was full-on princess, into everything that went along with that, while the other wanted no part of it.

Even so, the two loved each other dearly, and Roishin's heart broke for her sister in that moment. The crying blonde had no idea Roishin had been ultimately responsible for Garratt's death. Nobody did, save for those who absolutely must.

The story would be that, after deciding to abdicate and abandoning his family, Garratt had been killed overseas, his body not found.

All of this was true, save for one minor detail.

⁂

Roishin and Laigen sat on a bench in the rose garden, baby Lorenzo in Roishin's arms. She gazed down at her new nephew, just a few months old. He had the dark hair and dark eyes of his father, though as he got older either of those could change. She lightly traced a finger along a chubby cheek, his skin so soft.

"It's amazing. Our family is growing," she said softly, not wanting to wake the sleeping babe.

"It is," Laigen agreed, the pride of a new mother upon her lovely face. "Roishin," she continued, voice gone from the softness of wonder to the quiet of devastation. "Since hearing about what Garratt did to Elsie, I've been thinking about little else." She met the eyes of her younger sister. "And then seeing just how brutalized she truly was by him…" She shook her head. "I'm horrified by what he did."

Roishin nodded, looking back to the infant she held. "It was a truly horrifying night, Laigen. I won't lie." She let out a heavy sigh, so sad by everything that had happened, how profoundly all their lives had been changed. "I never thought he was capable of doing something like this."

Laigen was quiet for a moment, but when she began to speak again, her voice was so soft that Roishin had to really listen to hear it.

"I had a dream the other night," she began. "Although, now I realize it was my mind's way of bringing back a memory I guess I blocked out." She glanced over at her son, that little smile returning as she touched his arm as if to ground herself, somehow.

"What happened?" Roishin asked gently.

"When I was about two, one night I heard the most horrible sound. Woke me up. Our parents were still alive, so I thought maybe it was them. It wasn't. Garratt and I shared a bed, but he wasn't there." Laigen grew quiet for a moment, staring off into a past Roishin didn't want to visit. "You see," she continued after a moment. "We had a lot of cats that used to be around, sleeping beneath the house and whatnot, and one was pregnant."

Roishin could see that Laigen was struggling mightily, so she cradled a sleeping Lorenzo with one arm and reached over with the other to take her sister's hand. Immediately, soft fingers curled around Roishin's.

"The next morning," Laigen continued, though it was clear she was forcing herself to finish the story. "That cat and her babies…"

Roishin squeezed her fingers lightly, trying to let her know she understood and Laigen didn't have to say it. "Garratt?"

Blowing out a long, shaky breath, Laigen nodded, meeting Roishin's eyes. "Aye." She looked down at their hands, which rested in her skirt-covered lap. "I knew he had a temper, saw it many times. But he'd never hit me, ever. I used to see him beat up on a bag of grain or something, you know? Seemed to be how he got out his aggression, what I thought was frustration."

"Maybe that's why he loved the military so much." Roishin shrugged. "Literally paid to brutalize. It was not only expected, but rewarded."

Laigen held her gaze for so long, Roishin was beginning to feel uncomfortable.

"I never even thought of that," Laigen finally said, looking a bit horrified. "But I bet you're right." She looked out over the gardens. "Is Elsie okay? I mean, *really* okay?"

"I think she will be," Roishin said honestly. "She's strong. She has a lot of support."

Laigen's smile was beautiful. "I can't believe how big Mariota has gotten. She's so beautiful."

It was Roishin's turn to smile with a mother's pride. "She is."

"You stay close to her?" Laigen asked. "I know you and Elsie were close when you were growing up."

Roishin nodded. "Still are." She wished so badly she could be open and honest with her sister, but it just wasn't possible. She did have to wonder, however, how much Laigen had seen or put together, if anything. If Garratt had, had she, as well?

"I'm glad, Roishin," Laigen said softly, giving the hand that held hers a little squeeze. "Really glad." She studied her little sister for a long moment, a serene smile on her lovely face. "I'm so proud of you. I know Garratt always thought it wasn't right that you were able to go off to school and all that. I always thought it was wonderful. And," she added, indicating the blue cloak Roishin wore. "I assume that 'schooling' was the Order of Ankou, right?

You're part of that?"

Roishin stared at her, stunned. "How'd you know that?"

"Well, I assumed. I'll never forget it, the day Mamaí and Daidí got married. I was what, four or five? But the woman who performed the ceremony, she was of the Order. Dressed like you, short blond hair, though. Oh," she blew out with wonder. "She was so beautiful. I wanted to follow her around everywhere. She almost seemed to, I don't know, float or glide, somehow." She gave her a smile. "Silly thoughts of a little girl, but she was so magical to me. I wish I could remember her name."

"Enori," Roishin said softly, endless love and reverence for the woman she shared her life with in that one word.

"Aye!" Laigen exclaimed, wide-eyed. "Do you know her?"

Roishin felt she could tell her sister this, as she knew how completely she supported their parents. "She's my life partner, Laigen."

The noblewoman blinked a few times, as if trying to understand what that meant. "What is that? As in, the Order? You're a priestess, too?"

Roishin smiled and shook her head. "No. I am part of the Order, yes. I mean, like our parents. That's how we are."

Laigen's eyes widened as realization hit. "She's a lot older than you, isn't she? I don't know how that works in a situation like yours." She smirked. "Old men marry young women all the time, but…"

Roishin smiled. *If you only knew.* "It all works out," was all she said. Laigen wasn't around that much, so no real reason to freak her out further, she thought. "And, how are you, Laigen? How's Reinaldo?" She smiled at the memory of the man she'd only met during his initial visit to sweep her older sister off her feet. Clearly it had worked.

The smile that spread across Laigen's lips made Roishin very, very happy. It was a smile of genuine affection and caring. "He's wonderful. So proud of his son." Her laugh was like little girl laughter, almost a giggle. "He sings to him all the time when he doesn't think I'm around."

"I am so happy for you, sister," Roishin said softly, meaning every word of it. Though she and Garratt had a wonderful life with Fallon and Cateline, it hadn't been an easy start, and sadly, one that had gotten Garratt killed. She leaned over and kissed Laigen's cheek. "So happy."

Laigen tightened her grip on Roishin's hand, the smile on her face growing a bit sad as tears welled in her blue eyes. "It's just us sisters now," she whispered. "We all have to stick together. Protect the next generation."

Roishin brought their joined hands to her mouth, leaving a kiss upon Laigen's fingers. "I'm working on it," she said softly.

Chapter One

The Shadows

Pushing the hood of her heavy wool cloak back just a bit, she glanced up into the sky. They still had enough daylight to get back, but she was getting a little nervous. Her gaze fell to her twin brother, Laird, at his voice.

"We got plenty of time, Terryn," he said, the same shade of slate-gray as her own eyes looking back at her.

Nodding in acknowledgment but not necessarily in agreement, she looked away. The two continued on toward the stream. It was just far enough away that it wasn't their water supply, luckily, as she wasn't so sure it was currently drinkable. Littering the gurgling waterway was a whole assortment of useful items, though.

As she looked it over, Terryn gasped quietly, a hand coming to her mouth. Exactly like she'd seen in her dream. She felt Laird's gaze on her again. She shyly met it but looked away. It was only because the two had shared a womb that he knew—she knew that. She couldn't dare say it out loud or they'd all be in danger.

"Look at these tires!" Laird exclaimed. He climbed up onto one, which lay on its side in the water. He raised a hand to shade his eyes as he dramatically looked out over the landscape, like a pirate surveilling his watery kingdom.

Terryn grinned. "Idiot," she muttered, amused.

She picked her way through the pieces, parts of what looked to be a vehicle of some sort—a large one. She'd seen pictures of them in the stolen books, her greatest treasures. Even Laird knew nothing of those. But most had seen tires before, in their varying sizes and materials they were made of: rubber, wood, and even metal. They were leftovers from the war, so it was said.

"These would be amazing to help fortify, Terryn," he said, hopping down from his perch and walking all around the huge tire with its deep tread.

She glanced over at him from where she'd moved on. "And, are you planning to drag it behind you there, Laird?"

He looked at her, looked down at the tire he stood next to, kicking it with the toe of his boot, then back at her. With a sigh, he walked away and joined her. Shaking her head, she nudged him with her shoulder playfully.

She and her twin were the only two children of Blair and Ronan. Though down in the tunnels, it didn't much matter. It truly was a "takes a village" mentality in survival.

Like her, Laird was a dreamer, though in very different ways. His was that of making up fanciful tales, which had entertained the two of them their entire nineteen years on the planet. For her, it was more literal. And now, as she hopscotched her way from boulder to boulder, mangled truck part to mangled truck part, she was yet again deeply unsettled.

In her dream three nights ago, she'd seen a huge truck literally fall from the sky and crash into the ground just beyond the stream. It had nearly exploded into pieces upon contact. And now, as she looked at the scattered remains, she *knew* it was the truck from her dream. She truly hoped, however, that she wouldn't find what else she saw in slumber.

"Oh, man…"

Her eyes closed for a moment as her brother had wandered off again. And, from his tone, her fears were

about to be realized. She hopped off the large chunk of…
something she'd been standing on and splashed through
the water until she reached him.

Lying face down was a large man, his girth wrapped
in a cotton T-shirt and denim pants. She knew the
material from the color—she'd read it in a book. But she
was amazed as she saw it in real life for the first time. She
wanted to touch it but didn't dare. It had several places that
were stained with blood and who knew what else.

The man wore one work boot, the other she noticed
lying in the water. Laird was looking down at his own
boots and back to that on the dead man.

"I think it'll fit," she said quietly to him.

He met her gaze, bottom lip tucked in under his top
teeth. Finally, he looked back down to the boot and, with
a grunt of exertion, managed to get the sturdy leather off
after untying the laces. He tromped through the water to
the other one and grabbed it before heading to the rocky
shore to plop down and exchange his footwear, which was
worn and likely didn't even fit correctly anymore.

They'd been taught early in life: if it doesn't belong
to someone else, grab it. Well, this man was very dead and
no longer needed it. Fair game.

Terryn turned her attention back to the man. His
bald head was covered in a thousand tiny cuts, the blood
no longer flowing but dried and crusty, along with other
dried substances that she was pretty sure was brain matter
mixed with skull fragments. From the horrible scene in
her dream, the profound injuries made sense. His head
had become a battering ram for the large windshield.

She didn't even bother to lift his face from where it
lay in the water to see if it was the man she'd seen. She knew
it was. Instead, she continued past him. Her gaze swept to
the shore off to the left, something catching her eye there.

She headed in that direction, about fifty yards downstream from where her brother was changing his boots and where most of the crash site was.

Looking at the rocky shore, she saw what looked to be blood. There was no person nor animal nor anything else that would be the source. She definitely didn't think it was the dead bald man's blood.

Lowering herself, she squatted next to it, noting that blood was splattered on some rocks but most had soaked into the sand. It looked relatively fresh. Scanning the area, she noted there was an indention where it looked as though something had been lying in the sand right at the most blood-soaked point. She also noticed a partial footprint—looked like a boot print—leading away from the area.

Returning her focus to the blood, something told her to touch it. Chewing on her bottom lip for a moment, Terryn brought up a hand and brushed back long auburn strands that blew in her face, tucking them behind an ear. Using that same hand, she tentatively touched the crimson grains of sand.

A black swirl, like smoke rising from the campfire. Round and round until it began to straighten out, like an uncurling snake. Floating, all movement stopped until it surged at her, twin glowing eyes of icy white boring into her very soul.

Terryn gasped, scrambling backward until she cried out in surprise when her hands reached the cool water of the stream. Panicked, she jumped to her feet, stumbling as she jetted away from the rocky shore and across the stream. She lunged from rock to rock until she reached the opposite shore.

"Go!" she called out to Laird, who was just gaining his feet. "Go!"

Her cloak fanning out behind her along with her auburn hair trailing out like fire, she sprinted away from the stream. Her heart was racing, the sting of terrified tears pricking the backs of her eyes. True fight or flight, she had no idea in which direction she'd run, just knew she had to get them away from there.

Panting behind her, Laird gasped out, "Wait! Terryn, stop!"

She slowed, lungs burning from the exertion, tired from the miles they'd already walked that day to end up at the stream in the first place. She looked around, dread filling her. They were in what had become known as "the cemetery." It wasn't because they were surrounded by graves, but because they were surrounded by buildings that had been utterly destroyed during the war. The structures were more like skeletal remains than buildings of brick, stone, or wood.

Word was, they were all haunted and the ghosts could possess the living. She turned to Laird with wide eyes. "We gotta get out of here."

He ran a hand through shaggy brown hair. "I don't think we can make it back to the tunnels before nightfall, Terryn," he said. "You ran in the wrong damn direction!"

She nodded, looking around, the deepening shadows that grew across the ruins sending a chill down her spine, as well as the temperature that was already beginning to fall. She pushed her hair out of her face, trying to decide what they should do.

All around them were the ruins of the ancient city, destroyed by a war that was whispered about like children telling ghost stories around the campfire, though the elders refused to talk about it. Stories weren't passed down about it. Nothing was written about it.

It just *was.*

"We can head back that way," she said, nodding to the east. "At least get out of here, maybe make it to the forest?"

He shook his head, hands on hips. "No good. You know the rains will be coming soon, as they do every night. Not safe."

Blowing out a breath, she nodded. "Damn it," she muttered, angry at herself.

"What the hell happened, anyway?" he asked. "What got you so scared?"

What, indeed? "Look, let's find somewhere to spend the night, okay?" She indicated the space around them. "I think together we'll be okay. At least until sunrise, then we can head out."

He nodded. "Okay. I don't think we have a choice." He looked around, taking in all the devastation. "My god," he muttered. "It looks like a giant stomped on everything."

"I agree. Let's try and find something less destroyed than everything else for shelter to stay out of the rain."

As if on cue, the skies above began to rumble. The clouds were moving in menacingly, as happened every evening. Terryn was angry at herself. Why had she let herself get so spooked? And, for what?

No, she thought. She needed to stop berating herself.

She'd learned long ago that she had a gift, though she had to hide it, even from her twin. She trusted it even if she didn't always understand what it was telling her.

The siblings picked through the debris around them. From some of the items and rubble still recognizable, it looked like it had once been houses, part of a village. There were no personal effects left, of course. After so many centuries, anything like that had been scavenged or eroded away with weather and time. All that was left were the hollowed-out shells of life once lived.

For reasons she'd never truly understand, Terryn felt a kinship to these people, long dead. She felt a connection to them, as though they'd just perished recently and not more than five hundred years ago.

They climbed over a pile of fallen stones, as it looked like an entire wall of a house had been blown outward.

"So strange," Laird muttered behind her. "Like a bomb went off *inside*."

Nodding, Terryn ducked her head to look inside the house once she cleared the rubble. "I wish I understood better what happened."

"We'll never know," he said, both speaking in hushed whispers, like if they spoke too loudly, the sleeping dead would wake up.

"What do you think?" she asked, indicating the house. The structure seemed to be relatively intact enough to spend the night, other than the one destroyed wall.

He stepped inside, forced to hunch over a bit. Dirt and debris had blown in over the years, bringing the floor up several feet. He met her gaze and nodded. The two found themselves a spot in each corner, not separated by more than five feet.

The structure was small, likely not much more than just a one-room cottage. Terryn took it all in, looking up to see the ceiling overhead. She was stunned to see some timbers still in place, though many had rotted away or snapped.

She reached up and untied her cloak, pulling the heavy garment out from around her and laying it on the ground to lie on. Her long, auburn hair fell around her shoulders as she worked. Finally getting comfortable, she lay down, tucking her hands behind her head. Glancing over, she saw Laird was lying pretty much the same way, though his long legs were bent at the knee.

"I'm really sorry," she murmured.

He glanced over and met her gaze. "What happened?" he asked quietly. "What got you so scared?"

She held his gaze, easily able to see the stormy skies within, just like her own. Finally, she looked away. "Just had a weird feeling, is all."

"Terryn? Hey, look at me." When she did, he continued. "It's me, sis. I ain't gonna tell anyone, you know that."

She swept her gaze back up to the ceiling, able to see it all over again. "Laird?" she said, her voice holding a dreamy quality to it. She felt his gaze on her again. "Do you think it's true?"

"What's true?"

"What Old Man used to tell us, before he disappeared?" She glanced over at him again. "About the evil one."

He looked to the ceiling, jaw muscles working as he seemed to be contemplating what she was asking. Finally, he said, "I think he was just telling us stuff to scare us."

Disappointed, as she'd hoped he wouldn't just repeat what their parents and the others had said, she said nothing. Instead, she reached into the pocket of her baggy pants—hand-me-downs from Laird. They'd been cuffed at the hem rather than cut off. You know, in case the one and only son needed his pants back. But, the pockets were handy.

She felt the jerky she always kept in there, especially when she was out with Laird. The two had been known to take last-minute adventures since they were kids, and she'd learned to be prepared. She tossed him one of them, the food landing on his stomach.

"Thanks," he muttered around a bite of the tough, cured meat stick.

She gnawed on her own, enjoying the salty flavors that exploded on her tongue. Holding the meat between her teeth, she managed to wrench free a bite and chewed as she rested her hand that held the meat stick against her stomach.

"Are you having visions again, Terryn?" he finally asked.

"No," she lied, tucking the rest of her jerky back into her pocket. "Gonna get some sleep." She turned over onto her side, her back to him as she rested her head on her arm.

⁂

Gray eyes blinked open. She lay there for a moment, trying to figure out what had awoken her. Finally, she heard it. Humming. No, chanting? Sitting up, Terryn listened. It was pitch dark, yet she felt the scratchy wool of her cloak beneath her and the coldness of the ground beneath it. The smell of spent rain was in the air, and she felt her twin just a few feet away.

Pushing to her feet, Terryn walked carefully to where she remembered the heap of stone and debris that they'd climbed over to get inside. She rested her hands atop the rubble pile, the stones slick from the recent rains and moss that covered the top layer. Standing there, she listened again.

Yes, definitely chanting. Her eyes strained through the darkness, trying to see anything of the source. It was so low she couldn't make out what was being said, or even how many were chanting in unison. She only knew it was more than one person. As she listened, her own lips began to move, though no sound escaped.

She felt herself joining in the low, comforting rhythm, even as she spoke not a single word. Compelled, she inched her way along the stone with her hands until she felt the lowest point, where they'd climbed in. She heaved herself up and over the pile with a quiet grunt of exertion.

Climbing down the other side, she was now standing on the ground outside of the shelter she and Laird had tucked themselves into. Her lips continued to move along with the distant chanting. As if in a dream, she walked blindly through the darkness, somehow not stumbling or falling over the debris field that was the village.

The chanting got louder, to the point where she could feel the vibration in her gut, a deep, low rumbling that almost made her feel nauseous. Even so, she continued on. Her own voice began to join those she sought, somehow her lips, tongue, and teeth knowing how to move and shape the words that tumbled from her unchecked.

Making her way over what seemed like a mountain of destruction, she found herself looking down into the deep-set ruins of a building, perhaps once a temple. A fire danced and sparked at the center of four hooded figures. Their faces were nothing more than eerie shadows in the deep recesses of their hoods.

Their hands were raised and their voices low. They spoke in a language she didn't understand, even as her lips continued to move in perfect sync with their chanting. Male and female voices, and from the size of the figures, it seemed there were two women and two men.

Closer. She needed to get closer. She began to slowly make her way down the rubble she was perched upon. Slowly, slowly, careful not to create an avalanche of stones, dirt, and destruction. She felt the rumbled voices in her bones now. It called to her, carried her farther and farther down.

She honestly wasn't sure she could stop if she wanted

to. The pull to be with them was almost painful. She felt a need in her soul that made no sense to her, but still she made her descent. Heading back into the tunnels with Laird to her parents and all those who shared the space with them, like little termites living in the wall, wouldn't feel as home to her as this did.

But, what was "this"? She had to know, had to go home.

In her haste, she slipped, her fingers desperately trying to latch on to anything stable. But the large rock she grabbed gave way and sent her tumbling down the rest of the way. She rolled down the pile, grunting with each stab of a pointed stone or stick until finally she landed unceremoniously with a thud *on her back at the bottom.*

She lay there, dazed, her back and head hurting. The chanting stopped and, to her horror, all the hooded figures turned to look at her. Now, their backs to the flames, they were menacing silhouettes in robes. One of them walked over to her, their steps slow and steady. Reaching her, a hand was extended down to her.

She looked at it, the hand nearly invisible in the large sleeve of the robes the person wore, the hood still in place. They waited patiently until she took it and was pulled to her feet. Standing, she looked up into the blackness of where the face should be, completely hidden by shadow. Even so, she could feel an intense gaze on her.

"It's time to wake up," the quiet voice said, that of a man.

Terryn gasped, her eyes popping open.

Chapter Two

She brought the apple to her mouth, taking a large bite from the succulent fruit. They stood in a gorgeous orchard, which, only in Duras, held trees that bore pretty much any fruit Enori could ever want. The army of trees spanned half of the property, the other half filled with vineyards and gardens loaded with veggies.

In between sat a two-story farmhouse with a large, covered front porch that overlooked a huge yard lined with flowerbeds. It was gorgeous, there was no doubt. Roishin turned to look at the woman who was picking the perfect peach for herself. She glanced over to meet Roishin's curious gaze.

"Yes, my love?" she asked with a quirked brow just before she took a bite into the tender flesh of her chosen fruit.

"Well," Roishin said, holding up her apple. "You should have said this was what we were doing today. I would have brought the baskets."

Enori gave her an enigmatic smile as she took Roishin's free hand. She led them out of the trees and across the emerald-green lawn and to the front porch. "This is not why we are here today," she said. "Well, not the only reason." She grinned and took another bite.

Eyebrows drawn, Roishin drawled, "Okay."

"What do you think of this?" Enori asked, indicating the gorgeous property. Much like the beach house, it was extremely private, not another house as far as the eye could see, just acres upon acres of trees and rolling hills beyond them. It was stunning.

"It's so beautiful," Roishin admitted. "So quiet."

Nodding, Enori took her hand again, tugging her toward the front door of the house. Entering, Roishin saw it was empty, an open palate. The floors were wide plank wood, and a lovely fireplace was the centerpiece of the living room with an intricate mantel. Crown molding ran along the ceilings. Beyond the living room was a dining room and large kitchen.

Like the other rooms, the space was empty, only cabinets and counters to allude to the room's intended purpose. She looked to Enori for explanation but instead was led to the stairs to head to the second floor. They were met by four bedrooms, the largest sporting another beautiful fireplace, which was a smaller version of the one downstairs.

There was plenty of closet space in all four bedrooms and a traditional bathroom arrangement in the hallway. It was the only room in the house equipped. Enori looked at her shyly.

"What do you think?"

Roishin shrugged as she chewed the bite of apple she'd taken. "I think it's beautiful," she muttered around the food. "Who lives here?" She grinned. "They're even more of a minimalist than you are." She lightly squeezed Enori's fingers in teasing.

Enori chuckled. "Yes, well..." She looked down at their entwined fingers for a moment. Clearly she had something to say, so Roishin remained quiet, letting her gather her thoughts.

She brought their hands to her mouth and left a kiss. "Let's go sit down."

The two walked to the largest of the bedrooms and sat on the wood floor. Roishin thought that maybe a more relaxed environment would help with whatever Enori had to say.

Finally, Enori looked up from her lap and met Roishin's patient gaze. "You have heard us speak of the war," she began. "The one that started when I was a child."

Roishin nodded. "Aye. You were ten, about to be sacrificed. Right?"

Nodding, Enori took a deep breath then looked back down at their hands, still joined and resting on Roishin's knee. She seemed lost in memory as she continued. "You see, Roishin, there was a place called Bowhar, a crossroads between Duras, Brittany, and Ryarch."

"What is Ryarch?"

"The Druid realm." Enori indicated the house around them. "Much like Duras is home of the Ankou." At Roishin's nod of understanding, she continued. "Bowhar was a wonderful place, inhabited by Ankou, Druid, or humans, *enlightened* humans, alike." Her smile was beautiful, even if sad. "But, Bahutha wanted it."

Roishin swallowed, a bad feeling in her gut. She knew what he was capable of from the small encounter she and her family had with the God of Chaos when she was almost thirteen. "Oh boy."

Enori nodded. "Yes. He was gathering Breton children, girls before they began their bleed." She held Roishin's gaze. "You know how powerful a girl is at that time."

Roishin nodded. "Bad, bad memories."

Enori smiled but then grew serious again. "His intention was to sacrifice them. With each one slaughtered in his name, he would have grown more powerful, absorbing all that energy loosed in their death."

"My god," Roishin whispered, apple forgotten.

Enori nodded. "Much happened, but Ankou and

Macha, Queen of the Druids, banded together against him." She let out a long slow breath, Roishin able to feel emotion just under the surface. "He was stopped, but at a terrible cost."

Roishin rubbed her thumb along the back of the soft hand she held. "I'm sorry, baby," she whispered, able to see it in the beautiful eyes that met her own.

"He was stripped of his ability to have a solid form, which is why he must go from body to body now, possessing them."

"Like he did with Daidí?" Roishin asked.

"Exactly. But the Druid and Ankou Orders were torn apart. Anger over the final solution and deep suspicion of the other harboring the darkness or that they had allowed it to happen in the first place. Allowed the complacency." She shook her head. "Terrible time."

"It seems there still isn't a lot of partnership now," Roishin observed. "Is that true?"

Enori shrugged a shoulder. "The hatred has died down over time, but the alliance has not been healed." She gave Roishin a shy smile. "This is why we are here." She indicated the room they sat in. "You see, many years ago, Ankou sent me to form an alliance with the head priestess of one of the last Druid circles left on the earth plane."

Roishin listened, able to feel the sadness coming off the woman she sat nearly knee to knee with on that hard, wide plank floor. She released Enori's fingers, instead placing the hand flat on Roishin's thigh and gently rubbed her own fingers over it to soothe and comfort whatever Enori had to say.

"We fell in love," Enori explained. "She was my first love." She gave Roishin the most beautiful smile. "Only love, until you." The smile slipped from her lips. "But I failed, and she was executed, along with the other leaders in her tribe."

Roishin's heart fell. "Oh, Enori," she whispered.

"I was able to get her baby to safety, and that baby went on to have a baby, who ultimately, down the line, was the ancestor of Elsie."

Roishin's eyebrows shot up and she gasped. "She was *Mariota*?"

Enori nodded. "She was." She let out another long breath, as if relieved that she'd gotten it out. "Over the time you have lived with me, Roishin," she said, her voice softening to that of a woman deeply in love and content in that love. "I have come to understand that I have lived in the stone cottage because it reminded me of the last place Mariota and I had happiness."

Roishin nodded, trying not to outwardly react. She knew it was childish to feel jealousy in this. After all, look at how much Enori had dealt with regarding Elsie, who was still very much alive and in their lives.

"And though, yes," Enori said with an amused smile. "I do prefer a more simple life, but I have come to realize part of it has been almost penance, somehow. I have terrible guilt over not being able to save her."

Roishin brought Enori's hand to her lips. "Oh, sweetheart," she whispered, kissing her fingers.

Enori's smile was somewhere between sheepish and sad. "Before you moved in, I had no bed, no comfortable furnishings. I brought those in for you, so you would be comfortable and feel at home." She smiled. "So, this brings us to why we are here."

She pushed to her feet, gently urging Roishin to hers. Roishin felt the need to take this precious woman into her arms and just hold her for a moment. Enori responded, their hug tight and full bodied. With a kiss to Roishin's neck, Enori pulled away a bit, clearly having more to say.

"I want us to have a start at what *we* want, Roishin," she said softly, fingers playing in the short, dark hair at the nape of Roishin's neck. "I no longer wish to live in the past when my present is so wonderful." She left a soft kiss on Roishin's lips. "My future is even more so. With you."

Deeply touched, Roishin pulled Enori against her with her arms wrapping around her waist. "Is this what you want for us?" she asked softly. "This house?"

"Only if you do," Enori said, shrugging a shoulder. "I figure here, plenty of fruit." She grinned at Roishin's laugh at that. "Plenty of space for Mariota to grow into, because she will not be a baby forever. And, plenty of room for Isabeau, too."

"I love you," was all Roishin could say as she took her in a slow, deep kiss, letting her unending passion for this precious woman and her heart speak for her.

❧❧❧❧

Roishin's eyes were closed as she focused on the pleasure. Enori's hips glided gracefully over Roishin's and the phallus attached to them. She was deep inside the woman atop her, and it felt incredible. She opened her eyes and watched, Enori's face expressing the rapture she felt. With every thrust of her hips, not only was the phallus moving inside her, but it was also pressing against Roishin where she needed it most.

Her hands glided up Enori's abdomen until she was able to cup her breasts. She squeezed the hard, sensitive, light pink nipples before gently rolling them. A soft sigh escaped Enori's lips, atop the wonderful noises she was already making. Her own hands rested on Roishin's stomach, bracing herself.

Roishin watched her, studied her. Enori was so

exquisite, absolutely ethereal as the moonlight came in through the window of their new bedroom, illuminating her like the angel she was. She could feel her own pleasure beginning to build, and as much as she wanted to flip them over and pound into the other woman, she wanted Enori to control this.

They were an intensely passionate couple and made love at least once just about every day. The days they didn't, for whatever reason, they just held each other and would exchange light touches and kisses. Oh, the kisses. Whereas Enori craved her fruit, Roishin craved Enori's mouth. She craved her skin, her scent, to be in the very same air Enori was breathing.

Finally, Enori was reaching her limits and began to move her hips faster. Her back was arched and her head thrown back as she rode Roishin's hips hard, bringing them both to an intense and very verbal release. Enori's upper body fell until she lay upon Roishin, who was still buried deep inside of her.

Roishin held her, both breathing heavily as they tried to come down from their experience. After a long moment, Enori lifted her head, leaving a soft kiss on Roishin's lips.

"I love you," she murmured against them.

"And I love you," Roishin responded, running her hands over a smooth back and sighing in contentment.

"So," Enori teased. "Am I going to end up pregnant?"

Roishin grinned. "Not telling."

Enori's chuckle was throaty and very sexy. She left a final kiss before easing herself off the phallus and Roishin's body. Roishin climbed off the bed just long enough to unbuckle herself—harness and phallus dropped to the floor to be cleaned later—before climbing back on, Enori moving into her arms. They exchanged a few soft kisses before Enori rested her head on Roishin's shoulder.

"I really love it here," Roishin murmured softly, her hand lightly gripping the thigh that Enori rested across Roishin's. She could feel her spent wetness against her hip. "This house, the property." She leaned her head against the one which rested against her. "So peaceful."

"I love it, too," Enori admitted.

"Did you ever think you'd leave the cottage?" Roishin asked, running her fingers through soft, blond hair.

"There are a whole lot of things I never thought I would do before you came along, my love," Enori murmured.

"Yeah, I know," Roishin said with a dramatic sigh. "Came along and gave you sunshine."

Enori grinned, raising her head and stealing a quick but heated kiss. "You came along and gave me lots and lots of orgasms," she murmured against Roishin's lips.

"That, too." They shared one last kiss before Enori rested her head back down. "In all seriousness," Roishin said. "Do you feel okay, since we moved? I know we've only been here a couple days."

"I do," Enori said without hesitation. "Honestly, I know I will always love Mariota in a part of me, just like you with Elsie. But I needed to go, to let that part of myself rest and not live in a constant reminder of something painful."

"I'm proud of you, baby," Roishin said, stroking the back of the hand that rested on her stomach. "I'm so sorry you had to go through that." She left a kiss to her forehead. "I can't even imagine." She was quiet for a moment when something hit her. "Can I ask you something? And, you may not know this."

"Of course you can."

"I know there are a lot of reasons behind Ankou

wanting the child I had with Elsie. But…" She paused as she considered. "If Elsie is a descendant of the Mariota you knew, a Druid priestess, it stands to reason that Elsie is Druid, therefore so is *our* Mariota, as well as Ankou from my side. Right?"

Enori lifted her head, resting it in a palm as she looked down at Roishin. A soft smile graced her lips. Roishin met her gaze.

"I'm right, aren't I?" Roishin said, though she hadn't even fully stated her thought.

"When you were in Sursha to meet Cateline and Laigen upon their return from Spain," Enori said softly. "What Ankou wanted was to talk to me about this very thing. Macha wants to meet her."

Roishin felt a whole lot of butterflies bat at her rib cage. "Oh," she said dumbly. "That's a good thing, right?"

Enori nodded, her fingertip tracing along Roishin's collarbones and down between her breasts before her hand settled on her stomach again. "It is. Mariota may once again be the bridge between our peoples."

Roishin smiled up at her, a hand coming up to lightly brush Enori's soft cheek with the backs of her fingers. "Then maybe it wasn't all in vain, baby," she said softly.

❧❦❧❦

Roishin was making herself something to eat, Enori out on   a training mission. She was expecting her guest at any moment and wasn't disappointed. She wiped her hands on her trousers and headed to the front door. Smiling, she stepped aside and let him in.

"Welcome."

"Thank you." Ankou gave her a smile. He grew serious, gently turning Roishin's face this way and that with two fingers under her chin. "How has it all healed?"

"All right. I think this will scar." She lifted her shirt just enough to show the mark where the blade had gone in about two inches below her breastbone. Now, it looked like a small birthmark shaped like a crescent moon.

He grimaced. "Ouch. Listen," he said as Roishin dropped her shirt back into place. "This is why I'm here."

"All right. Can I get you anything? I was making some supper." She nodded toward the kitchen.

"Nope, but I'll happily sit with you." He followed her deeper into the house. "Love this. And," he added with amusement in his voice. "Endless fruit."

Roishin laughed. "That woman and her fruit. Sit." She walked back to the counter where she'd been making herself a sandwich. "She's gotten me to really love it, though, I have to admit."

He chuckled, taking a seat at the kitchen table they'd taken with them from the cottage, along with the couch and love seat, since it had been brought in for Roishin anyway. She brought her plate to the table and set it down before grabbing herself something to drink from the fridge they now had. She was quite excited by that.

Roishin didn't need a house that was exactly plopped down from the twenty-first century, but she was learning it was nice to have some fun conveniences—to Enori's chagrin.

Sitting across from Ankou, she met his gaze. "So, what's wrong? I can see it in your eyes."

"The situation with the trash truck that day," he began. "When you and Ava were on the surveillance mission."

Roishin nodded sagely. "Aye." She still felt terrible over that one, no matter how many times Ava hugged her and told her it wasn't her fault *and* that she was fine.

"Where did you send it?"

She paused as she was about to bring one half of the halved sandwich to her mouth. "I'm not sure," she said. "Honestly, in the heat of the moment, my intention was to get it away from everyone and everything."

"And Garratt," he pushed. "Where did you take him? What was the intention? Exactly."

Confused on the questions, she responded honestly. "The same. To get him away from anything and anyone that might get hurt in our fight. I knew it was going to be ugly. And, if by some chance I failed and he got away, I didn't want him finding his way back home." She studied him. "Did I do something wrong, Ankou?"

He smirked, reaching over to her plate and snagging the large cheddar cheese crumb that tumbled from the filling of her sandwich.

"No," he said, tossing it into his mouth. "Yet again, my daughter has left me bemused and shaking my head and asking myself, 'How did she do that?'"

Chapter Three

The crypt beneath the large cathedral was dark and a bit creepy. The group of five was led by the two women in cloaks, one blue with gold stitching, the other dark gray. Both women held a candle tucked into a brass candleholder. The halo of light that blossomed from the lit tip of their candles glazed the stone walls of the ancient tunnels as they proceeded.

Roishin followed behind the woman in the blue cloak, Elsie the woman in the dark gray, the baby in her arms. They passed by crypt after crypt of the sleeping Surshan ancestors of centuries past. It pained Roishin to pass that of her much-missed daideó, Carthac, his crypt resting next to his beloved wife, the first Roishin.

Just down from them was the uncle she'd never met, Ailfred. He was a man whose loss Roishin knew still was a wound for Fallon to this day, twenty-five years after his death. And then, of course, Livia's crypt and finally, the one that sat empty, Garratt's.

They made their way to the center of the crypt, the maze of tunnels coming together to a bit of a rotunda. Roishin had never realized it before, but her family crypt was set up much like the Crystal Palace and all its spokes jutting out from it.

She suspected that wasn't by accident and wondered how far back Ankou went in her bloodline. And, this would be on Carthac's side, not Roishin the elder's side, she realized with interest.

At the center of the stone floor was a symbol inlaid

in the stone. Roishin gasped when she realized it was the triskelion, which had been the broach Enori had given her so long ago that she'd ultimately given to Elsie, whose own mother had also given her one. She wanted to look to Enori for answers but knew this moment wasn't the time.

Set upon that inlay was a stone altar-type structure. A religious tome could be set upon it, candles, or even, as would happen today, an infant. The two cloaked figures stopped and turned, one on either side of the altar—one the High Priestess of the Order of Ankou, the other the High Priestess of the Order of the Druids, one arriving from Duras, the other Ryarch.

The pale skin and hair of one absorbed the candlelight and turned her eyes nearly translucent, while the mahogany skin of the other and dark eyes seemed to reflect the glow. Roishin thought the dichotomy was beautiful. Elsie placed a sleeping Mariota upon the stone altar, after Roishin had spread out the small blanket she'd been given to carry for this purpose.

Anise, the Druidess, handed Roishin her candle, and Enori handed hers to Elsie, the two moms standing across from each other. Roishin met Elsie's gaze for a moment. She could see the unease in the sapphire depths, turned a golden gray in the candlelight. Roishin gave her a small smile of reassurance. She had no idea what was going to happen but knew it was immediately important.

The two priestesses reached over the baby and joined hands. Again, that beautiful combination of the dark skin and light, a true symbol of the rejoining of two worlds and two peoples. Softly, the two women began to chant, each in her own language and each her own words of significance to her god. Even so, somehow it seemed to meld, become one.

Roishin felt the energy around them begin to

change. It was palpable. The cool, dank air of the crypt began to warm, almost as though a large fireplace had been lit, though its flames unseen. She felt a hum, though it wasn't heard. It began in her stomach, almost making her feel nauseous, then it spread to her bones. Her entire body was nearly vibrating with it.

Mariota began to whine a bit from where she lay atop the covered altar as if she, too, were feeling it. The chanting got faster, both women's eyes open and unblinking as if lost in the power of their chant and the energy produced by the sacred words. It was hypnotic, and Roishin found her own eyes growing heavy, a trancelike state overtaking her. Her body began to sway with the chanting, the very flame upon the candle she held flickering to an unheard beat that matched the rhythm of Roishin's heart.

Suddenly, with a caress of breeze across her face, the candles went out, the smell of acrid smoke teasing her nostrils. A soft blue glow filtered in, no seeable source. Roishin could just barely see the outline of Elsie standing across from her, though she could see no details of her face or hair. She basically just knew from the size and shape of the silhouette that it was her.

To her left, where Enori had stood, was a larger hooded figure, nothing more than a dark shape. To her right, Anise was also replaced with a larger hooded figure, though not as large as that to her left. This figure had a smaller shape perched upon its right shoulder, and the caw that echoed in her head made her think it was a raven.

In unison, a male and a female voice began to speak. "Child of my blood. Child of my Order. Child of above. Child of below. You are blessed."

The figure to her right leaned down, seeming to place a kiss upon Mariota's forehead. When they stood erect, the figure to her left did the same. It was in that instance

Roishin caught just the barest glimpse of a skeletal hand.

The man's voice said, "This child may cross the borders of Duras."

The female voice said, "This child may cross the borders of Ryarch."

They both said, "She is part of me."

All went dark again. Roishin gasped softly when the flame of her candle seemed to light itself, sparking to life, as did Elsie's across from her. The princess was blinking rapidly, as if she'd just been pulled out of sleep. No doubt she'd been in the same trancelike state Roishin had. Their gazes met for a moment before both looked to Mariota.

Roishin smiled as the baby lay cooing on the blanket, not a care in the world. She seemed calm and content. There were two marks upon her forehead, however. One was red, the other blue, and the lines crossed to form an X. Looking to her left, she was relieved to see Enori once again, who briefly met her gaze.

"Mariota has been accepted and blessed by Macha," Anise said softly.

"Mariota has been accepted and blessed by Ankou," Enori added.

Anise leaned down and placed a kiss on Mariota's forehead, followed by Enori doing the same. The marks were gone, and the two women shared a smile before looking at the expectant mothers.

"It is done," Enori said, looking from Elsie then to Roishin, giving her that special look reserved only for the woman she loved. Roishin returned it.

She had to admit, watching Enori in her official capacity as the head priestess of the Order was quite the turn-on. The immensity of Enori's knowledge and abilities, the complete trust she had earned from Ankou, was incredible.

When she worked with Enori, which was often, they were in another time and another place, playing the necessary roles to get the job done.

So, to see her as she was today, performing the ceremony, all that awe that Roishin had felt for her "angel" as a child came back to her full force. She was breathtaking. And, as she looked at her in that moment, Roishin knew that Enori was her best friend, her confidante, and her lover. She also knew she wanted her to be her wife.

Enori met her gaze and held it. Eons filled with love and trust passed between them in that moment. As if able to read Roishin's thoughts from a few seconds ago, the softest smile brushed full lips, and Enori gave her a small nod.

⁂

Taking the open door back to Caisleán Thiar, the five dined in Elsie's private chambers—those of the prince, which she'd taken over upon Garratt's death. She'd told Roishin she couldn't bear staying in the princess's chamber any longer after the attack. As it had been during Roishin's childhood, that space would be turned back into the family chambers.

"What are you chewing on?" Anise asked with an exaggerated gasp and smile. The baby in her lap giggled but kept the large medallion the priestess wore tucked into her hands.

Roishin sat back and watched, charmed by how wonderful Anise was with Mariota. "Do you have children of your own, Priestess?"

Anise glanced up at her from the little one sitting in her lap. "I do." Her smile was big and bright. "Three boys, but it's been a long time since they were this young." She smiled down at the infant who was still trying to chew her way through the medallion. "Enjoy this age, ladies," she said, sparing a glance at all three women who sat with her. "It doesn't last long."

"I truly appreciate you doing this with us today, Anise," Enori said softly. "It has been too long."

Anise reached across the table, Enori taking her hand. The two women shared a look of deep friendship. "It has," the Druid said softly. "We mustn't wait this long again."

Enori held her gaze, squeezing the other woman's hand in affection. "Agreed."

Roishin watched the two women, wondering what the story was there. She was about to ask when Anise turned her attention to Elsie as she and Enori withdrew their hands from the hold.

"What is your gift, child?" she asked. "You carry it from your mother's line." A statement.

Elsie met her gaze and nodded. "Aye. I see things," she said quietly, almost as if feeling ashamed.

"Such as?" Anise asked, sipping from her goblet of wine as she continued to hold and play with Mariota.

"In people," Elsie explained. "I can look at them and know if they are good or bad, I can read intent sometimes." She gave her a small smile. "Sometimes it frightens me when it's accurate."

Anise nodded as she smiled. "The Sight is an unsettling thing, isn't it?" Elsie bore a relieved-looking expression as she nodded, and Anise asked, "Do you possess the Second Sight, as well?"

Roishin was fascinated as her head went from one to the other. She didn't know this about Elsie, though in retrospect, it made a lot of sense. She thought back to those dark days with Bahutha when none of them knew what was going on. Somehow, Elsie had been the glue holding them all together.

Now, Roishin wondered if the then-servant had known something was wrong, or even what it was. Even the moment of their first kiss…which had happened because Elsie knew somehow she had to break the spell that damn mist had on Roishin.

"I don't know." Elsie glanced over at Roishin and then Enori. She smiled. "I sit here with giants," she said quietly, again taking in her companions. "I feel so oddly… normal."

A loud bark of laughter escaped Anise's lips. Roishin chuckled while Enori smiled. "Oh, love," Anise said. "Give us time. We'll get you to your *unnormal*, too." She left a kiss on Mariota's head before she pushed to her feet and walked over to Roishin. "Take your daughter," she said. "Before I kidnap her."

Chuckling, Roishin happily took the bundle, who finally let go of the medallion. "Thank you so much for today," she said to the woman, accepting a one-armed hug from her.

"Of course." Anise squeezed her arm as she released her before walking over to Enori. The two shared a long, heartfelt hug before she moved on to Elsie. "I will see you soon," she said quietly to her before she, too, received a hug. She looked to Enori. "Walk me out?"

The two priestesses walked out of the chamber together, leaving Roishin with Mariota in her arms and Elsie standing close by. She looked to the princess. "How are you?" she asked softly, indicating the room around them.

"It's been hard," Elsie said, meeting her gaze. "In some ways, moving in here has made it easier as I've begun to make it my own, but in other ways it's like I can feel him here. This was *his* room." She smirked. "As often as he was here. Does that make sense?"

Roishin nodded, looking around. "It does."

She noted Mariota's cradle had been brought in and the furnishings from her bedroom, minus the bed, had replaced the bulky, more masculine furnishings Garratt had decorating his space before.

Looking back to Elsie, she smiled. "I have endless respect for you. I honestly don't know if I could have come back here."

Elsie raised her chin a bit, almost as if in defiance. "Garratt may have beat me physically, but he will never beat me emotionally or mentally."

"No," Roishin said softly, shaking her head. "He will not."

"Did he say anything to you?" Elsie asked, her voice quiet. "Before…" She shrugged. "Before."

"He said a lot of really ugly things," Roishin admitted. "Honestly, the man I dealt with that day…I didn't know him. I'm beginning to believe none of us ever did."

Elsie hugged herself, looking down at her feet for a moment. "I'm so sorry, Roishin. I cannot even imagine how you must have felt having to do that to your own brother."

"Hey." Roishin lifted Elsie's chin with two fingers. Looking into those sad eyes, much of the bruising now gone, she was easily able to see the broken woman she'd cradled that night all over again in her memory. "I'd do it again." She gave her a reassuring smile. "You did nothing wrong here."

"That's what Isla keeps saying," Elsie said quietly.

"And she's right, and you need to listen to her." Roishin gave her a big grin. "I knew I liked her."

Elsie's smile was that of a schoolgirl with a crush at

the mention of Isla's name, though Roishin could tell she was trying to hide it.

"Hey," Roishin said softly, "If you're happy, let yourself be." She waited until Elsie looked up at her. "Don't hide it, especially when you don't have to." She indicated the privacy of the spacious bedchamber.

⁂

The wonderful waterfall shower they'd had at the old cottage remained with them. Roishin had simply closed that open door and created a new one out of their bedroom. It was the ultimate master bath. After her shower, she stepped into the bedroom naked, still drying herself. Enori was hanging up her cloak in the closet.

"So," Roishin said, using the towel to squeeze the excess water from her hair. "Today." When Enori glanced over at her in question, Roishin asked, "Why?"

Enori stared at her, a brow quirked. "You're standing there like that and you expect me to answer a question?"

Roishin grinned and nodded. She should have known better.

Enori turned to face her, head slightly cocked to the side and a look burning in those light blue eyes that could incinerate Roishin where she stood. Without a word, she made her way to Roishin, every single thing about her screaming sensual intent in that moment.

Roishin swallowed.

Fingers of one hand found their way into damp, short dark hair, Enori's lips mere inches from Roishin's. "Today was Anise and I coming together," she explained softly.

The fingers of her other hand slipped between wet folds, making Roishin gasp. She began to speak again as her fingers slowly stroked a hardening clit.

"Ankou and Macha cannot come to the earth plane like you and I can." She gave Roishin a sexy little smile when Roishin gasped, talented fingers finding a particularly sensitive spot to press against. "So, we had to create a pathway for them to enter together to bless Mariota," she murmured a hair's breadth away from parted lips. "And to accept her into their embrace."

Roishin's eyes fell closed as the pleasure was quickly building. She cried out and fell forward as her orgasm snuck up on her. Only Enori's strong hold around her kept her upright. She was panting as she tried to recover. Soft words of comfort and love were whispered against her lips as the fingers were removed from between her legs.

She left a soft kiss on Roishin's lips before she pulled her into a full-body hug. Roishin held her, just letting herself melt into it. She felt a need coming off Enori, a need to be close, to be held. Roishin was all too happy to oblige.

After long moments, Enori murmured into the embrace, "Anise fought in the war with us."

Roishin said nothing, simply rested her head against that which lay upon her shoulder. It was her turn to comb her fingers through soft hair, but with a very different intent than had been Enori's moments before. "She's been around that long?"

Enori nodded. "She is as much to Macha as I am to Ankou and is what is known as an Ancient." She sighed in contentment against Roishin's neck. "She helped save my life."

"I thought you can't die?"

"I was very young then," Enori murmured in explanation. "Ankou had not blessed me yet."

"So glad he did," Roishin whispered into blond hair. "I owe her a great big thank-you the next time I see her."

She smiled at the little chuckle muffled against her neck.

"You will have your chance very soon. We are meeting with Anise and Macha in the coming days." She lifted her head and looked up into Roishin's face. A soft smile upon her lips, the vixen gone, Enori brushed her fingertips over Roishin's cheek. "Can we go to bed?"

"Of course." Roishin kissed her full lips. "But now I need a shower again."

Enori grinned before taking Roishin in another kiss.

Chapter Four

Not entirely sure what had awoken her, Elsie's eyes blinked open. She looked to her left, for some strange reason expecting to see someone there. When she found only empty space in the bed next to her, her gaze swept the bedchamber. The huge space was awash with shadows, which danced with the flickering flames in the fireplace.

Her eyes settled on Mariota's cradle and the figure that stood next to it. The figure wore a cloak, and for a moment she thought it was Roishin. That thought flew out of her mind when she realized that, yes, it was a woman, but the lowered hood revealed long red hair that took on the firelight, making it look as though she had a halo of fire around her head.

It was then that Elsie also noticed a large black raven perched atop a chair near the woman. Its dark, beady eyes reflected the firelight as it studied Elsie, who still sat in bed.

"I've wanted to come visit you for a long time now," the woman said, her gaze still looking down at the sleeping inhabitant of the cradle.

Elsie wasn't sure if she was talking to her or the baby. The woman lifted her head and glanced over at Elsie. She was breathtaking. Her hair was like a mane around her head, framing a face with beautiful feminine features though a proud, strong jaw. She had piercing light amber eyes. It almost looked like they were made of the very fire reflected in them.

The armor she wore over her torso was made of leather and metal, made to fit a woman's body. The leather trousers she wore were fitted, showing off muscular thighs, tucked into the tops of leather boots just below the knee. One hand was down at her side, the other resting upon the pommel of the sword belted at her hip.

Her dark gray cloak was swept off one shoulder, revealing a muscular arm, though this woman was all that—woman. She had an air about her of someone wild and free, just blown in off the winds of time. She smiled, which softened the chiseled features.

"Aye," she said. "I'm here for you both." She seemed to be responding to Elsie's unasked question. Her voice was soft yet held a quality of strength to it. It wasn't hard to imagine her belting out orders to an army of men.

Turning back to the cradle, she carefully lifted a sleeping Mariota out. She held the infant to her bosom in bracer-clad arms. Lowering her head, she pressed her lips to the baby's forehead, so incredibly gentle. She whispered something, which Elsie wasn't able to hear.

Mariota's eyes opened and stared up as the redhead raised her head. The look in the baby's eyes was one of awe. She didn't cry, didn't fuss, just stared. Another kiss was left before the woman placed Mariota back into her cradle, her touch extremely tender, almost motherly.

"Who are you?" Elsie asked. Her gaze went back to the raven when it cawed at her.

The woman turned to her once the curtain was pulled back into place on the cradle. Head slightly cocked to the side, she stared over at Elsie. She was studying her, that penetrating gaze seeming to look into the princess's very soul.

"It's astonishing, really," she said. "Just how much you look like her." She walked over to the bed and sat upon the side. Her intense study continued. She took in Elsie's face, and her long, blond hair loosed around her shoulders and down her back. "I see her strength in you," she continued, *words soft, reverent.*

Elsie swallowed. "Who?"

The woman smiled. She reached up and tucked some golden strands behind an ear. "The very woman you named your child after."

Elsie swallowed again, nervous with the proximity of this strange woman. Her touch was a mixture of maternal yet decidedly sensual. Her entire essence was very heady and confusing.

"You knew Mariota?" Elsie managed.

"Of course," the woman murmured, giving her a smile. "I made her." The hand that had tucked the hair behind Elsie's ear now rested upon her cheek. "Just as I made you."

Elsie felt her heart rate pick up and her body respond, even as she had no idea who this was or why she was there. She pushed that away, knowing that wasn't her true desire. It was as if this woman had an effect on a person that they couldn't control, though Elsie wasn't entirely convinced that was this woman's intention.

"I'll return," the woman said, leaning forward and leaving a lingering kiss on Elsie's forehead. "Because," she murmured against the skin. "It's time to wake up."

Gasping, Elsie's eyes flew open. Hand to chest, which was pounding, she lay there. She took in long, slow breaths to try to slow her racing heart. She stared at the underside of the canopy of her bed, trying to reconcile the strange dream she'd just had. It had been so incredibly real.

Her hand moved up to her forehead, touching the smooth skin there. She swore she could still feel soft lips pressed to the center. Of course, she felt nothing there, and her hand flopped back down to the bed. Blowing out a final breath, she sat up. The fire was burning down, morning on its way. Soon enough Agnes would arrive to wake her and help her get her day started.

She pushed the covers off her body and climbed out of bed. She smiled when she heard the quiet babbling begin from the cradle. Mariota was awake and beginning her morning chatter to herself. What did she talk about? Elsie wondered, not for the first time.

Reaching the cradle, she was about to pull back the curtain when something caught her eye. Walking over to the chair nearby, she saw the single black feather that lay there.

※ ※ ※ ※

Elsie sat before the mirror in the boudoir as Agnes stood behind her, braiding her hair for the updo it would be placed in that day. Her gaze caught Isla's reflection as she stepped into the room just behind the lady-in-waiting. It was hard to keep the smile from coming forth, but Elsie knew it was in her eyes.

Returning to Caisleán Thiar had not been easy on many, many levels, but one of the biggest issues had been the knowledge that Isla would be going back down to her own chambers. During her time at the king's residence, Isla had shared her bed every night, and Elsie had known she could easily get addicted to her presence.

She had.

Her first night sleeping alone had been awful. Yes, largely because of what had happened. She had been so tempted to move her and the baby in with Fallon and Cateline, as had been offered. But no—she was determined. As she'd told Roishin, she would win, no matter what. She'd overcome too much in life to quit now.

Plus, and mostly if she were honest, she wanted to show Mariota what it meant to be a strong woman. Her daughter was born with a target on her back and a heavy responsibility on her small shoulders. Absolutely, Elsie would show her love, affection, and all the wonderful things a mother should. But she'd also show her how to rule.

She felt a new energy and strength coursing through her body this morning, and she intended to capitalize on it.

Her dream came back to her, the warrior woman. She had no idea who she was still, but she decided to take her bearing and her presence to heart. She'd said Elsie had the strength of her great-great-grandmother, and though Elsie had obviously never met her, she'd always admired her. So, though just a dream, Elsie decided to tuck the words into her heart and do all she could to make the first Mariota proud.

"Here you are, milady," Agnes said, finishing up the intricate do.

"Thank you, Agnes," Elsie said, pushing up from her chair once the young woman had stepped away from her. She gave the young woman an appreciative smile. "See you this afternoon."

Unlike many women of royalty or nobility who kept their lady-in-waiting with them around like a shadow all day for whatever may come up, Elsie allowed her lady to enjoy time to herself. It had been difficult enough to accept the need for servants upon marrying Garratt and assuming her new role in the royal family. Over time, she'd found what worked for her needs versus her conscience.

And frankly, she wanted to do as much for herself as she could. Certain things weren't possible, such as the intricate outfits and their various pieces and parts that needed a second set of hands. Her hair, for certain, as she did not possess eyes in the back of her head nor the natural skill to master such things herself.

Also, she had to admit, it gave her unfettered time with Isla. It had become clear the two were dear friends and companions, especially after the events involving Garratt. Despite the many obstacles associated with being the "weaker sex," it was easier to get away with a woman as your close confidante because, as the emotional creatures that they were, the bonding between women was expected and accepted.

She couldn't even imagine how difficult it would be being a man attracted to other men. The expectations were so different between the two genders. So often it was unfair and deeply shortsighted toward women, but in this area, they certainly had the upper hand.

"My goodness," Isla murmured, cutting into Elsie's thoughts as she walked into the room once Agnes had taken her leave. "Looks quite serious, your musings."

Elsie met her eyes, loving the teasing little twinkle in their brown depths. "It is."

"Oh? Care to share?"

"Nope," Elsie said, a teasing grin on her lips. She laughed at the quirked eyebrow she got. "Fine." She sighed dramatically but then grew serious. "I was essentially just thinking that I'm grateful to have you in my life." She lightly ran her fingers up and down the side of the bib portion of Isla's sleeveless tunic that covered her dress. "I wondered if you'd like to spend the day with Mariota and me," she asked shyly.

"Would that be an official request, milady?" Isla asked softly, a bit of teasing in her voice.

Elsie smiled and shook her head. "No."

She honestly didn't know why she felt so shy in that moment. She felt like a schoolgirl with the worst crush upon her tutor. Roishin was Elsie's only experience with physical love. And, despite the many years' worth of built love she and Roishin had for each other, let alone having a daughter, they'd only been together sexually on three occasions.

Now, standing in her boudoir with Isla, the princess felt like a downright virgin. She could see the returned desire in Isla's eyes, could feel the buzz between them. Elsie knew it would be very easy to sweep Isla across that final line, which had started at employee, then shifted to friend, and finally could shift to lovers.

But Elsie wanted more than that. She didn't want just a beautiful woman in the castle that she could call to her bed at will and then send back to her duties. Even if the want was mutual, that wasn't at all what appealed to her. She wanted something real, something much deeper than the physical.

The castle in which she lived was a huge structure, a fortress of safety and comfort, and she was grateful for it, but what she most craved was a home. She looked into the warm brown eyes, which had lost the teasing flirtation of moments before. They instead were looking back at her with a deep understanding. It was almost as if Elsie had said the words out loud, had voiced her deepest needs and desires.

Isla reached up and cupped the side of Elsie's neck with warm fingers. She leaned in and placed a soft, almost chaste kiss upon Elsie's lips. It was the first time Isla had ever initiated any sort of affection that wasn't born of concern or comfort.

"I would love to spend the day with you and the baby today, Elsie," she said softly.

Elsie smiled, reaching up and taking the hand from her neck and holding it securely within her own. Her smile grew big and bright, as did Isla's. "Then I think we should begin with breakfast."

"Which," Isla said, her lips quirked into a grin. "Should be arriving…" There was a knock to the chamber doors. "…right about now."

Elsie burst into laughter. She stole a quick kiss before the two headed out to get their day started.

❧❧❧❧

A wonderful, quiet day of reading and knitting in Elsie's chambers was coming to an end. Both women lay on Elsie's bed, a sleeping Mariota on her tummy between them. Elsie, resting on her right side with head cradled in her palm, watched her daughter. She was so in love with the child, some days it frightened her.

"She's getting so big," Isla said softly. She mirrored the princess's position on her left side. She gently rubbed the baby's back with her hand.

"She is," Elsie agreed. "I think of my life before her, and honestly," she said, meeting Isla's gaze. "I absolutely cannot imagine my life without her ever again."

"You are such an amazing mother, Elsie." Isla smiled. "I watch you with her, so loving, so dedicated."

Elsie beamed. "Thank you." She studied the other woman. "You're amazing with her, too. I know she loves you."

Isla smiled shyly, her hand moving from the baby's back to the soft blond hair at the back of her head. "I love her, too," she nearly whispered, sparing a glance at Elsie before returning it to the infant between them. "Want me to put her down?"

"Certainly." There were few that Elsie would allow that privilege. Really, outside of Roishin and Mariota's grandparents, nobody else. She leaned down and left a kiss on her daughter's forehead. "I love you, my sweet," she whispered. "Sweetest of dreams."

"Come on, little one," Isla murmured, gathering the baby into her arms. She left little soft kisses on her head as she carried her to the cradle.

Elsie watched, charmed. She knew Isla's history and the babies she'd lost while married to Martin. It pained her, as she could so easily see what an incredible mother she would have been to those babies. But then, she had to remind herself, their life would have been awful and likely violent. And, if Isla had three additional mouths to feed after Martin's death, would she ever have been able to support herself and them? She knew it had been hard enough with just herself.

She was pulled from her thoughts when Isla walked back over to the bed, Mariota snug in her cradle. She climbed on, resuming her previous place. "I suppose I should head downstairs," she said softly, so as not to wake the baby. It was quite clear by her tone, and by the fact that she didn't move, that leaving was not what she wanted to do.

Elsie studied her, dread in her heart of the moment she would leave. "Do you want to?"

Isla looked down at the quilt they lay upon, her fingers lightly running back and forth over the spot in front of her. Shaking her head, she looked shyly at Elsie. "No." She shrugged her shoulder. "It was such a wonderful day, I don't want it to end."

Elsie smiled. "It was. I loved having you here. I mean, all we did was work on the blanket for the bed and some reading. Quiet, peaceful." Her smile grew. "But somehow you being here, being part of it, made it so special." She reached out and covered Isla's hand with her own, their fingers automatically entwining.

"You know," Isla said softly. "Since the day I married Martin, I hadn't felt safe. Initially because of the horrors of who he was, but then even after he died, the constant fear of survival." She looked deeply into Elsie's eyes. "It wasn't until I met you that I finally do. Feel safe," she finished quietly.

Elsie said nothing, easily able to see the truth in Isla's eyes. She very much understood, and in that moment, she knew she'd do anything to keep this precious woman feeling just that—safe. Scooting over the foot or so of distance that separated them, she took her hand from Isla's and cupped her jaw.

"You *are* safe," she whispered. "I'll never let you face anything like that again." The air between them was heavy, though she could feel a bit of anxious energy coming off the woman mere inches away from her as well. "Would you stay tonight, Isla?" she asked softly, absolutely no expectation in her mind. She gave her a small smile. "I really miss having you here."

Isla nodded, looking almost relieved. "Aye."

Elsie placed a kiss to soft lips. "Let's get ready for bed," she murmured against them.

"Do you want me to get Agnes, have her help you?" Isla asked.

"Will you help me?"

"Of course."

"Then, no." They shared a shy look before climbing off the bed. "It's late, and she's probably fallen asleep anyway."

They went to Elsie's boudoir to begin the arduous task of undoing all that Agnes had so efficiently done that morning. Isla looked at her, amusement in her eyes. "Where do you want me to start? Where does Agnes start?"

"She starts with my dress," Elsie said.

Isla nodded dutifully. "Then I shall, too."

Elsie swallowed and nodded, her heart beginning to race. Maybe this wasn't such a good idea, she thought.

Chapter Five

Elsie raised her arms as the tunic was raised and lifted over her head. Isla set it aside then returned to the princess. Their gazes met briefly before Isla focused on her fingers, which deftly made progress on the row of buttons down the front of Elsie's dress. Normally, Elsie did this task as Agnes took care of her tunic, be it rehanging it or putting it in the basket for washing .

She would have happily done it herself this night, too, but Isla had beaten her to it. She was doing her level best to keep her breathing even and steady, even as her heart was racing. Isla's fingers were so close to her breasts, despite being under layers of clothing. She could see that Isla's pulse point was pounding at her throat.

The dress unbuttoned, Isla met Elsie's gaze briefly before she eased the garment off her shoulders. Elsie watched as brown eyes took in her bare upper chest and cleavage, far deeper than it was ordinarily, due to breastfeeding. Elsie said nothing nor did she move. She could see the intense curiosity in Isla's eyes.

Of course, Isla had seen women in any manner of undress before, especially with what she did for her job. Hell, she'd seen the queen half-naked. But this was a very different situation, and Elsie understood that.

After a long moment, Isla swallowed and then helped tug the sleeves off Elsie's arms so the upper half of the dress could pool around her hips, the bulk of the chemise beneath not allowing it to fall fully from her body.

Isla was nearly standing breast to breast with her as

she gently pushed the garment downward. Finally, it fell to the floor. Isla met her gaze again before she moved away, bending down to gather the dress after Elsie stepped out of it. As Isla hung the dress and tunic, Elsie began on her own hair. It was much easier to take down than put up.

"Do you want to borrow one of my sleep gowns?" she asked Isla. "Or, you can sleep in your chemise." She shrugged when the other woman met her gaze from where she was handling Elsie's dress. "Entirely up to you."

Isla chewed on her bottom lip. "Are you sure you don't mind? I can head downstairs and grab—"

Elsie walked over to her once the dress was hung up and gathered the material of Isla's tunic, pulling it upward. "I don't mind," she said softly. Isla lifted her arms to allow the garment to pass. She began to work on the buttons of Isla's dress.

"You don't have to do that, Elsie," Isla murmured.

Elsie smiled, looking her in the eyes. "And, neither did you."

Isla looked away, but not before Elsie saw the little smile touch her lips. She watched what was revealed as she worked the buttons. She'd seen Isla in her sleep dress many times while at the other castle, but those were made to reveal nothing and cover all. But now, her eyes were hungry as flesh became visible.

The dress unbuttoned, Elsie pushed the garment off pale shoulders, marveling at the delicate structure that was her upper chest, shoulders, and throat. It was so beautiful, the skin creamy. Her gaze dipped into demure cleavage that literally made Elsie's mouth water. She yearned to see her, to touch her.

But she only allowed herself a moment to enjoy before she respectfully looked away and continued her task. She squatted down, Isla using her shoulder to brace herself as she stepped out of the dress. Elsie stood again, lovingly handling the garment as she walked over to where her own dresses were hung, doing the same with Isla's.

"I'll brush mine out while you take yours down?" she said, walking to the vanity table to grab her brush for her unbound hair.

Isla said nothing, simply nodded. She seemed a bit overwhelmed, so Elsie thought something simple would be good to help cool the situation, as the temperature was certainly beginning to warm. She turned away from the other woman, hoping that would give Isla a chance to take a breath and calm her anxiety.

As she carefully brushed out her long, blond hair, Elsie thought about the woman standing ten feet from her. She knew she'd have to be careful with her. It was clear that Isla was extremely interested, but she seemed…scared? Elsie got the feeling that her only experience with sexual physicality was not a pleasant one.

And in truth, it had been a short time for Elsie since Garratt's attack. Luckily, she'd been able to see how wonderful sex could be. It was indeed a wonderful thing with the right person, something which Isla didn't seem to know firsthand. They had time.

Her hair finished, Elsie turned and smiled at Isla sweetly. "Here you go." She held out the grooming instrument, Isla taking it.

Elsie left the boudoir to give Isla some space. She peeked in on Mariota to see that she was sleeping soundly. The fire had been banked not long before the trio had lain on the bed, so it was time to turn down the bed and climb in. She did just that, sighing in contentment as she got settled on her side of the bed.

What a strange thing, she thought. *Her* side of the bed. As if this was something that happened every night.

She did have to admit, she had slept much better with Isla lying next to her than she had alone. Yes, some of that was likely her fear after what had happened, but she knew it was more than that, too. The natural way the other woman had about her, her calm energy.

She glanced over when she saw Isla padding over to the bed. She was stunning. It was so hard not to stare. Her body was absolutely beautiful, and her long, chestnut hair was brushed down to a shine. She spared a timid glance at Elsie before she climbed beneath the covers. She lay on her back, looking like she was barely breathing.

Elsie reached over beneath the covers, lightly taking the hand she found there. "Isla?" It took a moment, but Isla finally glanced over at her. "I'm not going to hurt you," she said softly. "Or force you into anything."

Isla held her gaze and, with those simple words, seemed to relax. She turned on her side, facing Elsie. She kept hold of her hand, almost like a child with a rag doll that was held close for comfort.

"You must think I'm quite childish," she finally said.

Elsie mirrored her position, now both lying as they had been when the baby was between them. "No," she said easily. "I think you're an incredible woman, so beautiful, yet you've been through a lot." She rubbed her thumb over the back of Isla's hand. "I'm so glad you're here, Isla." She smiled. "In every way."

"You're the most beautiful woman I've ever seen," Isla whispered.

Elsie felt those words straight to her heart. She smiled. "Can I give you a kiss?"

Isla nodded. "Please."

Elsie pulled her hand from Isla's and gently urged her to roll to her back. She scooted up beside her, holding her upper body up on her forearm. Looking down into Isla's face, Elsie gave her an understanding smile. She lightly brushed her cheek with her fingertips before lowering her lips to Isla's. The kiss was soft, gentle, non-demanding. She kissed her that way a few times, a light touch only to return for another.

Intending to move away, she stayed when Isla's hand came up and moved into Elsie's hair. She gently urged her down, Elsie complying. It was a gentle play of lips caressing, experiencing. Isla sighed softly as the kiss deepened a bit. In response, Elsie used her tongue just to barely swipe at the underside of Isla's top lip.

A little gasp of surprise came from Isla, but she didn't stop the kiss. Elsie lowered herself, her breast just barely pressing against Isla's. Another gasp escaped Isla's lips, but it was followed by a soft sigh when she seemed to realize what was touching her. There were just two thin garments separating their heated skin.

At the first stroke of Elsie's tongue against Isla's, the dressmaker whimpered softly, her fingers burying themselves deeper into Elsie's hair. It was clearly a very new world opening up for Isla, and she was extremely receptive to it. Elsie had a feeling she'd reach her limit, overstimulated by a lot of new sensations, but she was pleased she no longer seemed to frighten the woman she kissed.

Many moments later, Isla used the hand that had been in Elsie's hair to gently push against her shoulder. Understanding, Elsie left a final soft kiss on her lips then lifted her head to see a very flushed Isla. They were both breathing hard.

"Can I hold you?" Elsie asked softly. Nodding, Isla was about to turn on her side to present her back when Elsie stopped her. "No. Come here."

Elsie moved to her back, urging Isla to move over

and cuddle up next to her. Initially Isla was stiff, but as she relaxed, she moved her body as close to Elsie's as she could as she rested her head on her shoulder.

"I don't know what to do with my arm," she murmured.

Amused, Elsie grabbed her hand and gently eased it to rest against Elsie's other side, Isla's arm stretched out across her midsection. "Is this okay?" she asked, fingers lightly combing through long, chestnut hair.

Isla let out a contented sigh. "Very okay." She scooted in even closer, making Elsie smile and hold her tighter. "I never could have dreamed it could be so wonderful, Elsie," she whispered.

Just wait, she thought. "What could be?"

"Touch," Isla said. "Kissing." She buried her face in Elsie's neck. "So warm," she murmured.

Elsie's eyes closed at the exquisiteness of all of it—holding this woman, introducing her to a new world of love and pleasure rather than hate and pain. She felt a kiss on her neck and then a pause, almost as if Isla was waiting to see what Elsie would do, or perhaps even afraid she'd done something wrong.

In silent invitation, Elsie moved her head just a bit, exposing more of her neck to what seemed to be a curious woman. She was glad she'd guessed right when she felt another kiss. She caressed the skin of a soft shoulder to let her know it was okay, okay to continue, okay to stop. Apparently stopping wasn't what Isla had in mind.

She readjusted herself so she was resting on a forearm, much as Elsie had done several minutes before. Elsie responded to Isla's kiss, letting her control it. She seemed more relaxed being in control, being allowed to move things at her own pace. Elsie did, however, gently urge her to move on top of her. She wanted to feel her warmth covering her body.

They both sighed at the feel of their breasts fully pressed together, the bodice of their chemises the only thing between them. The kiss was slow, Isla still seeming to be trying to get her feet under her. Elsie didn't care. She just wanted to be close to her, to feel her.

She slid her hands down Isla's back, stopping just before the swell of her shapely behind before making their way back up. She could feel the warmth of Isla's back, and as much as she wanted to feel her naked against her, she knew that would come in time. After many minutes, the kiss came to a natural end.

Forehead resting against Elsie's, both once again breathing hard, Isla murmured, "I'm sorry. I just couldn't help it."

Elsie smiled, again trailing her hands over Isla's back, but this time in comfort. "You don't ever need to apologize, Isla. Ever." She looked up into Isla's eyes when she raised her head. "You also never need to ask."

Nodding, Isla stole a quick kiss, as if testing that theory. She grinned and moved off Elsie and back in against her. She held her tightly, almost possessively. "I love kissing you." She gave a rueful snort. "Never, ever did I think I'd say such a thing."

Elsie smiled, leaving a kiss on Isla's forehead. "After Martin, I can understand."

"I never thought I'd want to be touched again, Elsie," Isla said, her voice flat. "I honestly didn't. But you know what's funny?"

"Hmm?" Elsie traced her fingertips over the softness of the forearm resting across her belly.

"That first day, when I came in to measure you for your wedding dress." A tone of almost wonder was in her voice. "I was so taken by you, I almost couldn't do my job."

She chuckled softly. "I worried you'd fire me."

"Why?" Elsie asked, remembering that day well. "You were so sweet that day. So incredibly kind."

"I was afraid you'd see it all over me." Isla readjusted her head to a more comfortable position. "I now realize I was completely attracted to you."

"I was to you, too," Elsie admitted.

"Really?" Isla said, sounding stunned.

"Aye." Elsie left another kiss to her forehead, letting out a contented sigh. "So glad you're here," she whispered.

✺✺✺✺

Though very glad to see her and accepting the tight hug and kiss to the cheek, Elsie felt a little sheepish and nervous. She had trouble meeting Roishin's gaze as the hug ended. She spared her a glance then looked away before she walked over to Mariota, who was all packed and ready for her time with her other mother.

"Everything okay?" Roishin asked.

Elsie didn't say anything for a moment until she turned around to face her. She chewed on her bottom lip before she finally spoke. "You once offered to create a door...For Isla."

Roishin nodded. "I did," she hedged, watching Elsie carefully.

Elsie couldn't take the scrutiny from those intense, deep green eyes, so she once again looked away. "I wondered if maybe...perhaps...well, if..." She cursed silently. Damn it! She had absolutely nothing to feel bad about. So, why did she feel so damn guilty?

As if reading her mind, Roishin took a step toward her, a hand to her shoulder. "Hey," she said softly. "Elsie, look at me."

It took a moment, but finally she did. She saw nothing but compassion and understanding in those eyes.

"Our daughter is almost eight months old," Roishin began. "And, there was a nine-month pregnancy before that." She smiled. "That's a lot of time for us both to work on getting our own lives. We've done an amazing job, Elsie. Building a friendship and a mutual respect built on the love we have for each other and always will." She took Elsie's hands in her own. "All the while, we've been working on our own respective lives." She shook the hands she held to emphasize her coming point. "You have a right to be happy, to love, and to *be* loved the way you deserve to be." She added. "By someone who's actually here."

Elsie felt tears of relief and appreciation prick the backs of her eyes. She used her thumbs to caress the backs of Roishin's hands in affectionate gratitude. "Did you feel guilty?" she asked quietly.

Roishin nodded enthusiastically. "You bet I did!" She smiled. "I cried the night I realized what was happening between Enori and me. I felt horrible, Elsie. So guilty, even though we'd decided a long time before that that we needed to go our separate ways." She brought Elsie's hands up to her lips and left a kiss to both. "Be happy, sweetheart."

Elsie released her hands and took Roishin in a tight hug. "Thank you," she whispered into it, feeling so much weight lifted from her shoulders.

"I'll happily make you a door," Roishin murmured. "Just tell me where to start digging."

Elsie burst into laughter.

Chapter Six

She walked through the dimness of the maze of stone, not needing the light of a torch. She knew every turn, bend, and nook like the back of her hand. As she meandered her way deeper into the mountain to her family home, Terryn heard the typical sounds as she passed those where others lived: conversation, a baby crying, the soft grunts and groans of quiet passion, snoring, and finally, a man retching.

She rolled her eyes at that last one, as she knew that meant it was going to be a rough night, as the man retching was her own father, and that retching was from too much "escape." Lovely.

She turned right and brushed the hanging curtains that served as the front door aside enough to step past them and into the little cubby that was essentially the family room of their little piece of heaven. It was a squarish-shaped room with a small firepit tucked into its own nook, the fire within weak at best as nobody had deemed it important to keep it going.

Their father had made furniture out of found pieces of wood and other debris. It worked, for the most part, and was also where they ate during the rare times they took meals as a family. Mostly they ate with everyone else in the largest cavern in the system. It served as a communal dining room but was also where any community meetings or any other large event took place.

"Thanks, all," she muttered, irritated because so many times she'd been tasked with making sure the fire was banked to show the way home for Laird or their father. Their mother, Blair, wasn't always a well woman and didn't leave the family area all that often.

Terryn had finished her penance for keeping her and Laird away that night and for "keeping your mother absolutely terrified!" as their father had roared upon their return the next day. So now, she had to help serve dinner and then help clean up the food mess for the entire community until further notice. And Laird's penance? Nothing. In fact, he'd gotten himself an "atta boy" for getting the wayward pair home safely.

How sweet.

Just beyond the living room was a short hall that opened up into three separate rooms, as it were, though one was significantly smaller than the other two and could barely be called a room. The one to the left was where their parents slept, each with their own sleeping nook carved out of the stone. The other nooks were used for storage, six in total.

The room to the right was where Terryn and Laird slept, a similar layout to that of their parents' with two sleeping nooks, one for each of them. There was, however, only one additional nook. Laird used that for his personal belongings since he was taller than Terryn was. She could stuff her clothing at the end of hers, as her feet didn't nearly reach the end as his did.

The final space in their family home was used for bodily needs, where her father was currently liberating his stomach of too much hooch. Many of the men in the compound took fruit that was about to rot and stuffed it into a barrel with water and sugar and let it turn into something noxious.

Apparently to them the short-lived escape from their dim reality was worth the bellyaching later. Most of the women in the tunnels who later paid the consequences for that choice by the men would heartily disagree.

Terryn was about to step into the bedroom she shared with her brother when she heard her mother's voice call her name in question.

"Yes, it's me," Terryn responded.

"Come in here," Blair said. "I need to talk to you."

Doing as asked, Terryn turned left and headed into the candlelit room. Her mother was reclined back against pillows in her nook, blankets pulled up to just below her bony shoulders. Her hair was red like Terryn's, but whereas Terryn had the deep rich auburn of her grandmother, Blair was more of a carrot top , the strands thin and a bit frizzy.

"Did you finish?" the older woman asked, looking down at Terryn as her bed nook sat nearly five feet off the stone floor.

"I did." Terryn crossed her arms over her chest. "Why am I the only one being punished, Mom?" she asked. "Laird was there with me."

Blair said nothing, her silence telling her daughter all she needed to know. Blair, along with most of the other women in the compound, had given up their voices pretty much at birth. Those who tried to speak up were punished severely and harshly, or simply banished. Terryn had seen it many times.

It was only to her twin that she spoke her mind to any real extent. Even with Laird, she knew he loved her and supported her, but that only went as far as his conditioning allowed.

She knew at heart he believed like he'd been taught to: men were the superior voice in the world, so it was best if she didn't forget it. Well, screw that! Yes, she had to be careful, she knew that. But her mind never stopped, nor did the questions that populated it. Somehow, someway she'd get out of this community.

"How are you feeling?" she asked her mother, pushing her thoughts away.

Blair shrugged. "Good as can be expected, I guess."

"Do you need anything, Mom? Water, go to the bathroom?"

Blair shook her head. She gave her daughter a tight smile. "Go on to bed, now."

Terryn nodded. "All right. Good night." She was about to leave when she turned back to her mother at her name. "Yeah?"

"Go make sure the fire is nice and bright for your brother," Blair said.

Beyond irritated but saying nothing, Terryn nodded like a good girl and headed out to do her mother's bidding. She headed back the way she'd come to the living room. Walking over to the firepit, she studied it. Glancing over her shoulder to make sure her father wasn't coming, as the retching had stopped, she looked back to what wasn't much more than embers.

Tucking her bottom lip beneath her top teeth, she held her hand out a couple feet above those embers, fingers just slightly spread. She could feel the barest bit of warmth in the little alcove that held the firepit, but as she focused on the orange glow of the embers, she felt the warmth begin to increase, though it wasn't coming from an external source.

She brought her fingers into a loose fist, palm down. She could feel the heat inside the loose cage of fingers and palm. She had no idea what she was doing, just that a strange gut instinct was guiding her. The heat in her hand began to intensify, almost painfully so. Turning her hand over, she opened her fingers.

Literally biting her tongue so she didn't cry out in

shock, a small ball of fire glowed from her palm. It burned, but not like a painful burn as if she'd stuck her hand into an active fire. No, it was an internal burn, as if the underside of her skin burned, *buzzed*, all the way up into her arm. It was a strange itch that she knew couldn't be scratched.

She'd been feeling the urge lately to do this, whatever "this" was, but had no understanding of what was happening.

Panicking, she frantically waved her hand over the firepit, as if trying to dislodge something sticky from her fingers. To her stunned horror, the fireball shot toward the stone wall near the firepit alcove in an arc of fire from her hand. Even still, the original fireball never left her palm. She stared down at it before once more waving her hand to extinguish the small light, much as she would were she holding a torch.

She gasped loudly when a stream of fire shot into the firepit, which came to life with a dramatic *whoosh!* Eyes wide, she whipped to her left when she heard the screech of the curtain slide across the rod at the entryway of their home.

Laird cried out in startled panic when the curtain his hand held lit up. He was quickly able to beat the fire out with his hand before it spread. Eyes huge, he looked from her hand to her eyes before he turned and disappeared into the darkness beyond.

"Laird!" she cried.

Desperate, she clapped her hands together, the fireball vanishing. Rolling her eyes, she ran after him, finally catching him two left turns and three stairs down. She grabbed his arm, nearly yanking him off his feet. He whirled on her, face filled with rage.

"Are you crazy?" he hissed, yanking his arm from her.

"Please," she begged, breathing hard from the chase. "Please, Laird."

"You'll get yourself killed, Terryn!" He grabbed her hand and nearly yanked her off her feet as he took them to a storage area that wasn't often populated. Shoving her inside, he followed. "What the *hell* were you doing?" he demanded.

Tears rolled down her cheeks, both in fear of what could happen to her if he told anyone and in fear of what she'd done. She still felt the buzz in her hand, even as it was beginning to ease. She ran that very hand through her hair, then slapped it against her thigh.

"I didn't mean to," she said. "Mom told me to get the fire lit for you."

"Yeah?" he exclaimed. "And you nearly lit *me* on fire, Terryn!" He seemed to calm when he heard her sniffle in the darkness. "Look," he said, voice softening. "I'm worried about you. I think maybe you should go talk to Raif."

Terryn froze at the name. "Why?" she asked, voice hard.

"Because he seems to know about…well, everything. Maybe he'd know what's wrong with you. The dream stuff, and now this." He tugged on her hand in the darkness. "I'm really, really getting worried, sis."

"No." She began to back away from him, but he grabbed her hand again, stopping her retreat. "Let go, Laird."

"I'm not gonna say anything about this," he said quietly. "But you've got to get this under control. I'm not gonna allow our family to be hunted because of you."

Deeply hurt and afraid, she pulled her hand from his, Laird letting her go this time. "Don't touch me again," she said, then turned and felt her way out of the darkness and back to the hallway to head home.

The huge cavern was awash with people, chatter and body odor all concentrated in the large but enclosed space. Row after row after row of tables, bench seating on either side, the people sat thigh to thigh as they ate and drank. A smattering of lit candles were centerpieces, and lit torches mounted to the walls provided much of the illumination.

It was mostly the men who were seated stuffing their mouths, the women serving. The only reason this wasn't Terryn's usual position was because she already had a job working in the tailor shop with some of the other women, making and mending clothing. So, now she was doing double duty, and frankly, she was pissed.

Nothing she could do about it, she followed orders. Currently, she was carrying a huge, heavy clay jug filled with ale around to the seated diners, refilling mugs. She reached between two men to grab a mug to fill when a hand was suddenly placed on her behind. Squeezing her eyes shut for a moment, she mentally counted to three so she wouldn't dump the contents of the mug on the head of the man who dared to touch her.

Glaring at him, she got a grin in return. "Kindly remove your hand," she said.

The man's grin morphed into a glare right back at her and he pushed up from where he was seated. He had an easy eight inches of height on her. "What did you say?"

Crap. She didn't have to deal with this nonsense in her regular job, so she wasn't entirely sure what to say.

"Sit down, Greg," demanded a deep voice

Terryn turned to see Raif, the leader of their community, suddenly at her side. The man who had been so bold with her immediately stood down, but his eyes were hard when they looked at the much smaller woman again before retaking his seat. She was relieved, but only for a moment, as Raif spoke again.

"I need to speak to you, Terryn."

Fingers of ice began to walk their way down her spine, nearly taking her breath with them. She swallowed and nodded. "Aye,"

"When you finish with that," he said, indicating her jug of ale. "Find me."

Watching the big man walk away, she took a shuddering breath and continued her rounds. When she was finished, she delivered the empty jug to the kitchen with a quick explanation of why she needed to duck out and went in search of Raif.

He was a man of more than six-and-a-half feet with shoulders wide enough that he had to turn a bit to pass through some doorways. He was a fierce fighter, and more than one man had been fool enough to challenge his leadership. His head was shaved, save for the hair needed for the thick braid that trailed down the center of his scalp and halfway down his back. A heavy beard finished his look.

When Terryn found him, he was sharpening his sword in his chambers, where he lived with the two women he called wife. She stood just outside, waiting for him to notice her. Oh, how she did not want to be there in that moment.

Raif made her incredibly uncomfortable. He'd never done or said anything to her to make her feel that way, it was just something about him that unsettled her. He was usually polite, perhaps even charming, but in the same way as a snake oil salesman might be. There was something beneath the surface that wasn't to be trusted.

"Come on in," he said, never taking his eyes off his

task.

Taking a deep breath to center herself, Terryn entered the cave-like room. It was pretty much like every other one she'd ever seen, just a slight variation in size or layout. Word had it, long ago the tunnels had actually been for the dead, the sleeping nooks intended for bodies to rest in for eternity. After the war, supposedly, it had been overtaken by the living.

She basically stood at attention—didn't look around, showed no interest other than listening to whatever he had wanted to tell her. He glanced up at her before he set the sharpening stone aside. She did note the sword was massive, a so-called Claymore, or so she'd read. Either way, it was nearly as tall as she was, she noted as he pushed to his feet with the blade in hand.

He walked over to two massive iron hooks jutting from the stone wall and carefully, almost lovingly, lifted the sword to rest in their welcoming arms.

"How old are you now, Terryn?" he asked conversationally, his back to her as he adjusted the sword in its cradle.

Completely taken off guard by the question, Terryn stood there for a moment. She was still deeply worried that Laird had said something, or that their conversation had been overheard. Was this question just to box her in somehow? Stalling tactics?

When he glanced at her over his shoulder, she remembered there was still a question on the table. Clearing her throat, she responded. "I'll be twenty on the Summer Solstice."

Nodding, he smiled and turned to fully face her. He placed massive hands on his hips as he looked at her. Well, more aptly, looked her *over*. Finally, his deep-set gaze met hers. "Do you have a man?"

Pure ice speared her heart, dread bleeding down her spine. "No," she said honestly.

He nodded as if she'd just verified what he already knew or suspected. "Don't you think by now you should be contributing?"

Confused, she blinked. "I do contribute, Raif. I work in the—"

"No." He grinned. Though incredibly intimidating and huge, he actually carried a great deal of charm and charisma, no doubt why he led the community when not even forty years old. "No," he said again. "You see, Terryn, one of our greatest assets as a community against the others is our numbers."

More dread as understanding crashed through her. *Contribute.*

"As it is," he continued. "Last winter we lost a goodly number of our old folk when that sickness swept through the colony. If I remember correctly," he added, raising heavy eyebrows to emphasize his point. "You lost your grandmother."

That loss still raw, she looked away and nodded. "Aye."

He walked over to her, using two fingers to bring her chin around to look up at him. "I know it's tough. I lost my father, too. But we must keep going and we must continue to repopulate." He held her chin in his fingers. Though his touch was essentially gentle, it was firm. "Understood?" He smiled and dropped his hand. "Us men are doing all we can, but we can't do it alone."

She swallowed.

"So," he said, moving away from her. "You have until your twentieth birthday to find a man and begin your duty as an adult member of our community." He eyed her. "I do need a third wife."

Terryn's breath caught. Message heard loud and clear. And, as she looked at the hulking man, she knew she absolutely did not want that to be her future. She'd seen both his wives with bruising at various times, and one or the other was constantly pregnant. She gave him a small head bow of deference, then turned and hurried from the house.

As soon as she was out in the cool stone corridor, she felt the tears threaten. She hurried away, blindly running, just to get away. The tears were falling now, and she couldn't stop them. All she could do was get away. Get away from Raif, get away from Laird, and get away from her parents.

She wanted to get away from the trap she felt slowly closing around her. It hadn't even occurred to her that she was in any sort of danger in this way. Yes, she'd heard of forced or so-called "arranged" marriages in the community, but she had no idea she'd be threatened into one. She'd had looks cast her way, she'd been flirted with, and, such as the idiot at dinner tonight, she'd had men outright try to touch her.

But, wasn't that just something women had to put up with in general? Wasn't that just a symptom of the weak gender that was male, born lacking the brain power to control themselves? Or, better yet, to govern themselves where women were concerned. She ran. She ran down one corridor, turned in a random direction, and kept going.

Maybe, she thought in some part of her brain and heart, she'd run to the center of the earth and burn up in the molten core. Finally, she ran out of places to run and slammed her hands against a stone wall.

"Damn it!"

Turning, she slumped her back against the cold hardness and slowly slid down until she landed on her butt. She tucked her legs up against her chest and hugged them. She was in complete darkness, no idea where she was. She honestly didn't think there was any part of the compound she didn't know. She and Laird had spent their childhood exploring every nook and cranny.

But, as she sat there, the air so cool and seemingly empty, she had to assume not. In fact, as she sat there, she realized that wherever she was had an entirely different feel than anything in the compound. She used the sleeve of her shirt to wipe at her eyes and her face as she pushed to her feet.

She listened, trying to get a feel for where she was. Sniffing the air, she didn't smell food, didn't smell unwashed bodies nor firepit fires. She didn't smell the black smoke swirling from a candle or torch. She smelled…nothing. Nothing but cool, undisturbed space, as if a body hadn't entered this area for centuries.

Turning, she came face-to-face with the wall she'd been leaning against. Her hands rested on the cool, smooth stone. Something. She felt…something. She felt it deep inside, her bones alive with it. A humming. A vibration, almost. She felt life on the other side of the wall. She felt…

"Time to wake up," she whispered.

Chapter Seven

The night was calm and cool. There were no real seasons, per se, though Terryn had heard many of the elders talk about how there used to be things called winter, spring, summer, and autumn. Now, it was cold in the mornings, cold in the evenings with rain, and then, if you were lucky, the sun would peek out of the gray skies above during the day. Many times, Terryn saw the exact color of the clouds in her twin's eyes.

Tonight was no different. The rain had already come, leaving the air smelling fresh. More would come, though. The skies were already beginning to rumble distantly, out in the beyonds. Terryn wondered what was out there. Her little journey with Laird, as scary as it had been at the time, had been fascinating. She wanted to return to the cemetery. She knew there were many other communities like theirs, scattered about.

They'd always been told the other people were dangerous, criminals with murderous intent. Women weren't safe and they needed the men of their community to protect them.

Yet, then why had some women been shunned and banished for not following the rules? If it was so dangerous and scary, wouldn't their community want to protect them at any cost? And why were so many women of their community, including her own mother, not treated right? Was *that* "protection" by the menfolk?

These were questions that one dared not ask. Terryn had never even heard another woman raise them. Well, not one that still remained in the protective arms of the tunnels, that is.

Terryn tore her thoughts and gaze from the distant night and returned her focus to her task. Dinner was over, the women who had served it finally getting to eat their fill, and cleanup had been done. So now, she was outside dumping the scraps into the fenced-off compost pile. The contents would later be used to fertilize the gardens.

With a grunt, she lifted the heavy basket overhead so the scraps would clear the top of the fence. The contents slid down onto the pile with a sickening plop, making her lip curl in disgust.

"Good eve."

Startled, Terryn cried out, nearly throwing the basket at the man staggering over to her. She could just barely make him out in the torchlight mounted at the mouth of the tunnel entrance. He looked to be perhaps thirty. His light brown hair was long and matted with blood, and he had dried blood caked around his nose and mouth.

His clothing was basic, though his boots were those of a warrior. He didn't seem to have any weapons on him, and he was holding his left arm against his side, left hand cradled against his chest. Concerned, she walked over to him.

"Are you all right?"

He gave her a weak smile. "I guess that depends on your definition. Might I get some water from you? Perhaps food?"

"Can you wait here?" she asked, knowing better than to alone make such a momentous decision of bringing in a stranger into the closed colony.

He nodded. "Aye."

She turned to head back inside but stopped. "What's your name?"

"Garratt."

Nodding, she pulled open the heavy, thick plank wood door with a grunt and hurried down the long, main tunnel that a person had to traverse to reach anything of merit. She dropped the basket next to the wall and sprinted to the little niche where the guard had his post. Ducking her head in, she saw the man on duty was there. He and another guard were playing chess.

"Excuse me." When they looked at her, she explained. "There's a man outside, says his name is Garratt. Looks pretty beat up or injured somehow. He wants food and water."

One of the men pushed to his feet, eyeing her as he grabbed his sword. "He armed?"

Terryn shook her head. "Not that I saw. He's alone, too."

She knew better than to follow so stepped aside as the two men headed out. She watched them go, then walked to where she'd left her basket and headed to the kitchen to put it where it belonged. Once it was stowed away properly, she was about to head home when the two guards showed up in the dining hall.

As the only person in the kitchen, they turned to her. "Fetch some water and some bread," one of the guards instructed.

Nodding and hiding her irritation, Terryn did as asked. She gathered the items and carried them out to where Garratt had been seated at one of the tables. The guard on duty went back to his post while the second one stayed. Terryn glanced at him as she set the plate of bread slices before Garratt and a mug filled with water pumped from the well that was housed at the back of the kitchen.

He glanced up at her and nodded his thanks. Turning to the guard, Terryn asked, "Want anything?"

The man waved off her offer but said, "Grab Raif."

Nodding, Terryn headed out. She was glad to finally leave the kitchen and just *maybe* be done with her night, but she wasn't looking forward to seeing the big man again. His demand and warning to her a week ago still fresh in her mind, she'd done her level best to keep her distance.

Her steps slowed as she neared Raif's uncovered door. She heard things from inside that space that she wasn't entirely sure what to do with. Living where she did, it was just a fact of daily life that you'd see or hear something you didn't want to see or hear. But she'd grown to know those sounds—man and a woman.

What she heard was two distinctly female voices that sounded very much like they were in the throes of pleasure or passion. She started when one cried out in a high-pitched whimper. Deciding she needed to come back later, Terryn turned around only to nearly run right into the barrel chest of Raif.

She looked up at him with wide eyes while he grinned down at her. Saying nothing, he gently urged her to turn around and walk the few steps to the open door. Her heart was racing, both in fear as well as acute confusion. Her body was responding to the sounds of the two women in ways that made her profoundly uncomfortable.

"Watch them," he whispered into her ear, his hands resting on her shoulders from where he stood behind her.

Terryn swallowed hard, wanting nothing more than to run, but she knew that wasn't an option. Just inside, Raif's two wives were both naked, lying in a nest of pillows and a quilt on the floor near the firepit, which was aglow. The blonde lay on her back, legs spread. The one with dark hair had her head between her legs, mouth in a place Terryn would never in a million years think a mouth should or would be, let alone the mouth of another woman.

Their clasped hands rested on the blonde's pregnant belly. She was clearly very much enjoying what was being done to her, and for her part, the brunette's noises seemed equally enthusiastic. The blonde's swollen breasts were beautiful, heaving with her quickened breathing. The nipples were rigid and a dusky rose color.

Terryn was mesmerized. Forgetting for a moment just exactly who she was looking at and just who they *belonged* to, her gaze swept over the women's bodies. They were beautiful, particularly the blonde's breasts, which again she was drawn to. She couldn't see those of the other woman as she lay on her stomach on the floor. The arm that wasn't attached to the hand holding the other woman's was wrapped around one of the spread thighs.

"Want to join them?" Raif whispered into her ear.

That shot her right out of her daze and into the very real here and now. She whirled away from him, shaking her head vigorously as she backed up. "Someone, here, in the dining hall," she sputtered. "Ethan told me, find you. Go."

With those words, she took off, not stopping until she reached her own home. Pausing at the closed curtain, she did her best to calm her heavy breathing. She rested her forehead against the cool stone outside of the archway entrance. Her heart was racing, and she knew it had much more to do with what she'd just witnessed than the sprint she'd just made.

Terryn closed her eyes, unable to get that visual out of her mind. She didn't know either woman other than by sight, though she thought the brunette's name was Edith. They were both beautiful and a handful of years older than Terryn and easily ten years younger than Raif, if not more. Again, she saw the brunette one's mouth between the other's…

How…? Do…? Why…?

She pushed away from the wall, slid the heavy curtain aside just enough to step around it, and stepped inside. The room was dark, only a bit of light coming from the candle lit in her parents' room. Shaking her head, she headed in deeper to their home.

"Where were you?" her father, Ronan, barked from his bunk.

She peeked her head into the room. "A man showed up while I was throwing out the scraps for the compost pile. I had to stay late and get him food."

Her father, a generally angry man, glared at her. His brown hair, the same color as Laird's, was thinning, his hairline not much more than a V dipping over his forehead. "Who?" he asked.

She shrugged. "Name is Garratt. That's all I know."

With that, she headed to her own room, her twin not in bed. She wondered what was keeping him out so late recently, but she honestly didn't much care in that moment. She didn't light a candle but instead quickly changed into her sleep clothes in the darkness for privacy before climbing up the wooden ladder to her sleep nook.

With a sigh, she got settled, happy to be in bed, finally. The following day she had off, her first since she and Laird had wandered to the wreckage site she'd dreamed about. She was tired and needed a break from everyone and everything. She so often felt claustrophobic in her life and living in the tunnels.

The only fresh air she got since being punished was to dump the scraps for compost at night. She missed the sun—when it actually came through. Hell, at this point she'd even be fine with the normal cloudy day.

She wanted out. No, she *needed* out.

Sitting up a bit, she plumped her pillow before lying

back down, pulling her blanket up to just under her chin. Again, she saw those two women in her mind. Why did Edith have her mouth there? What was she doing? And why did the other woman seem to be enjoying it so much?

Terryn was confused. She'd never touched another person in any sort of way outside of a basic hug or a hand to an arm to get one's attention.

Even with her twin, affection wasn't common. She'd certainly never touched anyone in a sexual way. A man, that is, because that's who she *would* touch that way, right? But the two women, Raif's wives… That was sexual, wasn't it? It sounded sexual, and the hushed excitement in Raif's voice had also sounded like he was aroused. She'd heard that tone before in her father's voice to her mother across the hall.

That's what had scared her so badly. Her father had never done anything to her that was in any way inappropriate, but that tone… Knowing what it represented when Raif aimed at her had absolutely terrified her.

Terryn forced that out of her mind and sent her thoughts back to the two women.

Instantly, a warm sensation slithered its way down into her underwear. Curious, she sent her fingers down after it. Never, ever had she touched herself.

She'd heard Laird doing something in his bunk, which sounded a lot like the moans and groans from the men she'd heard who were having sex with women, though Laird had been alone. She'd heard it was called masturbation when it was done alone.

With basically zero privacy, she never felt comfortable to try anything. Besides, she couldn't really recall a time when she'd felt the need to explore or try something. Until now. She felt nervous, bad almost. Was she doing something wrong? She pushed that thought out of her mind as she focused on what she was feeling.

One thing she did know, there was an immense pressure between her legs that almost felt as if something were going to burst, but she had no idea what. She bit her bottom lip to keep in the gasp when her fingers felt the unbelievable amount of wetness between her legs, warm and thick. What was that? She knew she hadn't peed herself, nor was it that time of the month.

Her lips fell open and eyes closed when her fingertips brushed against something incredibly swollen and sensitive. Just one small touch sent a jolt of sensation through her entire body. It was like a bolt of—

"Hey, sis."

Her hand froze. Shame immediately infused Terryn's flushed body. She slowly slid her hand from her pants. She had no idea what to do with the wetness that covered her fingers and top part of her palm. Squeezing her eyes shut, she wiped them on the leg of her pajamas. She said nothing, hoping like hell he'd think she was asleep.

※ ※ ※ ※

The next morning, Terryn woke early. She climbed down from her nook, glancing in to see that Laird was still sound asleep. Keeping an eye on him from time to time, she quickly got dressed. She considered grabbing one of her beloved books, hidden underneath her clothing stuffed in her nook, but decided against it. She wanted to explore.

She quickly scribbled a note to him, as their parents were both illiterate:

Went to the sandpile. Be back before dinner.

She knew that nobody would be angry if she went

to the sandpile—a literal mountain of sand a lot of the younger people liked to hang out at that was close by—nor would they send Laird to fetch her.

It was her day off, and she was going to take full avail of that. She had grabbed three jerky sticks from the kitchen last night before leaving and had those in her pocket, as well as the canteen filled with water she'd also taken, strap slung over her neck beneath her cloak.

As quietly as she could, she tiptoed by her parents' bedroom, not even bothering to stop to pee. She'd do it out on her journey somewhere. She just wanted to get out.

She hurriedly made her way out of the family home and down the corridor that would lead to the exit. She smiled a greeting to a couple people she passed, hoping none of them would give her any guff about heading out by herself.

To her absolute joy, nobody asked questions nor really said anything beyond "Good morrow."

Once she was outside, she stopped and closed her eyes, inhaling the morning air. She didn't care that it wasn't an entirely pleasant scent. To her, in that moment, it smelled like freedom, if even just for the day. She pulled her cloak a bit tighter around her and was on her way. She slowed when she noticed a man lying on the ground, curled up on his side under a tree.

As she got closer, she realized it was Garratt. No doubt, he'd been given permission to sleep outside the tunnels until he could get a proper audience with Raif. Despite her passing on the guard's message the night before, the community leader had undoubtedly been quite busy, considering his excitement level when Terryn had booked it.

All night long, she'd had dreams that had left her very confused and very uncomfortable in her underwear.

Even now, as she made her way out into the day, she felt that strange heaviness between her legs. It was like an expectant ache, and she had no idea what to do about it. She'd dreamt of the two women doing that to each other again, and she even had vague memories of a dream where the blonde was doing the same thing to Terryn.

She'd woken with a gasp and a jolt of pleasure rolling through her like thunder. Her underwear were even more wet than they'd already been. That was when she'd decided to just get up. She planned to find a stream, though not the one at the crash site, and bathe. She smelled like…she didn't even know. What was it?

The thing that was even more confusing, though, was that her own smell was making her ache between her legs again. She just wanted to feel like herself once more.

As she walked away from the mountain, she took in her surroundings.

A thick layer of trees acted as cover for the tunnel entrance, save for a space out in front that had been cleared. But if a person didn't know where the entrance was, they'd likely never find it. She turned around, walking backward. The mountain was visible, of course. Even from the distance she was, which was maybe two-thirds of a mile, she couldn't see anything of the large door.

Her steps slowed as dark auburn eyebrows drew. How did Garratt know to go there, then? Maybe he'd lived there before? She knew people had come and gone over the years. Or, maybe he just headed for the trees to find shelter and stumbled upon the entrance. Well, upon her, anyway.

"The torch," she muttered. Right. In the darkness, no doubt that was easy to see, a veritable beacon.

Pushing the thought away, she turned back around and continued on her way. She was in a glorious mood.

She'd never set out without Laird before, and honestly, she wasn't clear about what was giving her the want to do it now. He was her twin, her best friend, and the closest one to her.

Lately, she'd begun to feel a bit of a need to distance herself from him. It happened from time to time and had throughout their lives. They weren't as close as Lola and Lisa, the identical twin girls who were inseparable in the compound. She loved Laird, but she needed to do this on her own.

She just wasn't entirely sure what *this* was.

Chapter Eight

*L*ong *and narrow, darkness all around, even though she knew she was making her way farther and farther, deeper and deeper. Tunnels. Reaching out, she felt, smooth, cold stone against her fingertips, gaps every now and then, as if doorways or entryways to adjacent tunnels. She didn't know because she just couldn't leave the main stretch.*

She stopped, hearing something. What was that? Footsteps? Yes, footsteps, and they were getting closer, coming up fast. She turned, only to nearly be bowled over by her. She couldn't see her, but she could feel her. She held her tightly, so protective of her.

"It's okay," she whispered into the hug. "It's okay." She rested her cheek atop her head, which fit nicely under her chin. A small woman. Her hair was soft, and she couldn't help but smile in relief. "My shadow," she whispered.

Gasping, Roishin's eyes popped open, and she looked around frantically when she realized her arms were empty. And then, once she realized she was in her own bed and it, too, was empty, she nearly panicked.

"Enori?" she called out, feeling like she was about to cry. Her chest was heaving, and she still felt like she was in that dark tunnel and she'd lost her.

"Are you okay?" Enori hurried in, her flowing white gown making her look like she floated down to the bed. Concern on her beautiful face, she cupped Roishin's cheeks. "What is it, my love?" she asked, running her hand through short dark hair that no doubt was sticking up all over the place. "You look like you are about to cry."

Roishin relaxed, nearly melting into her touch as relief washed over her. "I'm sorry."

"Do not apologize," Enori whispered against Roishin's lips before leaving a soft kiss there. "I was downstairs getting your coffee started." Another kiss left. "We have to be to Ankou's soon." Enori rested her forehead against Roishin's. "Bad dream?"

Roishin only shrugged a shoulder, as she was unable to speak for a moment. As so often happened, she found herself getting lost in the pure essence that was Enori. Her scent, her warmth, *her*.

"I don't think it was a dream," she murmured, pulling herself out of her haze. In some ways, she felt like a child— comforted after waking up disturbed. She let out a heavy breath and lifted her head, running her hand through her own messy hair. "An omen, maybe?" She shook her head. "I don't know."

"Well," Enori said, head slightly cocked to the side as she studied Roishin. A sexy little smile brushed her full lips. "If we had more time, I'd join you in the shower and make it all better." Her smile grew at the dark eyebrows that shot up at that. She left a couple more kisses before climbing off the bed.

❧ ❧ ❧ ❧

Still troubled, though there was no real discernible reason why, Roishin stood at the massive fireplace in Ankou's library. Her hands were tucked behind her back, and she wasn't seeing the flames nor was she feeling the heat upon her face. Instead, her mind was back in that tunnel.

"She's beginning to wake up, you know."

Roishin's head whipped to the side to see Ankou standing to her right. A small smile was upon his lips, even as he looked very serious.

"Come," he said, nodding toward Enori and the woman who stood with her. "Join us."

Roishin's gaze immediately went to her partner, as it always did, but then glided over to the woman she spoke to, who Roishin hadn't even noticed had joined them, so lost in her own thoughts had she been.

There was clearly a long history between them, as the woman held Enori's hands in her own. The look upon her face was almost maternal, certainly filled with affection.

She had a mane of fire-red hair, her features angular, strong yet definitely a woman. Her eyes were penetrative, even from halfway across the room, Roishin almost felt nailed to the spot when they swung her way briefly before returning to Enori. They were pale amber, adding to the imagery of the mane of hair. A female lion, though no lioness.

The breastplate she wore was metal, lined with leather around its edges and in its embellishments. Fitted black leather trousers ended in warrior boots. A fine sword was belted at her hip. The cloak she wore was dark gray and pushed back over one shoulder. A large raven was perched upon that shoulder, beady black eyes ever watchful.

She was tall, easily as tall as Fallon if not an inch or two taller, giving her a few inches on Roishin. She was, in a word, magnificent. As Roishin neared the two, her attention was back on Roishin. Her smile softened the harder features. She was beautiful.

"It's a pleasure to finally meet you," she said, her voice a bit accented. It reminded Roishin of Anise's accent. Subtle, but there, and unplaceable. "Macha."

Taken aback, Roishin took the proffered hand, giving as good as she got in the firm shake. "Roishin."

"But of course," the goddess and Queen of the Druids said with a winning smile. "You have done what this one has tried to do for centuries." She nodded toward Ankou then reached out a hand and placed it upon Roishin's shoulder, squeezing with affection. "Go raibh maith agat," she said softly.

Roishin responded with a nod. "A thousand 'you're welcomes' back to you." She chuckled. "Though, not sure why."

With a slap to Roishin's shoulder, Macha dropped the bracer-clad arm before crossing both powerful arms over her chest. "Pleasantries over," she declared. "Now to business."

Roishin felt better when Enori stepped over to stand next to her. She could feel her body heat. Roishin was incredibly confused, feeling almost like Macha was having a totally different conversation than mere "pleasantries." She decided to just see what was said next before asking any questions.

"Macha and I have been scratching our heads," Ankou began. "Wondering how you opened the door." He looked pointedly at Roishin.

She looked to Enori then back to Ankou. "To what?"

"To what is left of Bowhar," Macha explained. "The destruction left by the war, sealed to keep the evil inside."

"Bahutha," Ankou explained. "We still don't know how he escaped, but clearly," he said, nodding to all present. "We all know he did."

"Wait," Roishin said, holding up her hands. "Are you saying the door I opened with Garratt?"

"And the trash truck," Ankou added. "Yes."

"I believe the cave is there, also," Enori added,

looking to Roishin. "Where you and Elsie used to meet."

Stunned, Roishin looked from her back to the two gods who stood before them. "How? You said it was sealed."

"It was," Macha said. "There is only one way it could be done."

"Your shadow is within," Ankou added.

Eyes huge, Roishin stared at him. "What did you say?"

"Your shadow," Ankou repeated.

"We all have one," Enori said. "A person born at the exact moment that you are. Exact day, year, minute, second, and exact gender."

"And, since you are Ankou," Macha supplied. "This means she must be Druid to be your shadow. Just like you, as an Ankou, are her shadow."

"And," Enori concluded softly. "She is in Bowhar."

"She is powerful," Macha said. "She has to be, in order to unlock the door for you."

"Does she know she did this?" Roishin asked.

Ankou shook his head, his arms crossed and resting on his belly. "Not likely. If she's your age, she is young. If you hadn't had Enori or anyone else to teach you, Roishin, you'd likely not be able to do much of what you do. Or at least, you'd be very rough around the edges in your abilities."

"What if she had someone to teach her?" Roishin asked.

Macha shook her head. "I lost all my mortal Druids during the war. We locked it down so all the evil inside would die, Roishin. The darkness and evil Bahutha created could not be allowed to spill out into the world. Any of my Druids who had the blessing to live on," she explained, nodding toward Enori as an example, "would have vanished from the eyes of any humans who may have survived, to their own reality."

"Clearly," Enori said quietly. "There were mortal survivors."

❧❧❧❧

Roishin peppered her daughter's face with kisses. Mariota was in the middle of a veritable love fest from her mother, Enori, Ava, and Anise. All the women, including Elsie, stood in Elsie's bedchamber. She'd been kind enough to let them use the space as a jumping off point, as it were, to head for the most important mission of any of their lives: Bowhar.

This was not a door to be opened in the Crystal Palace, as it was not through Ankou or the energy of Duras, but Roishin herself. And, since Anise was joining them from Ryarch, it made sense to have a mutual meeting point in the earth plane world, since Druids, aside from Macha, could not go into Duras. So, Sursha it was.

With one final kiss, Roishin handed the baby off to Enori's waiting arms. Mariota squealed in delight, the two very bonded. No doubt the smile upon Roishin's face was goofy in her pride and love for her daughter as she stepped over to stand next to Elsie. Nudging her playfully with her shoulder, the two shared a smile.

"I can't believe how talkative she's getting," Roishin marveled. She chuckled as Enori had an all-out conversation with her, replete with gasps and wide eyes in excitement at whatever Mariota had to say, even if none of them understood it.

"You know," Elsie said quietly, the two moms watching as Enori shared the infant with Anise and Ava. The three women were in a huddle with the baby. "Soon enough she'll be talking. We need to decide how we want to be addressed." She smiled at Roishin. "Something tells me you don't want to be Daidí."

Roishin smirked and shook her head. "No. Only one woman could wear that title." She considered for a moment. "Well, do you want mam for you?" she asked, looking to the shorter woman. "Considering that's what you called your mother, or do you prefer mamaí?"

"You ask all the hard questions," Elsie muttered, making Roishin chuckle. "And then," Elsie added. "There's what she should call Enori, also."

Roishin looked at her, stunned.

"What?" Elsie asked. "Enori is every bit of a mother to our daughter as you or I, Roishin." She returned her gaze to the women. "I think she's an incredibly important force in Mariota's life," she continued softly. "Just like she has been in yours." Her smile broadened. "In all of ours."

Roishin was truly struck speechless by the incredible generosity of spirit and heart Elsie was showing in that moment. Finally, she nodded and was able to meet the patient, beautiful sapphire gaze.

"You truly will make an incredible queen someday," she whispered with reverence.

Elsie's smile was soft. "Well, hopefully I won't have to. Hopefully, by the time it's Mariota's turn, she'll be grown and long into adulthood and can take her rightful place herself."

Roishin wrapped an arm around Elsie's shoulders and left a kiss on the side of her head. "Agreed."

"Is this dangerous?" Elsie asked. "What you're about to do?"

Roishin considered the question for a long moment before she responded. "I'm honestly not sure."

Elsie moved away enough that Roishin's arm fell back to her side. The princess faced her, eyes hard.

"Please do not make me stand at your grave," Elsie whispered, emotion tingeing her words. "Please." Her gaze bored into Roishin's. "Your daughter needs you here, and I absolutely do not want to have to speak to you through a mirror."

Roishin smiled, but only because she was so touched by the little bulldog standing before her. She was surprised she hadn't received a matching poke to the chest with each word.

Nodding, she said, "I promise." The two shared a tight hug, Roishin giving the smaller woman a squeeze and another kiss to the head before she released her. "We need to get going."

She turned away from Elsie after they parted, the other three women already turning toward the two moms. Ava held Mariota as if it was Pass The Baby, musical-chairs style, and when it was time to stop, the young woman had ended up with her.

She left a kiss on the happy infant's cheek before handing her over to Roishin so she could give Elsie a hug.

"Thanks for the baby time," she said playfully.

As Roishin stood back and watched, it made her so happy to see her life in Duras and those who shared it converge with her life in Sursha. She hoped that someday Elsie would either be able to visit Duras, or perhaps a new Bowhar could be established, where the two peoples could easily intermingle and live in harmony as they once had.

Anise gave the princess a tight squeeze before it was Enori's turn to hug Elsie. Roishin had noticed that, since the night of Garratt's attack, the two women that she loved most in all the world had seemed to have found a sisterhood. There was true and genuine affection between them, and it warmed Roishin's soul like nothing else could, except her own child.

Their hug was tight, softly spoken words between them meant only for the other, before with a squeeze to Elsie's arms, Enori stepped back. Roishin accepted the final hug from Elsie, their daughter babbling between them.

"Be safe," Elsie murmured.

Nodding, Roishin passed Mariota to Elsie, the baby whining a bit when she realized her other mama was leaving. "I love you, little one," Roishin said, kissing the baby's head. "See you soon." It broke Roishin's heart as Mariota began to cry, her little arms reaching for her. She felt a knot in her throat.

"She'll be okay," Elsie said. "I'll distract her."

"Okay." A final kiss to the baby's heated, tear-streaked cheek, and Roishin stepped away. Hardest damn thing to do.

"You know what?" Elsie said, excitement in her voice as she turned away from the women, her focus solely on Mariota as she headed for the door to her bedchamber. "Let's go see Isla!"

Still whimpering, at least the little hand stopped reaching for Roishin over Elsie's shoulder. Once the two left the bedchamber door, which closed softly behind them, Roishin's head fell.

"It gets easier," Anise said softly, a hand to Roishin's back. "Before you know it, you're running after *them* for attention."

Roishin smiled, grateful for the kind understanding. "Thanks, Anise. Just hate to see my baby cry."

Anise squeezed her shoulder then looked to the other two women waiting for them. "Come on," she said. "We've got a job to do."

Knowing the older woman was right, Roishin snapped herself out of her mother's guilt and into work mode. She knew Mariota was more than fine in Elsie's very capable arms, and they had a mission to get to.

"All right," she said, clapping her hands together. "So, where do we need to enter?" She looked to Enori and Anise, both of whom knew Bowhar before and during the war.

"You said it was essentially sand dunes where you fought Garratt, correct?" Anise asked.

Roishin nodded. "Aye."

"And, the trash truck wasn't there?" Ava said. "In the sand?"

Roishin shook her head. "No. There was absolutely *nothing* there. It was like being on another planet."

Enori and Anise met gazes. "The borderlands," Enori said, Anise nodding in agreement. She looked to Roishin. "A small strip of land that essentially connects Bowhar to Brittany," she explained. "Awakened humans were able to cross there."

Eyes wide, Roishin looked to Ava, who looked just as surprised. "Okay," Roishin drawled. "Is that where I should make the door, then?"

Anise shook her head. "It's so far from anything useful, especially now that you say there's nothing there. There used to be outposts there, people who lived in the area who basically hopped back and forth between the earth plane and Bowhar. Can you find the truck, do you think?"

"Find the driver, Roishin," Ava said quietly. "Connect with him." She gave her a look of understanding. "Plus, I'm sure you don't want to see the body of your brother again."

Roishin nodded. Very true. Looking to the other two for agreement, nods all around, she focused. She remembered his face, would never forget it. That quick glance before the truck plowed through the door she'd made. She saw him again: bald head, double chin, bulbous nose, and hard, small blue eyes.

She reached out to find his energy. Though he was likely dead, some would still remain with him until his body was fully decomposed and bones turned to dust and blown away. Roishin felt a small surge in her stomach and knew she'd found him.

Glancing over her shoulder to make sure they were all still alone in the huge bedchamber, she created her door.

She and Enori shared a quick look, an entire dialogue of conversation within it before Roishin took her hand. The chain began as Enori took Ava's and Ava Anise's to keep their energy contained during passage.

Roishin took a deep breath. *Here we go.*

The group stepped through the door…

Chapter Nine

… and to a small, moving stream of water.

Not far in was the prone body of a man. It wasn't pretty, his body already beginning the natural processes of breaking down. His white T-shirt and jeans were discolored from any number of bodily fluids, both from the initial impact as well as decomposition and elements of nature.

Enori's gaze ran the length of the stream and its rocky shore on either side. The water was littered with large rocks and parts from the truck, which literally looked as if it had been dropped from a hundred-story building. As horrible a scene as it was, not to mention the man who lost his life in the incident, it made her shiver to think of all who would have perished had Roishin not acted that day and the truck had been allowed to slam into traffic.

She knew that day had rested heavily on Roishin, especially with the grave wound Ava had sustained. Again, if Roishin had not intervened, it would have been one more tragedy to add to a tragic day. She glanced over to see Roishin looking down at the man, her expression troubled.

"We need to give him a proper funeral," Anise said softly.

Roishin nodded. "Aye."

Ava moved over to her and wrapped an arm around her waist. "You did what you had to do, Roishin," she said softly. "I was there. A whole lotta people would have died if you hadn't."

Roishin nodded, never taking her gaze off the man.

When she did, she glanced up and met Enori's unwavering gaze. Enori tried to send as much love and comfort in that moment as she could.

"Let's gather some wood," Anise said. "Make a funeral pyre."

The area was dry, rocky land with the stream cutting through it, gurgling its way into an area of large boulders and small foothills. The foothills gave way to a small wooded area, perhaps a few dozen trees at best. Enori took it all in, including the heavy gray skies overhead. To the average person they looked like storm clouds gathering, but she knew better.

Once upon a time Bowhar had been a beautiful place, bustling with commerce and residents. Much like Duras and no doubt Ryarch, a place she'd never been, Ankou energy not being compatible with Druid, and vice-versa. Thus had been the beauty of Bowhar. Elsie or Roishin could take Mariota to their respective homelands, as she carried both their blood, but one or the other mothers would be left behind.

If Roishin and Elsie had remained a couple, they could have happily raised their daughter together in Bowhar. Enori had known many stories such as that. She herself had been part of such a household of mixed energies. But that wasn't something she needed to think about right now. Couldn't.

Now, it was all gone. What broke her heart the most, however, was the barren landscape that had become Bowhar. In Duras, at every turn was a new landscape. A new era or a new climate. It was an endless carousel of choice.

What made it that way was literally the magic of the energy of those who populated it. It was the magic of collective desire, collective cooperation, and collective harmony that made Duras what it was, and what had made Bowhar what it had been.

Until Bahutha.

He had destroyed the dream and incited a war. Standing there now, more than five hundred years later, Enori could see where the dream had ended and the nightmare had begun. Frozen in time, the earth sharing her scars.

"Are you okay, baby?" Roishin asked softly, coming up beside her and pulling her to her side with an arm around her shoulders.

Enori could only nod, far too overcome to speak. She leaned her head against Roishin's shoulder, needing her warmth and presence. She felt Anise step up on the other side of her, a hand rubbing her back for a moment before the older woman spoke.

"We've got to rebuild this," she said. "We have to do whatever we have to in order to bring it back."

Enori swallowed down her emotions and nodded. "Yes. We must."

"Come on, Roishin," Ava said. "Let's gather some wood."

Roishin moved to kiss Enori's cheek. "I'll be right back," she murmured.

Enori nodded, turning her head to catch the kiss on her lips before the two youngest of the group headed out for their task. Snapping herself out of it, Enori and Anise joined in, the group gathering enough wood from fallen tree limbs to make a small pyre for the man's body. Anise could handle the rest.

Once the wood had been gathered and formed into a foundation, Roishin glanced over to the body near the stream thirty yards away. "How are we going to get him over here? I, uh…" She swallowed. "Not sure he'll stay in one piece."

"Watch and learn, Ankou," Anise said.

Enori was most interested to see how Roishin would react to this, as she didn't think her love had a lot of experience with Druid fire. A small smile curled her lips in anticipation.

Anise moved so she was standing at a perfect distance between the stream and the wood structure. She brought up her arms, the long, draping sleeves of her dark brown dress revealing her hands, palms up.

In both palms, marble-sized balls of light appeared. Steadily they grew, and it became obvious that they weren't just light, but firelight. When they were the size of basketballs, she brought her hands together. The balls of flame joined and exploded upward into the darkening sky.

Roishin gasped, and Enori was pretty sure she would have clapped in delight if the situation wasn't so somber. Enori rested her head on Roishin's shoulder, a strong arm around Enori's middle beneath her cloak automatically pulling her closer.

The stream of fire was brought down until it split in two once more and arched toward the dead man. As if with the gentleness of human hands, the two streams eased beneath him and the two flames extended, wrapping around the length of his body in a coil. Anise raised her hands, controlling the streams of fire.

As she did, the man's body was lifted, cradled in the fire streams, and moved over to the bed of gathered limbs and branches. She eased him down, his body already beginning to smoke from the fire wrapped around him. Once he was rested upon the wood, he was fully alight, catching the wood beneath him on fire.

Anise clapped her hands together, the fire coming from the palms extinguishing as the body continued to burn. The four women stood together in silence as the flames popped and sparked, sending a light into the darkening night around them.

"You know what bothers me the most?" Roishin said softly, her head resting against Enori's.

"What?" the Ankou priestess asked.

"His family will never have any idea what happened to him. He literally just vanished."

Enori nodded. "Yes," she agreed, never taking her eyes off the body, fully engulfed. A humanoid figure, but no longer distinguishable. "I am sorry, my love." She knew this would weigh on Roishin for a long time, and there was nothing she could do or say to make it better. Unfortunately, it was part of their job, though that knowledge didn't make it any easier.

"Evil!"

Enori whirled around to see two men running at them, one with a sword raised and the other clutching an axe in his hand. Roishin instantly grabbed Enori and pushed her behind her with one hand as her body twirled around, the other hand whipping through the air, as though she just backhanded someone.

The man's axe went flying, sending him staggering backward with the sudden action. The man with the sword kept coming. Anise sent her hand out, a chain of fire whipping around the man's neck. He stopped, eyes shooting open in stunned shock before his entire face crumbled as he grasped desperately at his neck. He was gasping for air.

He dropped the sword and then to a knee.

"Hold him," Enori said, walking over to the sword and picking it up. "But do not kill him."

The chain around the man's neck seemed to loosen, but just enough for him to take a partial breath. He was still clearly unable to get back to his feet, no doubt Anise's fire coil effectively leaving him too paralyzed to do much.

Shouldering the heavy weapon, Enori walked to the other man, who seemed frozen to the spot in terror. He looked down at her with huge brown eyes that reflected the flames of the funeral pyre several yards behind Enori.

"Kneel," she said.

When he just stared wide-eyed at her, she cocked her head to the side, staring him down. When he still didn't respond in any way, Enori gathered the energy over his head, using it to literally weigh him down until he had no choice. With a grunt, he fell to his knees.

"You're gonna kill me, aren't you?" he gasped. "You're a witch!"

She smirked. "I have been called worse. And it was not I that came running at you with a sword or an axe, now was it?" She lightly tapped the confiscated sword against her shoulder for effect. Smelling fresh urine in the air, she noticed the crotch of his trousers growing dark in color, his fear getting the better of him. "Who are you?" she asked, ignoring the unpleasantness. "Why did you try and attack us?"

"Because you're evil," he said, a snarl lifting his lip at that last word.

"Oh?" Enori lifted an eyebrow. "What is my name?"

He spit at the ground at her feet. "I don't care to know your name."

"You do not know my name, or that of any of my sisters here." She indicated the other three women. "So, how do you know I am evil? You do not know me."

"I know your kind," he insisted. "The stories all talk about your kind," he said. "How you started a war and destroyed men like me. *He* tried to save mankind."

She stared into his eyes long and hard. "Who?"

"His name is sacred," he spat. "Or, evil like you will curse him. Again."

"Bahutha?" she asked.

His eyes grew wider. "You dare speak his name."

Lowering the sword, she stuck it into the ground next to her with a grunt until it stood on its own. Looking deeply into his eyes, she took his grizzled chin between thumb and fingers, forcing him to look up at her as she leaned down a bit. "You are a fool to worship him," she said softly, knowing she would affect him.

She purposefully used her greatest power to bring him to heel, as she could tell he was growing angry, and a man in rage fueled by ignorance was a very dangerous animal. He swallowed, and she could see the bulge grow in his trousers. He was nearly trembling as she used the backs of her fingers to glide along his jaw.

"Where did you come from? How many are there like you?" she asked, her voice soft, lulling him into a haze of sensual bliss. She used a fingernail to run down over his bobbing Adam's apple as he swallowed.

"The tunnels," he managed in a whisper, sounding like a man who was barely holding on before he orgasmed. "Maybe two hundred of us."

"Where?" she asked, her lips mere inches from his. "Where are these tunnels?"

He swallowed again. "Three miles," he gasped out. "Beyond the trees."

"Thank you," she whispered, her hand falling away as she stood fully erect.

He cried out and fell to his hands and knees, and it was very evident what had just happened as he panted, trying to get himself together. A new stain had flowered on the crotch of his trousers. His head hung, the strands of greasy brown hair hanging to curtain his face.

Enori turned to see her audience of four staring, mouths hanging open. She looked to the other man, who eyed her. She wasn't entirely sure if he was looking at her with hope or with dread.

She met Roishin's quirked eyebrow with a little smile. *Your turn later.*

"What do we do with these two?" Ava asked.

"If they do not return," Enori said, turning to look at both men. The one frozen with the fire chain still around his neck, the other man still on all fours, trying to recover from his ordeal. "I have no doubt a search party will be sent out looking for them."

"And," Anise added. "If we send them back home, a search party will be sent out looking for us."

Roishin said nothing, simply walked to where the man's axe had landed. She grabbed it and held it up before her eyes for inspection. Smacking the broad side against her palm, she carried it with her as she walked back to the other women. She studied both men, the one who had survived Enori's brand of interrogation now looking up at them.

She met Enori's gaze. "If we're damned if we do, damned if we don't..." She shrugged. "I say then let's at least be damned with information about the enemy."

"Agreed," Anise said.

Enori looked to Roishin. "Can you get us all to the cave from here?"

Initially, Roishin looked at her in confusion, but then it dawned on her from her expression. Nodding, she looked to the two men then back to Enori. "Definitely."

Enori nodded to the sword. "Let us leave this here." She smirked, looking back to her companions. "It will be found, and questions will be asked."

"Is that a good thing?" Ava asked, uncertainty in her

voice.

"I think it's brilliant," Roishin said, glancing from Enori to Ava. "Let them wonder. If they think there's an uprise of 'evil,'" she said, using finger quotes. "Then it'll throw them off-balance."

"And," Anise added. "There has *got* to be others here." She looked to Roishin. "Like your girl, who are either in hiding or hiding in plain sight."

Roishin nodded. "Agreed." She looked to everyone. "Ready?"

Anise looked to the man with the fire chain and, with a wave of her fingers in a come-hither motion, he lurched to his feet and stumbled in her direction, as if an invisible rope connected to that fire had been yanked.

"No fucking way!" The man who had gotten the Enori treatment hopped up to his feet and began to run. He was quickly swallowed up by the shadows of the night.

Her anger with that man at a fever pitch, Enori threw a burst of energy at him, which plowed into his back and sent him sprawling, heard as he took a header with a loud grunt. Without a word exchanged between the two, Enori and Roishin walked over to him. He was whimpering as he began to try and crawl away.

"Why are you making this harder on yourself?" Roishin demanded. She looked at Enori. "Be right back."

Enori watched as she vanished through the door she made. The sky above began to rumble, the clouds above swirling ominously. A moment later, Roishin reappeared.

"Had to close the doors from the cave that led either to Duras or Sursha," she explained. She looked to Ava and Anise, who were already walking toward them, sword boy following dutifully. "After you," she said, indicating the door she'd made.

Enori watched the trio pass, the man looking as

though he were marching off to his own execution. Once they'd disappeared, she looked back to Roishin. "Ready?"

They worked together, intentions melding to lift the sprawled man. He gasped in shock as his body levitated above the ground. As though he were last week's garbage, he was tossed through the door, vanishing into the cave. Neither woman wanted to hurt him, but they had to make it very clear to him that to cooperate was his wisest course of action.

Left alone in the night, Enori cupped Roishin's face. She initiated a deep but quick kiss. "Well done, love," she whispered against soft lips.

Roishin grinned. "You, too. Let's go interrogate." Roishin stole one more quick kiss. "After you, milady."

Enori gasped and glared back at Roishin when her behind was pinched as she was about to step through the shimmering space before them. She was about to voice her indignation when she saw Roishin stop suddenly, looking out into the night. If Roishin had been a dog, Enori was pretty sure she would have seen her ears perk and her nose sniffing the air.

"What is it?"

Chapter Ten

*B*lue eyes blinked open. She lay there for a moment, trying to figure out what had awoken her. Finally, she heard it. Humming. No, chanting? Sitting up, Elsie listened. It was pitch dark, yet she felt the soft linens beneath her and the softness of the mattress beneath it. The smell of spent rain was in the air, and she felt Isla just a foot away.

Climbing off the bed, Elsie pushed to her feet. She walked carefully to where she remembered seeing the shimmering air, out of the way in the corner. Standing there, she listened again.

Yes, definitely chanting. Her eyes strained through the darkness, trying to see anything of the source. It was so low she couldn't make out what was being said or even how many were chanting in unison. She only knew it was more than one person. As she listened, her own lips began to move, though no sound escaped.

She felt herself joining in the low, comforting rhythm, even as she spoke not a single word. Compelled, she stepped through...

...and into the ruins of a village. The chanting got louder, to the point where she could feel the vibration in her gut, a deep, low rumbling that almost made her feel nauseous. Even so, she continued on. Her own voice began to join those she sought, somehow her lips, tongue, and teeth knowing how to move and shape the words that tumbled from her unchecked.

Making her way over what seemed like a mountain of

destruction, she found herself looking down into the deep-set ruins of a building, perhaps once a temple. A fire danced and sparked at the center of four hooded figures. Their faces were nothing more than eerie shadows in the deep recesses of their hoods.

Their hands were raised and their voices low. They spoke in a language she didn't understand, even as her lips continued to move in perfect sync with their chanting. Male and female voices, and from the size of the figures, it seemed there were two women and two men.

Closer. She needed to get closer. She began to slowly make her way down the rubble she was perched upon. Slowly, slowly, careful not to create an avalanche of stones, dirt and destruction. She felt the rumbled voices in her bones, now. It called to her, carried her farther and farther down.

She honestly wasn't sure she could stop if she wanted to. The pull to be with them was almost painful. She felt a need in her soul that made no sense to her, but still she made her descent. In her haste, she slipped, her fingers desperately trying to latch on to anything stable. But the large rock she grabbed gave way and sent her tumbling down the rest of the way. She rolled down the pile, grunting with each stab of a pointed stone or stick until finally she landed unceremoniously with a thud on her back at the bottom.

She lay there, dazed, her back and head hurting. The chanting stopped and, to her horror, all the hooded figures turned to look at her. Now, their backs to the flames, they were menacing silhouettes in robes. One of them walked over to her, their steps slow and steady. Reaching her, a hand was extended down to her.

She looked at it, the hand nearly invisible in the large sleeve of the robes the person wore, the hood still in place. They waited patiently until she took it and was pulled to her feet. Standing, she looked up into the blackness of where the *face should be, completely hidden by shadow. Even so, she could feel an intense gaze on her.*

"It's time to wake up," the quiet voice said, that of a man.

Blue eyes opened, and Elsie gasped. She was so startled back into wakefulness, her upper body partially lifted off the bed. She was breathing quickly, her chest heaving. She felt like she couldn't breathe, still able to smell the smoke from the fire in her…dream?

Sitting up, her head fell and eyes closed as she tried to get centered. She started when she felt a hand on her back, warm through the material of her sleeping gown. Glancing to her left, she saw Isla looking up at her from where she lay on her side of the bed.

It had been so wonderful since Roishin had created the door for them, Isla spending nearly every single night next to her. In that moment, Elsie was so grateful.

She smiled down at the other woman, Isla's sleepy features seen in the glow from the huge fireplace. "Sorry I woke you."

Isla shook her head and lightly rubbed comforting patterns across Elsie's back. "Don't apologize. Are you all right?"

Was she? Elsie was deeply shaken, and she had no real understanding of why. She kept seeing the destruction all around her, no idea where she'd been. And then those figures in the robes. Who were they? Why did they feel like home to her? She was pulled out of her thoughts when Isla sat up, their shoulders nearly brushing. Her fingers were so gentle as she brushed long, golden strands back from Elsie's face.

"Want to tell me?" Isla asked.

"I was in this place," Elsie began. "It looked like what

I'd imagine a war zone looks like." She stared off into the distance, seeing the ruins all around her. Even as dark as it had been, it was almost as though she *felt* the destruction more than saw it. "It was awful."

"I'm sorry," Isla said softly. "Was it here? In Sursha?"

Elsie considered for a moment then shook her head. "I don't think so."

She turned to look at the woman who sat next to her, the woman who was beginning to mean so very much to her. She brought up her own hand, brushing the backs of her fingers down the softness of Isla's cheek. As she looked at Isla, all she could do was marvel at her. For just a moment, she forgot all about her upsetting experience.

"You are so beautiful," she whispered, surprised the words had fallen from her lips out loud.

Isla held her gaze, the softest smile upon her lips. She took Elsie's hand into her own, fingers so warm and soft. "So are you."

As Elsie tried to shake off her dream, or nightmare or whatever it had been, she felt a profound need to be close to this woman. Since that first night, they'd shared some light kissing but had mainly just allowed themselves to get used to Isla being with her nearly nightly. Also, working to create a routine where Isla could get back to her own chambers before Agnes appeared in the morning.

Elsie definitely understood why Cateline and Fallon largely helped each other ready in the morning rather than having a servant to help them. She longed to have those mornings with just Isla and Mariota. She had considered talking to Isla about it a few times, but the words never left her lips. Was it too soon? Too much?

As it was, she hadn't even fully identified what was happening between them. She was afraid to speak it and felt Isla was, as well. But, in that moment, looking into her eyes, Elsie wanted more. No, she *needed* more. She really hoped she wouldn't scare her, but Elsie took Isla's hand and placed it on her right breast, outside of her sleeping gown.

Isla's eyes went from sleepy concern to wide-awake surprise to…was that desire? Elsie lightly squeezed the hand on her breast before she moved her own hand back to Isla's face. She cupped her jaw, lightly urging her to lean in.

She sighed into the kiss as the hand upon her breast squeezed lightly, as if Isla were exploring this new, forbidden territory.

Isla smiled into the kiss, Elsie groaning inwardly when she felt the material covering her breast become a bit saturated. "Guess I need to be careful."

Elsie was able to smile, Isla clearly not turned off or grossed out as her breast leaked a bit. "Sorry."

"Not at all," Isla murmured, returning to their kiss. "You being a mother is one of the most beautiful things about you, and one of the many, many things I love about you."

Elsie smiled as she pulled out of the soft kisses. "I want to see you," she said, looking into Isla's eyes, reading to see if there was any doubt or fear or anything else that would give Elsie the cue to stop. Instead, Isla looked down at her hand, which still lightly cupped Elsie's breast. "Isla, if you don't—"

Isla gently used two fingers to press against Elsie's lips as she met her gaze again. "Shh." A small kiss replaced her fingers on Elsie's lips. "I have some scars. I just want you to be ready for that."

She took a long, steadying breath, then raised herself to her knees on the bed. Gathering the material of her sleeping gown, Isla pulled it up and over her head, revealing an incredibly beautiful body. Elsie could only stare at the perfection before her. The firelight licked upon the smooth, creamy skin, caressing the undersides of small but beautiful breasts and shadowing hard nipples.

Rising to her own knees, Elsie took in the beauty before her. She brought her hands up and cupped Isla's breasts, the skin so soft yet firm. Her thumbs brushed over dark rose nipples, eliciting a sensual sigh from Isla's lips.

"Can I tell you something?" Isla asked, her own fingers beginning to tug up on Elsie's gown.

"Of course."

"I've thought about it so many times," Isla said softly, meeting Elsie's gaze. "What it would be like to be touched by you." She smiled shyly. "What it would be like to touch you." When the garment cleared Elsie's head, Isla's gaze was like fire licking its way up the length of Elsie's body.

Elsie smiled. "You're about to find out," she whispered.

Placing her hands on Isla's hips, Elsie initiated a slow, sensual kiss as she brought their naked breasts together. Isla gasped softly at the sensations, Elsie understanding completely. The first time feeling that was a wonderous experience, truly magical, and so much slid into place. Her fingers ran down Isla's back, the woman she kissed stiffening a bit.

"Am I hurting you?" Elsie asked softly.

Isla shook her head but moved out of the kiss, looking ashamed. Elsie caressed her hair, running her fingers along the long strands and their rich chestnut shade. "Can I see?" she asked softly.

Isla chewed on her lip for a moment before she turned and lay down on her stomach. Elsie sat on the mattress next to her, managing to keep her verbal reactions silent. She stretched out on her side next to the trembling woman. She suspected that the trembling was no longer about arousal but fear or shame.

Isla's back was a roadmap of scars, some raised while others were flush. It was a mixture of faded pink and white lines crisscrossed over the expanse. Tears sprang to Elsie's eyes and slowly slid down her cheeks at the evidence of unbelievable pain and cruelty before her. Isla had told her a few stories about how it had been with Martin, but to see this, she now understood just exactly what Isla had survived.

She ran her fingers down the length of Isla's back. Lowering her head, she left a trail of kisses in the wake of the featherlight touches. "Never again, Isla," she murmured against the scarred skin. "Never again."

She moved away and urged Isla to turn over, which she quickly did, lying on her back. She, too, had silent tears trailing down her cheeks. Her eyes remained downcast.

"Never again, Isla," Elsie said once more. She cupped her cheek, thumb wiping at one of those tears. She looked into her eyes when Isla finally met her gaze, hoping that her own showed what her heart wanted to say. "You're with me now," Elsie murmured, giving her a kiss that demonstrated that fact.

Isla returned it, almost seeming desperate, though Elsie wasn't sure what that desperation spoke of. To put that horrible and ugly past behind her? To be loved? To have a much different future than was her past? Elsie intended to make all those things Isla's reality, as well as her own.

She scooted closer to her, sighing at the feel of Isla's softness against her. Now, more than ever, she wanted to show this incredible woman how beautiful physical love could be between two women. It didn't have to be about pain or abuse. It wasn't *supposed* to be.

Leaving Isla's mouth, Elsie couldn't wait to explore

the beautiful body before her. She hummed in contentment as she began to explore a soft neck. She left hot, wet kisses, loving the taste of Isla's skin. Her hand cupped her left breast as her mouth moved down to her right. When Isla sighed Elsie's name as the princess slowly ran her tongue over that nipple, a little shiver of arousal flowed through Elsie's body.

Isla's back arched a bit, offering herself to Elsie's mouth and touch. Her fingers wove themselves into long, blond strands, gathering Elsie's hair to one side and out of the way. Appreciative, Elsie lightly sucked the nipple into her mouth rhythmically before laving it with her tongue.

She lightly tugged and twisted the other nipple with her fingers, loving the soft noises Isla was making. They were both aware that they had little ears across the way asleep in the curtained-off cradle, so they kept sounds to mostly breathy moans or whimpers.

Wanting to give the other breast equal attention with her mouth, Elsie moved atop Isla, her lower body resting between spreading thighs.

As Elsie engulfed the left breast with her mouth, she could feel the growing wetness of Isla's arousal painting the skin of her lower stomach. To know that the precious woman she was making love to was excited, was feeling pleasure and enjoying what was happening to her, turned Elsie on immensely. She felt her own arousal grow in response, her body thrumming.

She wanted more.

After lavishing the breast with attention, she began to continue her kissing and tasting. She honestly wasn't sure what it was, but she was being pulled farther down Isla's body. She could smell her desire, and it called to Elsie like a siren's song. She kissed and licked her way down along Isla's beautiful body.

She nuzzled the soft skin of the insides of Isla's thighs with her face, leaving kisses along the way. Presented with the beautiful, swollen, and pink source of Isla's desire and need, Elsie left a kiss in the volcanic wetness. A long, deep groan escaped the dressmaker's throat, making Elsie look up the length of Isla's body. Isla's back was arching and her hips were slowly rocking. She was the absolute picture of a woman lost in sensuality.

She honestly had no answer to the question of what made her do it, but Elsie touched her tongue to what she thought was the pleasure point of a woman's body. It was the small, hard nub on her own body that Roishin had used her fingers and her own pleasure spot on to send Elsie into erotic bliss.

Isla gasped before another groan escaped her lips. Deciding she liked that reaction, Elsie did it again, though this time with a long swipe of her tongue like she'd done over hard nipples. She registered the taste on her tongue, and though it was unexpected and like nothing she'd tasted before, she understood it was the taste of Isla's need, her desire.

Moaning in sympathy, Elsie licked again. She wrapped her arms around Isla's thighs and got comfortable. She listened for what seemed to make Isla feel good. Luckily, she was a very responsive woman, and Elsie learned her noises and body language as she loved her with her mouth.

Finding the rhythm that seemed to please Isla, whose hips moved with her ministrations, Elsie was losing herself. Her own sex was pulsing in time with her tongue between Isla's legs. She felt she could stay there all night. She groaned in appreciation when she felt Isla's fingers in her hair, the other woman's pleasure clearly building.

Finally, a deep, languid groan escaped Isla's lips, her body growing stiff and her fingers becoming talon-like in

Elsie's hair. After several moments, her body relaxed, her breasts heaving as she tried to catch her breath. Elsie lifted her head, very proud of herself in this new favorite thing she'd discovered.

She moved back up to lie beside the woman who lay with her eyes closed, soft whimpers emanating from her with every heavy breath. Elsie gathered her in her arms, Isla clinging to her after a moment as if just gaining awareness that she was being cradled against Elsie's chest.

Unable to help herself, Elsie murmured, "I love you, Isla."

Isla's eyes opened, and she stared into Elsie's, a look of absolute wonder filling them. As if it took a moment for those words to really penetrate, as well as their meaning, a slow, beautiful smile spread across her lips. She tucked blond strands behind Elsie's ear.

"I love you, too, Elsie." She left a soft kiss on her lips. "So much." She kissed her again, but this time the kiss deepened. She pushed Elsie off her and to her back, following.

Elsie loved the feeling of Isla's body on top of hers. She loved the warmth and softness of her body, the solid weight. It made her feel so safe and so loved. She could feel that love coming off Isla in waves crashing straight to her heart.

She was careful as she ran her fingers down Isla's back this time, and though Isla stiffened a bit, the kiss didn't end. In fact, it deepened even more. After several moments, the two were left breathless.

Isla looked down into Elsie's eyes. "I don't know what I'm doing, but I want to do what you did. Can I?"

Elsie grinned and nodded. "I've never done that before," she admitted. "Nor have I experienced it."

Isla's eyebrows shot up. "Really?" At Elsie's second

nod, a sexy little grin graced Isla's lips. She left a final kiss before she began to explore.

Elsie's eyes closed, and her hands and fingers caressed Isla's shoulders and upper back as the other woman's mouth worshipped her neck. It felt so good. What admittedly made it feel even more amazing was knowing that Isla would still be there in the morning. That they could be in each other's presence whenever they wished to during the day, then have their nights together, too.

Never did Elsie think such a thing would ever be possible. Never did she ever think she'd find a love like this, one that had been based off friendship and mutual attraction. Based off a mutual need and want. Based off a love that grew from a tiny seed planted the day Isla had shown up to measure her for her wedding dress. The most dreaded moment of Elsie's life in Sursha had actually brought her one of her greatest joys.

Her lips fell open as Isla gently and carefully licked Elsie's left nipple. Knowing this was Isla's first experience with that, Elsie opened hooded eyes and watched. She could see how much Isla was enjoying what she was doing, even as she had to show some restraint due to Elsie's swollen breasts, filled with mother's milk.

Her every touch, every lick and kiss made it clear she was exactly where she wanted to be and with *whom* she wanted to be. Elsie saw a freedom in her expression that she'd never seen before, almost as if this night, the pleasure, and those three beautiful little words exchanged had unchained Isla from a very difficult life prior to this.

She was watching Isla come into her own, whatever that may be. It was magnificent to see—and certainly to experience.

As she made her way down Elsie's body, it was like Isla was born to make love to a woman. She was passionate yet so gentle at the same time. To Elsie, it felt as though Isla already knew her body, what she liked, and where she liked to be touched. And, at the first touch of her tongue to where Elsie needed her most, Elsie's head fell back into the pillow and her legs fell open in invitation.

Isla followed Elsie's example from moments before and wrapped her arms around Elsie's spread thighs, holding her open for her. Her tongue was driving Elsie to the edge, and when Isla sucked her into her mouth, Elsie exploded. Her cry was louder than she intended, her back arching and fingers gripping the sheet beneath her.

She was gasping, feeling lightheaded from her quick, high-pitched panting. Slowly, her body relaxed, and she was able to get herself somewhat under control. As Elsie had done, Isla climbed back up and gathered Elsie against her. They held each other, something new begun.

Chapter Eleven

Her gray eyes bulged and her mouth hung open as she watched, hiding within a small stand of trees. She'd seen the whole thing, from the heart-stopping fire show from the woman in the dark gray cloak to the way the blonde in the blue cloak handled the two men. She knew the men were from her community but wasn't sure of their names.

On top of all that, those *women* literally brought two huge, armed *men* to their knees, then they made them disappear! How? And, as she watched, the two women with short hair in the blue cloaks kissed! Terryn's mind was blown. It looked like they were about to disappear, too, but stopped.

Terryn's heart began to race for a whole new reason when the one with the dark hair began to look around. Her gaze settled in Terryn's direction. *Oh, crap!*

Just when Terryn was about to take off and run back to the tunnels, where she'd been headed when she'd found herself drawn back to the stream, the brunette vanished again. And then the blonde did.

"Oh my god," Terryn whispered, a hand going to her forehead as she felt like she'd utterly lost her mind.

About to turn to book it, she stopped dead in her tracks, nearly falling back against the tree she'd been hiding behind. Her scream was muffled when a hand was suddenly clapped over her mouth. The deepest green eyes she'd ever seen were boring into hers—the woman with the blue cloak and short dark hair. She just…*appeared.*

Terrified, Terryn stopped struggling, stopped trying to scream. After all, she'd seen what these women could do. The woman before her, who looked to be her age, quirked a brow as if to ask, *You gonna behave?* When Terryn nodded vigorously, the hand was removed.

Terryn stared at her. Her first impression was that this woman was gorgeous, and her second impression was, *I know you.* She knew she'd never met her before, never seen her before, but she just…knew her. And, from the slow look of shock spreading on the woman's face, she seemed to feel it, too.

"Well," the woman said, a little smirk quirking her lips. "Guess this ended up being easier than I expected."

Terryn tensed again. "What?"

"Finding you."

Terryn swallowed. "Why were you looking for me?"

The woman in the cloak glanced around, looking uncomfortable. Finally, she turned those intense eyes back on Terryn. "Come on," she said, holding out her hand. "Let's go talk where it's safer."

Terryn looked down at the hand then up to the woman's face. She knew in that moment she pretty much had the option of going with her, wherever that was, or face her wrath. And, from what she'd seen, she was sure she didn't want to take that chance. Swallowing again, she took the soft hand, which gently wrapped around her own.

Before them the air seemed to shimmer, almost as if a million tiny little stars had collected in front of them. Terryn gasped, as she'd never seen anything like it. The woman took a step toward the shimmering air, tugging Terryn behind her. She took a step…

…into a cave. Terryn gasped again, her eyes nearly bulging out of her head. It was a completely enclosed cave, no entrance. There was a fire burning in the corner, seemingly free-floating above the stone, and there were a few natural rock features, but that was all the cave contained—except, to her shock yet again, the women she'd seen with the one who held her hand now, and the two men from the tunnels.

The men were on the ground, sitting side by side. Their wrists were bound by something that looked much like the collar of fire Terryn had seen around the one's neck, their hands resting in their laps. Both men looked pretty much terrified, and when they saw her, the man who had been carrying the sword didn't much react, no recognition in his brown eyes. The other man, however, looked at her with surprise. Clearly, he recognized her.

Terryn's gaze left them and looked to the four women, seeing them better in the firelight. The woman who had brought her there was tall, no older than her own early twenties. The blond woman was breathtaking. Her cerulean gaze met Terryn's with curiosity in their beautiful depths. She, too, looked to be in her twenties and stood next to the first woman. The two were clearly together.

The woman in the dark gray cloak was older than any of the others, looking to be in her fifties, perhaps. Her black hair was very short, and her skin was a shade lighter than chocolate, something Terryn had only seen a few times in her life. The woman's brown eyes were studying Terryn with intense interest, which made her feel quite squirmy.

The last woman, also young, perhaps just a year or two older than Terryn, was also quite beautiful. Her shoulder-length hair was very dark brown, nearly black, as were her eyes. Her skin was pale, making the dark color of her features all the more stark in contrast.

That woman looked very confused, looking from

Terryn to the brunette in the blue cloak. "Um, Roishin?" she said.

"Everyone," the one called Roishin said, stepping away from the blonde and over toward Terryn. "I'd like to introduce you to my shadow."

Terryn looked at her, confused. "Your shadow?" She looked to the other women to see they all seemed to know exactly what Roishin was talking about.

The woman with the dark gray cloak and big smile walked up to her. She grabbed both of Terryn's hands. "You and me have a lot of work to do, little one." She lightly squeezed. "You're waking up now."

Terryn's eyes widened at those words. She could only stare at her. "I…I don't understand," she whispered.

The woman smiled. "Yes, you do." She squeezed her hands again before releasing her and stepping away.

"What is your name?" the blonde asked.

"Terryn."

"This is Roishin," she said, indicating the woman who had already been identified as such. "I am Enori, this is Anise, and Ava." Each woman nodded as she was introduced. "Who are they?" she pointed to the two men.

Terryn looked at them. "I don't know their names, but they both are from the tunnels."

"Are you from the tunnels?" Roishin asked. At Terryn's nod, Roishin looked to Enori. The two didn't say a word, but an entire conversation seemed to pass between them. Roishin looked back to Terryn. "Were you out with them?"

Terryn sent a glance to the two men, noting they were listening to every word. Feeling nervous, she shook her head. "No." She didn't want to divulge anything in front of them. She was already going to be in serious trouble. She felt that intense green gaze on her. Chancing a glance, she saw that Roishin was studying her.

"Come with me." Roishin placed her hand on her shoulder and nudged her to walk with her. They walked to the farthest side of the cave away from the others and stopped. Roishin positioned herself so Terryn's back was to the men. "Tell me about those two," she said, voice not much more than a whisper.

"I've seen them, but I don't know them," Terryn said honestly. "They're part of the guard."

Roishin nodded. "Who's the leader in the tunnels?"

"A guy named Raif."

Roishin studied her so long that it was beginning to make Terryn uncomfortable. "You don't like Raif." A statement.

Terryn shuffled her foot, biting her lip as she wasn't sure what to say. Finally, she shrugged a shoulder. "What I think doesn't matter." She looked up when Roishin said nothing.

Roishin looked past Terryn, chewing on her bottom lip as if in contemplation. "Do any new people move into the tunnels? Or are they born in?"

Terryn hugged herself. "Yes, some do move in, but they have to be approved by Raif first. We have a guy who just showed up last night, in fact." She shrugged again. "When I left this morning, Garratt was sleeping outside because he was waiting for Raif to see him." She started at the look on the woman's face before her. She had never seen that color of pale on a human face before. "What's wrong?"

"Garratt?" Roishin said, her tone somewhere between a whisper and a gasp. "What does he look like?"

Terryn tried to remember. "Um, a little taller than you, I guess. Lighter hair, but not as light as Enori's. Long. He was bloody."

Roishin fell back against the wall, looking like the wind had been knocked out of her. "Oh god," she muttered. She brought up a hand and rubbed the back of her neck. After a moment, she asked, "Did you talk to him?"

"Garratt? A little. I had to get him some food and water."

Roishin focused her gaze on Terryn's, that intensity back. "How easy is it to get into the tunnels?"

For a moment, Terryn felt herself stiffen. She may not like where she lived or her situation, but it was home, and those who lived there were all she had. "Why?"

"What if I told you that you're like us?" Roishin asked, her voice barely above a whisper, for Terryn's ears only. "Like Anise."

Terryn studied her. Though she felt the strangest connection to this stranger, she was still extremely leery. She'd seen very few people outside the tunnels in her life, and this group of women was making her incredibly nervous.

"What do you mean, like Anise?"

Roishin took Terryn's hands, holding them palm up. Her gaze flicked from those hands to Terryn's eyes. "You've made fire," she murmured. "Haven't you?"

Gasping loudly, Terryn pushed Roishin away, needing some distance from her as her shock nearly folded the legs beneath her. She braced herself with a hand to the cold stone, her other hand on her stomach. She felt like she was going to throw up. This had to be a dream. A weird, weird dream. Her eyes squeezed shut when she felt Roishin step up behind her.

"We want to help get you out, Terryn," Roishin whispered in her ear. "Anise can help you become who you're meant to be." She paused. "She's like you."

Feeling tears of uncertainty and fear welling in her

eyes, Terryn turned to look into the understanding gaze of Roishin. "What do you want from me?"

"We need to get someone inside," Roishin responded. "We need information."

Terryn looked at her for a moment before shaking her head. "Who?"

Roishin shrugged. "Who would make sense?"

"What do you mean?"

Roishin looked to the three women. "Ava," she called out, waving the youngest of the three women over. She walked over to them, looking from Terryn to Roishin, dark eyebrows raised in question. Roishin looked back to Terryn. "An old woman?"

Terryn didn't even have time to think or consider when Ava faded away, replaced by an average-looking older woman with a matronly bun and kind blue eyes. The beautiful body of the twenty-something morphed into the plumper visage that stood in Ava's stead.

Fresh tears came to Terryn's eyes, her mind overwhelmed with everything she'd witnessed that night.

"Or," Roishin continued. "An old man?"

The old woman faded away and was replaced with a man who could have been anyone's grandfather. Unable to take her eyes off the "old man," Terryn fell back against the wall, a hand to her chest.

"It's okay," the old man said, giving her an understanding smile. He turned to Roishin. "Honestly," he said, his voice gruff and deep. "Probably need to be what would make sense to be around Terryn." As the words were said, the image faded and Ava returned.

All three women's attention was garnered by a *thud*. Turning, they saw one of the men had fainted, his head banging against the stone floor when his upper body fell backward, dead weight. The other man didn't look like he was far from also going. A lot for the human mind to take in.

"Um," Terryn said, swallowing. "Will he be okay?"

"Oh yeah," Roishin said dismissively. "Just passed out. So, what would make sense?"

Terryn smirked, hugging herself. "Raif is after me to get married, or he'll take me for his third wife by force, so if you can turn into some guy that I don't actually have to deal with…" she said flippantly.

Ava looked to Roishin and shrugged. The grin Roishin gave her in return made Terryn very nervous.

Ava looked back to Terryn. "What's your type?"

❧❧❧❧❧

Twenty minutes later, Terryn was taken back through what Roishin had called a door, back out into the night. They were very close to the tunnels, hidden from sight. She looked to Roishin, no idea what to say. *I had a good time? Sweet dreams?* She hugged herself.

"So," the cloaked woman said. "We have a plan. Right?" At Terryn's nod, Roishin smiled. "It'll all be okay, Terryn."

When Roishin took her in a hug, it was the strangest feeling. Terryn felt so safe and warm, as though she were receiving a hug from her long-lost best friend. She returned the embrace, relishing the comfort for even just a moment.

"You and I are connected," Roishin said softly, pulling out of the embrace but holding Terryn by the shoulders. "If you're in danger, just imagine my face and look around wherever you are. I'll know you need me, and I can find you. Okay?"

Terryn nodded. She had absolutely no idea what to think about anything that had happened that night, from the moment she'd first seen the women to the moment she was in.

Swallowing, she spoke. "So, two days, right?"

Roishin nodded. "Aye." She gave Terryn one more hug, then turned toward the door.

"Roishin?"

The cloaked woman turned and looked at her expectantly.

"I'm scared." Terryn gave her a small smile, feeling like such a child next to this woman, though supposedly they were the exact same age, down to the second. Her so-called shadow.

"I know," Roishin said. "It's a lot to take in, and we only told you a small part of it." She gave her a winning smile. "Be ready."

Terryn nodded. "Okay."

She watched as the other woman stepped into the shimmering air and vanished. Letting out a long, shaky breath, Terryn turned toward the trees that would take her to the entrance to the tunnels. She had to hope like hell that she could get to her room unseen and undetected. The night around her was dark and cool.

She hurried through the maze of trees, noting Garratt was no longer camped out. Either he'd been accepted inside or ordered to leave. She hadn't been told why Roishin had such a seemingly visceral reaction to the mention of the man, but   it had clearly shaken her world. Reaching the entrance, she pulled the heavy door open.

She was relieved that it hadn't been locked yet, no doubt because the two guards were still out and were expected back. Lucky break for her. She hurried along the long tunnel, heart racing. She quickly decided to duck into the kitchen, hoping some of the ladies were still in there cleaning up.

"Raelene!" She gasped, running over to one of the women she'd gotten to know a bit.

The blonde turned and looked at her from where she was wiping down the cooking surface. "Hey, Terryn. You okay?"

"If you're asked, I was in here for the last little bit talking to you. Okay?" Terryn looked at her with wide, pleading eyes.

"Yeah," the young woman said. "Sure." She looked around then back to Terryn, concern in her eyes. "Everything okay?" she asked again, quieter.

"Yeah," Terryn said, forcing a smile. "My day off and I was out at the sandpile, and wouldn't you know it, I fell asleep." She absolutely hated to lie and was pretty bad at it, but she had no choice.

Raelene looked at her with a question in her eyes but didn't ask. "Don't worry," she said, giving her a smile. "I've got your back."

Relieved, Terryn returned the smile. "Thanks." She turned to head out but stopped at her name. "Yeah?"

"Here." Raelene hurried over to a covered bowl on the counter. She grabbed one of the wheat rolls within. Tossing it to Terryn, who caught it, she said, "These were served with dinner, so your folks will know you were here."

Terryn's smile grew. "Thank you so much." She raised the bread in salute, then hurried out of the kitchen and home.

Chapter Twelve

"Ankou!" Roishin stood at the center of the library, hands on hips.

The fireplace was cold, the beautiful room empty. Growling, she was about to head out on a hunting mission when the fireplace suddenly whooshed to life, startling her. She also noticed the figure sitting before the fireplace that hadn't been there a moment ago.

She felt her stomach roiling for what she had to talk to him about. Swallowing, she just decided to say it. "Garratt is alive."

She felt like she was waiting on pins and needles while he said nothing. She saw his fingers tapping a staccato beat on the arm of the chair in which he sat. Finally, he spoke.

"In Bowhar?"

"Aye, but the people there now call it the Shadows."

"Matters not what they call it." His voice was low, anger tingeing it. "Did you see him?"

"No. Terryn told us."

"Your shadow," he said, a statement.

"Aye."

"Then, why exactly did you tell me you had completed the mission, which had been given to Enori?" he asked, remaining seated. His upper body and head were hidden from view by the tall sides of the wingback chair. One leg was crossed over the other at the ankle, and he kept up that infernal finger tapping.

Roishin rubbed the back of her heated neck with her hand. "He was badly wounded, but he was sent flying.

The impact of landing should have killed him, Ankou. Essentially, as if he'd been thrown by a catapult."

"Yet," he said with a sigh as he pushed to his feet. "He lives."

"And yet," Roishin admitted. "He lives." She met his hard gaze. "Something or someone in there had to help him. Garratt is just a human. He would not have been able to survive that fall."

Ankou clasped his hands behind his back and began to wander around the elegant space. He walked to the large stained-glass window and looked out. He was quiet for a long time, Roishin respecting it. Clearly he was thinking, the index finger of his right hand twitching a bit behind his back as if in an attempt to continue the nervous tapping.

"When you sent that truck into Bowhar," he began quietly. "You believe that driver was intentionally headed for you and Ava?"

This had been covered, so Roishin wasn't sure why the line of questioning. "Aye."

"You believe there was more to it than simply a rogue trash man?" he continued.

Not really liking where this felt like it was going, she said again, "Aye."

"And," he said, his back still to her. "You said those kids were going to try and connect with Bahutha?"

"Aye. The one kid claimed he'd come to him in a dream." She crossed her arms over her chest. "Ankou, we've covered this."

"We have." He turned to face her, eyes normally brown now nearly black. "He can heal, you know."

She blinked at him. "Who?"

"Bahutha!"

She started as his deep voice boomed in the room, a ripple of vibration pushing through her. It took her a moment to recover, but when she did, she said, "Are you saying you think he brought Garratt back to life?"

He smirked, shaking his head. "No. Only *you* can do that, Bringer of Life. But," he added, finger raised in emphasis of his coming point. The midnight irises of his eyes melted back to chocolate brown as his anger seemed to abate. "If Garratt had a single spark left in him, it was spark enough to reignite the light of life."

"You suspect Bahutha had possessed the trash truck driver."

He quirked a bushy eyebrow. "Don't you?"

She nodded, turning away from him. "Fuck," she muttered. She snorted bitterly as something came to her. "Back where you guys imprisoned him." She turned and looked at Ankou. "Isn't it? Damning those left in there with him. Again."

He eyed her. "Do not speak of what you do not understand, Roishin."

"I know what I saw," she responded. "Those people are living like goddamn rats in tunnels, Ankou. *Rats!*" Her anger was building. "And, do you know what they do to people like me?" she asked, fingers splayed across her own chest. "People like Enori. Ava. My *daughter*?"

He said nothing, though his jaw muscles were beginning to work.

"Hunt them down like goddamn dogs." Daughter and father stared each other down. "Twenty generations living on lies of who and what we are. They believe that Bahutha was the victim, was the one persecuted, no idea he began the war to begin with." Her laughter was sardonic. "They view him as some sort of Christ figure, Ankou."

Again, Ankou began to wander, his casual meandering manner in complete opposition to the energy Roishin could feel radiating from him. "Is there a leader in Bowhar now?" He spared her a glance. "The Shadows."

"Terryn said that in the tunnels where she lives, there is. It sounds like it's become very tribal, scattered settlements." She shrugged. "Guessing each one has a leader."

He nodded in acknowledgment. "You know," he said absently, moving to stand before the fire. "Garratt needed to be eliminated because he would raise an army."

Roishin stared at his profile for a long time, honestly not sure what to say. His tone wasn't accusatory, it wasn't angry, it wasn't happy. It just *was*. Even so, there was a heavy expectation in the air, almost as if he were thinking something and expected her to pick up the thread.

Terryn's face came to Roishin's mind's eye. A young woman, her shadow. An absolutely beautiful young woman with deep shadows in gorgeous gray eyes. A young woman with her whole life ahead of her, forced to live in the servitude of the patriarch. That was Roishin's world in the era she came from, yet she'd been able to escape that.

Nothing could be done in the earth plane, as time would have to catch up with the rights of women, but in Bowhar, that wasn't the way of the land. It wasn't how it was supposed to be, and a woman like Terryn should be living her true self, awakening to her gifts. Now, she could be executed for them, just like the very woman Roishin and Elsie's daughter was named after.

"Garratt was destined to raise an army and start a war," Roishin said quietly. "So, let him." When Ankou glanced over to meet her steady gaze, she added, "Let's get Bowhar back."

ༀ༅ༀ༅

Roishin was thoroughly amused as she sat on the

floor in the expansive living room with Mariota, who was lying on her stomach on the small quilt Ava had made for her. The eight-month-old was rocking back and forth, her little tongue sticking out of the corner of her mouth and little butt in the air as she was pulling one of her legs up beneath her body.

Roishin chuckled. "Any day now, this kid is gonna shoot off crawling." She reached out and rubbed her daughter's back. "How are you getting so big?" She outright laughed when Mariota glanced over at her, all big eyes and pink tongue. "You are too damn cute for your own good."

"Like mother, like daughter."

Roishin glanced up to see Enori walking into the house, followed by Ava. She sent her lovely partner an adorable grin for good measure. Enori rolled her eyes before sending her a sexy little side-eye as she headed toward the kitchen.

Forget about rocking as instinct to get the baby ready for her next step in mobility. She was now rocking in her excitement of seeing her bestie, Aunt Ava. Roishin pushed up to her knees and grabbed her daughter under the arms to bring her to her hip with a grunt of exertion.

"You are a chunky monkey!" she accused the squealing baby.

She grinned at her, leaving a kiss on her cheek as she followed the two bag-bearing women to the kitchen. She walked over to where Enori had set the bags she'd been carrying on the countertop.

The two shared a kiss hello before Enori took an ecstatic Mariota into her arms as Roishin began to unload and put away the groceries.

"Oh," she purred, eyeing some of the foods revealed. "Got me some good stuff, mama!" She grinned over at a chuckling Enori.

Ava rolled her eyes at the two in amusement as she set her bags on the kitchen table. "I'm pretty sure you two are constantly in heat for each other."

Roishin and Enori met gazes, then Roishin looked at Ava. "Pretty much."

"Shameless." Ava grinned, unloading the goods from the bags.

"You need to find love, Ava," Enori said, walking over to her so she could get some slobbery Mariota kisses.

"Hello, precious girl," Ava said, taking the squirming infant. She set the baby on the table and held her little hands in her own to keep her from falling off. "What do you think, Mariota?" she asked seriously. "Should I find love?"

All three laughed at the loud raspberry she got in response.

"What are you into?" Roishin asked, excited to try the flavored coffee creamer Enori had picked up for her.

She'd seen it during a mission once and had been curious ever since. She stowed it in the fridge, along with some of the other offerings that needed to stay cold. Later, she'd pick a whole array of fruit from their endless orchards for her lovely partner and peel and cut them up for her to easily grab and enjoy as a ginormous thank-you.

"Have you ever had a partner?" Enori asked, helping put away groceries as Ava kept an eye on the baby. "Here or on the earth plane?"

Ava shook her head shyly. "When I was in the earth plane," she said, smiling at Mariota's antics before continuing. "I was far too busy trying to understand why happiness was so unattainable." She looked at the couple. "You know?"

Enori gave her the sweetest smile as she walked over to Roishin and hugged her from behind. "I do."

Roishin smiled, covering the arms crossed at her lower stomach. She could feel Enori's heat all along her back and her head resting against Roishin's upper back. She glanced over at Ava to see that she was looking at them, a look of obvious wistfulness in her dark eyes. It hurt Roishin, as she knew what an extraordinary young woman Ava was. She'd become the couple's closest friend in Duras, and frankly, part of the family.

Something occurred to her. "Ava, are you into guys? Or girls?" She shrugged. "I've never heard you talk about anyone." She turned her head and accepted a kiss as Enori released her, the two getting back to putting away groceries.

"You," Ava said to the baby she'd picked up and held. "Are stinky." She looked to the other two women. "I'm gonna run upstairs and change her. And, as to your question," she said with a heavy sigh, heading out of the room. "I honestly don't know."

Roishin felt for her, as the other woman, right between herself and Enori looks-wise in age, looked so confused and almost disheartened. When Ava left the room, she turned to Enori, who was already looking at her.

"She's such an amazing person and would be an incredible partner to whomever."

Enori nodded. "I agree." She stowed the container of Roishin's coffee in the cabinet above the fridge, where all of the coffee paraphernalia was stored. It was easy for the taller woman to get to, and out of the way. "Ava has some ideas to show you," she said, closing the cabinet door and walking to the kitchen table where Ava's bags had been unpacked. "Some really wonderful options to use."

"That's great news!" Roishin leaned back against the cabinet, arms crossed over her chest. Her excitement from a moment ago deflated like a balloon, the heaviness of her day falling upon her shoulders once more. "I told

Ankou about everything this morning when I went to talk to him." She eyed the other woman, who was putting the last few items away from the kitchen table.

Enori spared her a glance but did a double take when she looked into Roishin's eyes. Clearly she saw something there, as she set the items in her hands down and walked over to her. Placing her hands on Roishin's hips, she met her eyes. She said nothing, just letting Roishin know she was there and was listening.

Roishin looked into her face, struck all over again at this precious creature who deemed her worthy enough to love. She'd never understand it, but she was forever grateful. She leaned down and left a lingering kiss on soft lips, just needing to feel her.

"I love you," she whispered against them. "Thank you for loving me."

Enori said nothing, simply pulled Roishin to her, holding her tightly against her. For a moment, she simply absorbed the other woman, every aspect of her: her scent, her warmth, her very essence.

"What is troubling your soul, my love?" Enori said as her fingers lightly ran through Roishin's hair.

Roishin smiled. "How do you read me so easily?" she murmured as Enori pulled out of the hug but stayed in front of her.

Enori smiled, lightly trailing her fingernail along Roishin's jaw before her hand dropped away as Ava's footfalls could be heard coming down the stairs, along with a babbling Mariota. "You forget, my love," she said softly. "You are part of me, and I you." She left a final kiss and then moved away.

"Everything okay?" Ava asked, reentering the kitchen, a freshly changed Mariota in tow.

Roishin crossed her arms over her chest and looked

to both women. "This mission is more important than ever, Ava," she began. "Enori said you have some really wonderful ideas."

"I do," Ava agreed. "I'd love to show you."

Roishin nodded. "Let's do it."

⁂

Later that night, long after Ava had left, the baby had been put to bed, Roishin and Enori had made love, and Enori had been left deeply asleep, Roishin was troubled. She stood out on the front porch of their house, folded arms resting along the top of the porch railing. She stared out at the expanse of their property. She could hear unseen insects and night critters calling out to each other or scampering here or there.

She felt like the weight of the world rested upon her shoulders, even as she knew it was the right thing to liberate Bowhar, a realm kept in captivity for five centuries. Once a mix of peoples—human, Ankou, and Druid—and now just a mass of confused humanity. She sensed that most of the Druid and Ankou had been bred out over the years, those still of the blood who hadn't been hunted, were in hiding, or were effectively asleep.

She thought of Terryn. She was beginning to wake up. Her Druid blood was beginning to warm in her veins, calling to her shadow. There had to be others, too. But how many? How many in those tunnels living side by side with fearful humans, an ignorant species of man taught over generations to fear what could possibly free them.

This would mean war. Again. This would mean war of humanity against those of the magic blood. Brother fighting brother, families torn apart as they were forced to pick a side. Forced to pick their fear over their blood—

literally. How many would die needlessly? Would Garratt rise against his kin?

She snorted bitterly. Of course he would. He'd already made his decision, long before that fight in the borderlands. Long before she'd thought she'd killed him.

A tear made its way down her cheek, tickling her skin as it lazily slid down to salt the corner of her mouth. She smiled as a second tear slid down when she felt her love's warmth along her back and strong arms wrap around her middle. She said nothing, simply turned in the circle of those arms and held the silent woman to her.

Chapter Thirteen

The matter is settled!" Elsie declared with finality. "Repayment will begin forthwith." She disregarded the look of angry disappointment on the guilty party's face. "If it is not," she added, looking the man squarely in the eye where he stood at the foot of the dais. "You will serve a term of no less than one month in the dungeon." She held his gaze, daring him to defy her judgment.

She was deeply satisfied when he looked down at his feet. She nodded her acceptance of the bowed gratitude for the farmer who had been given the rights back to his stolen property. As the two men were ushered away, Elsie's gaze fell on a man in the crowd. He wore the clothing of a typical villager.

He was of above average height and had a slender build, but what got her attention was the sable skin that covered his face and bald head. The whites of his eyes and teeth were brilliant against dark skin. His features were sculpted, and she could almost call him beautiful, though it was obvious he was a male.

But, as she looked at him, he seemed to glow faintly. It was as if a gold halo emanated from his body. She glanced around, wanting to see if anyone else was seeing what she was. The advisor standing closest to her met her gaze, a question in his. She looked away from him and to one of the guards. When he saw she was looking at him, he quickly hurried over to her.

"Milady?" he asked with a bow.

"That man," she said, indicating who had caught her attention. "Bring him to the antechamber beyond the throne room."

He bowed again then hurried off to do her bidding. She watched, noting the guard was not harsh to the confused man but was clearly firm in his request for the man to follow him. Forcing herself to take her mind off the man, even as he kept creeping back into her thoughts, she finished her duties.

☙ ☙ ❧ ❧

Nearly an hour later, Elsie was bustled into the antechamber where the servant awaited to take the crown she wore for her duties from her. It was his sole job to keep the royal finery safe, cleaned, and accounted for.

"Thank you, Alec," she said, giving the kindly old man a smile as he shuffled off. He'd held the same position since Carthac had been a young man.

The small room was made of stone walls and floor, a couple chairs placed for anyone who may be waiting there to enter the throne room, including her advisors waiting until they were called for when she sat upon the throne. Now, there was but one man waiting, save for the guard who stayed with the princess.

The bald man sat on the floor in the corner, his head bowed and large hands resting in his lap. For a moment she thought he might be asleep—until his hands moved, palms facing upward. As she watched, just for a split second, his palms began to glow then, startling her, he clapped his hands together and lifted his head.

Immediately, his light brown eyes found her, and he scrambled to his feet, only to drop to one knee and bow deeply in respect. "Milady," he said. Though he spoke

Gaelic, it was heavily accented, though she didn't recognize where from.

"Hello," she said, walking over to him. "I apologize for keeping you waiting."

He did not raise out of the bow. "I am sorry I have displeased you, milady."

Confused for a moment, she then realized that this poor man was just yanked out of the throne room for no reason and certainly no explanation. "Oh, no," she said, lightly touching his shoulder. "No, you didn't." When he looked up at her, confusion in his marvelous eyes, such a strange color, she smiled at him. "Please," she said. "Stand." When he did, she asked, "What is your name?"

"Jabari, milady."

"Why had you come today, Jabari?" Seeing the man up close, he was even more entrancing in facial structure, his sable skin smooth and beautiful. She couldn't tell his age, though the light brown eyes spoke of a soul that was ageless and had seen much.

"I came today to offer my spiritual guidance, milady," he said. Though his voice was deep and resonating, it was kind and had a soft quality. "The lady of the raven sent me to you."

All she could do was stare at him. "Macha," she whispered.

His smile was big and almost blindingly white against his skin. "Yes!" Then his eyebrows fell. "She told you I was coming, yes?"

All she could do was blink at him. She felt so overwhelmed by his energy. "I, uh…"

His entire expression changed in that moment, softened. He took her hand in his large ones. Though they were calloused and rough, the hands of a hardworking man, they were incredibly gentle.

"Perhaps," he said, voice quiet. "You can return my feather?"

Elsie gasped again, and as she looked into those light brown eyes, for just a split second she saw light amber eyes, just a shade lighter than those of the man before her. Swallowing, she nodded. "Aye," she whispered. "I still have it."

His smile broadened, and he lightly squeezed her hand. "I will return, milady. Tomorrow."

Elsie nodded. "Aye." She returned his smile before turning to the guard who had been standing quietly by. "Bruce, escort Jabari out, and assure upon his return tomorrow that he is brought in."

The trusted guard bowed deeply. "Aye, milady."

⁂

She sat dutifully on the stool as Agnes brushed out the long golden strands of her hair. After official duties, Elsie liked to get more casual than the opulence expected before her public. She honestly hated it. She wished to look more like her people when with them, as that was who she was at heart, but she did understand why it was necessary.

So, for now, her hair had been taken from its intricate updo and would be put into a simple braid down her back. She was in her chambers for the rest of the night and would also change into a simple dress. It was time to enjoy her supper and a quiet evening with Isla. The baby was with Roishin and Enori, and tonight she planned to explain all of it to her love.

As she sat there, she stared into her reflection in the mirror as Agnes stood behind her working on her hair. How would Isla take it? She'd done remarkably well with the doors, after her initial and understandably stunned reaction. Isla knew Mariota had not been Garratt's daughter. So, clearly there was a second parent out there somewhere, a *father*, as Elsie would understand it. She also knew that Elsie and Roishin had been a couple at one time and that their bond was still clearly intact, just changed.

So, how would she react to the news that they were one and the same? No, Mariota had not been conceived during a passionate random night during their relationship that ended in an accidental pregnancy. It was very much a planned event. But it was very much a planned event with another woman, one of which was half-human and half-goddess.

"All right, milady," Agnes said, stepping away. "Anything else I can do before I retire for the night?"

Elsie pushed to her feet. "No, Agnes. Thank you so much. Have a wonderful night."

"You as well, milady." Agnes gave her a quick curtsey then exited the bedchamber, closing the door behind her.

Left alone, Elsie considered what had happened with the man—Jabari—that day. She felt herself changing, though she wasn't entirely sure what that meant. She did, however, suspect his presence was part of that. Knowing about her great-grandmother, she'd always figured the small abilities she had were from her.

But now, as she'd seen Roishin's meteoric growth over the past half-dozen years, she realized it was deeper than that. It was in Elsie's blood like it was Roishin's blood, and Roishin had always felt it. Elsie understood that now. She'd had to leave, had to go home to be with her kind and learn and grow.

No, Elsie didn't believe she needed to go anywhere, nor was her place amongst the Druids as important as Roishin's amongst the Ankou. But she had a place like Roishin did, and, like Roishin, she was beginning to feel the call of her blood. She knew in her absolute soul that her place was in Sursha, and that her blood would help her in her destiny, and that it was *part* of that destiny.

She smiled when she felt Isla come up behind her, entering through the door Roishin had made from the dressmaker's chambers to Elsie's. Her arms snaked around Elsie's waist as she hugged her from behind, pressing their bodies together. Elsie leaned back into her, eyes closing in contentment.

"I missed you today," she said, her hands covering those that were clasped at her lower stomach.

"I missed you, too," Isla murmured against her neck.

Turning in the circle of Isla's arms, Elsie initiated a slow, thorough kiss that was returned, the two women left breathless. She cupped Isla's jaw after the kiss ended. She loved to look into the beautiful brown eyes, so open to her and filled with the love Elsie felt in her every look, every touch, every kiss, every action.

"How did it go today?" she asked, leaving one final kiss before she pulled away from her. Their supper would arrive soon.

"It went well," Isla said. "I have to say, though." She gave Elsie a look that made the princess chuckle. "I have never in my life had to measure around such a large bosom." She put a hand on her hip. "On a man."

Elsie burst into laughter as she walked over to the door when a loud knock sounded. She allowed the servants in with a welcoming smile as they carried in the couple's evening meal. She thanked them all as they delivered their goods then left as quickly as they came.

"This looks so good," Isla murmured, setting the table up for the both of them as they liked it.

"Agreed." Elsie took her seat across from Isla. She met the warm brown eyes that were already looking at her.

"I'm so proud of you, my love," she said.

Isla gave her a shy smile, even as her eyes danced with her excitement. "Thank you, mo leannan."

Word had begun to spread wide and far about Isla's amazing talents as a dressmaker and clothing designer because of the beautiful garments she'd designed and made for the princess, queen, and even a few for the king. She'd spent the day at the estate of a Surshan nobleman, discussing and measuring him and his wife.

As they readied their plates, Isla glanced up at Elsie. "What's wrong?" she asked softly. "You seem very worried about something."

Elsie chewed on her bottom lip for a moment as she buttered a piece of bread. Finally, she spoke. "I need to tell you something." She glanced up to see Isla's guarded eyes on her. She smiled, reaching a hand across the table to take one of Isla's. "My love," she said softly. "It's not about you and me." She looked deeply into brown depths. "You and I are fine, and I love you."

Isla released a long, soft breath. Nodding, she said, "All right. And I love you, too."

"I told you that Mariota is with her other parent tonight," Elsie began. At Isla's nod, she continued. "Mariota doesn't have a father, per se. That is, it wasn't a man that I conceived her with."

Isla stared at her for a long moment, her confusion evident. Shaking her head, she said, "I don't understand."

"I know," Elsie blew out. "What I have to tell you will sound crazy, but I assure you," she added with a small smile. "'Tis the truth." She let out another breath for courage. "You know that Enori and Roishin are of the Order of Ankou." At Isla's nod, she continued. "Roishin is more than just a priestess, Isla. She is a very special being, the *daughter* of Ankou."

Isla stared at her for a long moment, her shock at what she was being told clear in her eyes. "I…I don't…"

Elsie nodded. "I know. None of us knew this until she was twelve. She was always special, always something about her that set her apart, but none of us, including Fallon and Cateline, had any idea. It's a long story how, but Roishin is the actual daughter of Fallon and Cateline, along with Ankou." She shrugged, hoping what she was going to say would make some sense. "Essentially, Ankou blessed them with her."

Isla's gaze fell to where their hands were still joined and resting on the table. She seemed to be mulling over everything she'd just been told. There was certainly shock there, but Elsie also saw some recognition. If anyone really looked, Roishin was absolutely Fallon and Cateline; her physical features were both of them. Her physical size and build was all Fallon, and she held so many of Cateline's mannerisms, and even her voice was similar.

"And," Isla said at length. "Ankou blessed you with Mariota?" Her voice reflected the uncertainty of what she was saying.

"No. Roishin did. You've seen what she can do," Elsie said softly. She indicated the very door Isla had used not an hour before to enter the chamber from five full floors below. "But she also possesses the ability to save and create life. I've seen it with my own eyes." She thought back to that horrible day when Livia was killed and Roishin had to use her own powers to save her own life.

"Mariota is her child," Isla said, her voice small.

Elsie nodded. "Aye."

Without a word, Isla pulled her hand out of Elsie's and pushed back from the table. She looked as though she were going to be sick. Walking to the fireplace, she hugged herself and stood there.

Surprised by her reaction, Elsie also pushed back from the table and walked over to her. She didn't know what to do. Touch her? Keep her distance? Hug her? She moved so she was standing in front of Isla but didn't touch her, as the other woman had completely closed herself off physically. She wouldn't even meet Elsie's eyes.

"What are you thinking?" Elsie asked softly.

Isla gave her a rueful smile. "This may sound crazy, but somehow I knew it. I absolutely see you in Mariota and it's clear that you're her mother, but I also saw so much of Roishin. Her eyes. Her exact eyes." She shook her head. "I thought maybe a brother, someone I didn't know about, a cousin, something. But…" She briefly met Elsie's gaze. "When they're together, it wasn't an aunt with her niece or a cousin. It was a *mother*."

Elsie nodded. "Aye."

"I don't understand all of this, and honestly it is as you said, crazy, but the proof is there. I've seen it. My heart tells me you speak true, Elsie."

Elsie nodded. "But?" Isla's head fell, but not before Elsie saw a tear begin to fall. She took a step closer. "Talk to me."

"I can't give you that," Isla whispered. She snorted bitterly. "I couldn't even keep my own babies alive."

"Oh, Isla." Elsie gathered the other woman into her arms, relieved when she wasn't pushed away. She held her tightly, every bit of love she had for her in that embrace. "What I want and need from you, you already give me." She left a kiss to her neck before continuing as she held her close. "Mariota wasn't conceived in our relationship, Isla," she explained. "We already knew that our destiny wasn't together."

Isla sniffled, pulling out of the hug but staying in Elsie's personal space, which Elsie felt was a good sign. She brought her hands up and gently wiped at Isla's tears, then gave her a loving smile and left a soft kiss on Isla's lips, which was returned.

"Why was she conceived, then?" Isla asked, sniffling again.

"Because Fallon and Cateline wanted the Ankou bloodline to continue, as well as a true heir, as Garratt wasn't their blood son, as you know." She gave her a small smile. "If Roishin had been born to be with men, it wouldn't have been a problem, but since, like us, she's not…" She shrugged a shoulder.

"Fallon and Cateline know of all this, also?" Isla asked. At Elsie's nod, she took a long, steadying breath. Moving away from Elsie, she sat down in one of the two chairs before the fireplace. She was quiet for a long time, even once Elsie joined her there. "Can I tell you something?" she asked.

"Of course you can," Elsie said, still nervous of how this would ultimately go.

"My whole life," Isla began, looking into the flames. "My creativity, designing, it has always been with me." She smiled, though it was sad. "It would never hurt me, never leave me. Even during the darkest times with Martin, I'd leave my own body and just lose myself in creating in my mind." She glanced over at Elsie. "You know?"

Elsie nodded. "Aye. I do."

"I thought it was all I'd *ever* have, and then I met you. And you gave me the job here." She indicated the castle around them. Her smile was so beautiful, so filled with the hope she must have felt that day. "I was going to do everything in my power to not lose that job, that opportunity. And then," she added, looking into Elsie's eyes. "I got a friend out of it, too. It had been so very long since I'd had a friend. A real, true friend."

Elsie smiled, very much understanding that one. She said nothing, allowing Isla to continue uninterrupted.

"And then, to my shock, I realized I'd fallen in love with you." Isla looked away from Elsie and down at her hands, which rested in her own lap. "I was scared at that."

"Why?"

"Because I was so afraid I'd do or say something and make you fire me or push me away," Isla said softly. The look in her eyes when she looked at Elsie again broke Elsie's heart. "And again, I'd lose what meant everything to me. It would be taken away."

From the profound sorrow Elsie saw in those brown eyes, she thought she understood where Isla was going with this, where her worries lay. She moved from her chair to her knees in front of Isla. She took both of her hands in her own and looked up into that tortured face.

"Isla," she said softly. "Roishin and I had our time, and that is over. She is where she belongs, with Enori. And I am where *I* belong." She paused for effect, to make sure Isla was really hearing her. "With *you*. Here." She kissed the fingers of the hands she held. "Roishin and I will always be connected because we have a child together, but both of us have moved on to what our true destinies are."

"Are you sure?" Isla whispered.

"With all my heart," Elsie said in response. She leaned in and kissed Isla's lips. "My heart chose you, Isla," she whispered against them. "That will not change, and it won't be taken away from you."

With a relieved cry, Isla grabbed her in a bone-crushing hug. She buried her face in Elsie's neck. "I love you."

Elsie smiled, her hand cupping the back of Isla's head. "And," she murmured. "I love you."

Chapter Fourteen

It had been two days. In fact, it was winding down to the end of the second. Terryn was nervous with a capital N. She'd been relegated back to dinner duty after her "tardy reentrance" to the tunnels two nights before. Honestly, she was fine with it. It could have been so much worse, and from the eye that Raif and his goons were beginning to keep on her, she feared it would have been.

In fact, she feared it still could be. Raif seemed to have his sights on her. She needed Ava and the others to follow through on the plan they'd loosely devised that night in the cave. The tunnels had a strange unspoken law when it came to a man's woman. *He* could treat her any way he chose, but if another man were to do anything to her—flirt, attack, and, lord help him, rape—then that man could be severely punished.

Terryn had seen that punishment come in the form of a severe beating, banishment, and for the one man she knew who had raped a woman, publicly castrated and left to bleed out. She had the strong suspicion that Raif had made up his mind to bring her into his warped little harem. If Ava, as Mr. Mystery Guest, showed up and claimed her, Raif would have no rights.

She was dumping scraps into the compost pile, the night awfully damn cold. It hadn't rained yet, and it felt like the clouds were holding in the moisture until they were about to burst, almost as if all the heat had been sucked up in anticipation of the onslaught. She shivered as she lifted the heavy basket.

"Can I help?"

Terryn nearly lost control of the weight she was heaving up when she turned to look at the unexpected voice. "Crap," she muttered. Suddenly, a second pair of hands was stabilizing the basket.

"Ready?" asked the male voice, a smooth, very pleasant one. Not too deep but certainly not higher pitched.

"Aye."

Together they got the heavy, awkward load dumped into the pile. Once the basket was fully dumped and brought back down to rest at Terryn's feet, her companion rose up on his tiptoes to look over the fence.

"Man, that's gross." He grinned down at her.

Terryn met his gaze, eyes nearly coal black to match his hair, shaggy and draped across one of his eyes. He looked to be about her age, maybe a bit older. He was about four inches taller and had a slender, wiry build.

A very handsome young man. But, as she studied him in the light from the mounted torch, if she didn't know better, she'd think she was looking at Ava's twin brother.

She'd only been with the women that night for a very short time, including Ava, but this man had the same energy. It was a calm, laid-back air, yet a twinkle in his dark eyes belied his true identity. And, looking at him, being around him, it was a heady experience. She knew she didn't know him but felt like she did. It was like a fog fell over her brain, a memory of him that just wouldn't quite solidify yet made her feel comfortable around him.

"Jack," he said, holding out a hand in greeting.

Her gaze fell to that hand then rose back up to his eyes. "Hi," she muttered. She took the hand, which was warm and gentle as it wrapped around hers. "Terryn."

His grin was crooked and frankly, adorable. "Super nice to meet you. Again." He winked. He nodded toward the entrance. "Let's go in. Cold out here."

She had no idea what to say, what to think. "Uh, yeah. Okay."

Grabbing the basket, Terryn headed to the door, about to grab the torch, but Jack stopped her. "I got it," he said, his gaze meeting hers. She said nothing, just continued on as he took it in hand and lifted it from its holdings.

She grunted as she pulled the door open, Jack's hand taking hold of the edge of the door above her head to help. The two inside, he let the door go and it eased shut behind them with finality. Terryn's heart was absolutely racing as they walked down the long tunnel, patches of light meeting patches of dark only to meet another patch of torchlight.

The price for letting in a stranger would be hours of interrogation, and depending on the outcome, more punishment. This young man who walked beside her did not live in the tunnels; he was a stranger. Hell, she *thought* he was Ava's avatar but wasn't even positive about   that. Maybe she'd just let in a killer. What if he was a killer? Her mind began to somersault over the idea, even if it didn't feel right.

What if—

"Good eve…" one of the guards said, head peeking out from the guard post. He glanced at Terryn and acknowledged her with a nod of his head. His gaze returned to Jack, brows furrowing. "Shit, man, what was your name? It's right on the tip of my damn brain."

"Jack," the young man next to Terryn said. "Come on, man! You really can't remember the name of the guy who kicked your ass at dice?"

"Shit, you're right!" The guard held his hand up to Jack, who slapped it as the pair walked on.

Stunned, Terryn's head whipped in his direction.

She had endless questions but knew now wasn't the time. He met her gaze but then looked away. He had a little strut in his stride, coming off as a good-natured yet confident young man.

"Roishin says hello," he said softly, for her ears only.

A wave of relief washed over Terryn so forcefully that she nearly burst into tears. He led her to one of the deeper, darker patches in the blackness and stopped them. He placed his palm against the wall just above and beside her head as he bent down. To the casual observer, if they were seen at all it would look like they were kissing, but instead he whispered in her ear.

"I need a place to bunk down out of the way, no one else around. Also, can you draw me a map of this place so I can memorize it?" His breath washed across her ear and neck, making her shiver.

Terryn wasn't used to being this close to anyone, so she was struggling to not push him away. Swallowing, she nodded. "Aye. And I can show you where you can go."

He pushed off the wall and away from her. It took her a moment, as she had to remind herself that had been necessary, that amount of closeness. She didn't know what to do with it. She glanced up at him then hurried away from the little nook they'd been speaking in.

She could feel him beside and just behind her. She took him through the maze of dark tunnels, not worrying about letting Jack get his bearings, as she'd do as asked and make sure he had a map by morning. She took him deep into the system to that wall where she'd found herself at the end of the unused tunnel.

She knew nobody would bother him there. It was pitch black and colder than where they'd come from. She could, yet again, feel that strange hum in her bones as she had last time she'd been there. Knowing she could talk relatively openly to him, she explained.

"Nobody uses this part of the tunnels. I honestly don't know why, but I stumbled upon this. You stay here. I'm gonna go run and grab you a blanket. Do you have anything with you? Clothes, anything?"

"No," he said.

"Okay. I'll get you something."

She was about to walk away but stopped when she felt a gentle hand to her arm. She looked back, peering through the darkness. She was only able to feel him, but what was so incredibly strange in that moment was, unable to see him, she *felt* Ava. Again, she was about to walk away but stopped.

"Are you really Ava?" she whispered.

Terryn felt fingers touch her neck then her shoulder, finally sliding down her arm until they found her hand. It was wrapped in fingers that were clearly smaller than Jack's, then brought to the side of a face. There was no squared jaw or heavy brow. A decidedly feminine face with rounded chin, full lips, and longer hair, all of which her fingers were taken on a blind tour of.

"Wow," she breathed. Her relief was palpable and as great as her stunned shock at the whole thing.

Her other hand was grabbed and held, palms up. "Anise told me to show you this," her companion said, very much Ava's soft, *female* voice. Her hands moved to rest beneath Terryn's, almost as if to brace them. "Picture the flame, Terryn," she said softly. "It's already there, all you have to do is bring it to our reality."

Feeling nervous, as she remembered nearly starting her brother on fire accidentally, Terryn focused. Somehow, having Ava here, someone who knew what she could do, even if she had no idea how she'd done it, gave her courage to try. She remembered the words spoken a moment before and allowed her mind to visualize it, see it.

The skin of her palms began to heat up. She ignored the urge to shake them or run away from this. She had this opportunity and was going to take it. She saw it, imagined it, *knew* it. Gasping, her eyes widened when twin balls of light slowly appeared in her palms. They were no larger than two or three inches in diameter, but they were there.

She smiled, her gaze flicking across the span of their joined hands to a grinning Ava. The light reflected in the dark eyes, her face painted with light and shadow. The clothing she wore was Jack's clothing, though it hung on her much smaller frame, her exposed collarbones licked by shadow.

"Now what?" Terryn asked.

Ava met her gaze and gave her Jack's lopsided grin. Her hands still braced beneath Terryn's, she used her own to slap Terryn's hands together. The light vanished, plunging them into inky blackness once more.

⚜

Terryn had made her way to the tailor shop where she worked during the day. Going to her station, she dug out the clothing that she'd steadily been making for Laird for their upcoming twentieth birthday. Over the last several months, she'd gathered extra and scrap material and had been working on a new outfit for him. Slow, but steady.

The good news was he had no idea, so he wouldn't miss it. The bad news was, she now had nothing for his birthday, and the clothing would be big on Jack. She'd gathered the pants and shirt and the blanket she wrapped up in while working. In the cave where the shop was, it could get incredibly cold. She had hurried those items back to where she'd left Ava, who was now back to Jack. It was dizzying.

All that taken care of, she was now in her own sleep nook. Laird was asleep below her, three feet of stone separating them. Her mind went back to Ava/Jack. They needed to make a plan. The mission for Ava was to gather information, particularly on the Garratt guy.

Terryn had discovered that he had, in fact, been allowed into the tunnel's community. She'd seen him with Raif several times in the past two days. Garratt looked better, and he had been cleaned up and given fresh clothing.

He was a handsome guy and seemed nice enough. Terryn hadn't spoken to him since the night he'd staggered up to her to ask for food and shelter. She knew some of the women had an eye on him. New blood wasn't often allowed in, so when a new man or a new woman was brought in, the vultures began circling.

That, of course, made her think of "Jack." The whole point of Ava coming as a man instead of just as herself was so Jack and Terryn could appear to be a couple. This would get Raif off her behind about getting married and "contributing." Because, gosh darn it all, she'd finally have her man.

And hey, if she didn't get pregnant, well, she was trying, right? Also, it kept them together in close contact as Ava did her mission. It kept her safe, and Terryn could aid her with information while giving her cover.

How were they going to pull this off? She looked around her nook, noting how much space there was and wasn't. Most grown children simply moved their significant other into the family home for lack of space in the tunnels. There was enough room in her nook for Jack, though not any of his things.

But, with Laird sleeping in the same room, he'd

know that nothing happened between the two. That wasn't a length she was willing to go in this ruse. Besides, she doubted Jack even had…parts. She had no clue how Ava was able to transform as she was. Was she a shapeshifter? She'd read about that once.

While in the form of Jack, was she full-on male? She sounded male, and it wasn't just the deepening of Ava's voice—unless she was damn good at it. She'd felt him, had her hand held by his, and it was real. It had a different size and texture to it than Ava's smaller hand had. How was that possible? And if his hand was completely real, did that mean Jack had a penis?

She groaned and clapped her hands over her face at the idea of that. She believed in what they were doing and deep inside felt this was going to end up being bigger than she even understood. But the thought of having to have sex with a man just to make all this believable made her stomach churn.

Jack was a really good-looking guy, but she had zero interest in that. She had so many questions to ask Ava. Or Jack. Terryn also knew she'd have to put on the acting job of her life. Everyone in the tunnels knew her, had known her all her life. They knew her to be the quiet, fairly shy introvert that she was. She didn't interact with her peers, certainly not the male counterparts.

So, how could she possibly justify this new and very sudden interest in Jack? Maybe they could become really good friends, and maybe that, unusual in itself for her, could pass as interest. She dropped her hands back to her sides. Sending her right arm out she felt around, imagining Jack's body there. Could she do it?

Terryn had torn a page out of one of her beloved books to draw the map for Jack. It was of all the main areas he'd need to know how to reach: kitchen, dining hall, bathrooms, and waterfall for bathing. The entrance, guard posts that were placed sporadically through the tunnel system, and Raif's chambers. She'd also marked where her family lived in case he needed to find her. There were also the chambers where a lot of single men bunked together, though she wasn't sure if there was any space there or not.

At breakfast, she was seated with her family eating. She was nibbling on a thick slab of bacon when she saw Jack enter. He was wearing the clothing he'd come in, clearly wanting to hold off on changing into the fresh clothing she'd given him. He was carrying an apple, tossing it up into the air and catching it as he went.

She followed his progress with her eyes, noting he smiled at everyone he passed, chatted with a few of the guys like they were long-lost pals. She was incredibly impressed with him. Not a single person stared at him or seemed to think he was out of place. She thought she could tell by his lips that he'd said his name several times, clearly getting it out there. Ava was brilliant, she had to admit. Terryn had to remind herself that she was even behind the mask.

She saw those dark eyes wandering over the faces, and she wondered if he was trying to get a better idea of who was around him. Or was he looking for her? When his eyes settled on her, that question was answered. Terryn absolutely could not help but smile, amused. Suddenly, that subtle little strut Jack had become an all-out swagger.

"Who is that?" Laird asked her, his gaze finding the approaching young man.

"That's Jack," she said, as if it was so incredibly obvious.

"Good morrow!" Jack said when he reached the

table. He looked all four family members in the eye in turn, Terryn last. He looked down at the smattering of food on her plate. She was entirely too nervous about their situation to get much down. "You are appleless, beautiful lady," he observed.

Terryn glanced down at her plate then up to him. "I suppose I am," she agreed dryly.

With a lopsided grin, he polished the apple he carried on his shirttail then placed it delicately next to her plate. "An apple for the apple of my eye."

Her eyebrows shot up as she stared up at him. *Laying it on a little thick, aren't you?* His grin grew, and he winked before wandering off. She watched him go, admittedly amused if not bemused. She felt her brother's gaze on her.

Turning to look at him, she asked, "What?"

"Do you even know that guy?"

Chuckling, Terryn grabbed the apple and took a bite. "Not really," she muttered around the sweet fruit in her mouth.

Chapter Fifteen

If Ava hadn't been born in Duras but in the earth plane, she absolutely would have been an actress in film. Every chameleon is naturally drawn to acting, playing a role and mastering imitation, and not just the physical. They were watchers, observers, and masters of language and accents. They mimicked. They emitted. They became.

As difficult and ultimately soul-shattering as Ava's years living in the earth plane had been, she'd loved her time on the stage. Honestly, it had been the only thing that had kept her alive. An experiment that had nearly   cost Ava her life, had it not been for Roishin's instincts to take her home to Duras with her.

But even after all that misery and confusion, Ava hadn't had the fear she had in this mission. No, she wouldn't be there for years, probably not even months, but the tunnels were a very dangerous place, largely because there was nowhere else to go. There was no escaping the enclosed misogyny and entitlement and brutal tactics to keep women in place.

Even Eva's years in nineteenth-century America had afforded more rights to women than she was finding in the tunnels. It was definitely a good thing she'd come in as a male or she wouldn't learn a damn thing. She was on her third day and had managed to charm herself into the perfect job. She essentially bopped around from industry to industry as the go-for guy.

Need more wood to stoke that fire? I'll get it! Need

help steadying that pipe, fellas? Got two hands! Need more water, Miss Bessie? On my way! One lady had looked her squarely in the eye and had asked, "Now, how have I survived without you, Jack?" To which Jack had replied, "Well, now, you haven't. I was just here yesterday." A lie, of course.

Currently, she was carrying four large bolts of fabric into the tailor shop. The crazy thing about being a chameleon was that whatever the role, some of the attributes came with it. However, not all. As Jack, Ava was stronger than as herself, but in more, shall we say…delicate functions, little Jack was a no-show.

In the situation Ava had been put in, with her role as Jack there to spy, yes, but also be in a pseudo-relationship with Terryn, the consensus across the board was to delete that particular body part from the masquerade. The beauty of the chameleon was how *real* their incredible skill was. However, the energy they copied could not change or the whole thing was off.

Fingers or even a brush could be run through hair, but if scissors were added to the equation and the energy was altered, the ruse vanished. Every person, every animal, every living thing was nothing more than an elaborate illusion of energy. The chameleon simply copied and wore that energy like an outfit.

However, they had to be true to that energy at the time it was copied: hairstyle, facial hair style, and in Jack's case, if a flaccid penis had come with the persona, how his physicality had been in that moment was how it had to stay. Being in such close quarters with Terryn, or anyone for that matter, if Jack had gotten a wee bit excited and changed the state of his penis, the illusion would have disappeared. There were just too many unknowns to take a chance like that.

Normally, Ava would simply borrow the energy from someone she'd known or been around. In this case, and in light of just how important this mission was, all hands on deck had come up with her most elaborate ruse yet. Jack didn't exist, had never existed. He was literally Ava's own energy taken and folded in with who she would have been if she were male.

The head of the chameleons had gotten involved, along with Ankou and Enori's incredible ability to manipulate energy. All of it had essentially been tossed into a mystic's mixing bowl and thrown up onto Frank's projection screen. Ava had studied the resulting image from every angle.

Jack had a man's upper body, so she took it all in, absorbed that energy and understanding. So very different than her own body, which was obviously still beneath that coat of energy, easily recalled and reinstituted.

She'd played men before, but it had been short-term and no clothing was removed or changed for daily living, so details hadn't mattered. Now, she would have to live amongst these people, and she had to be able to pull this off. She and Terryn would both be playing roles, not really involved but would have to live as if they were. No situational details could be spared.

She'd spent the day with Enori and Roishin wearing Jack, getting his walk, his attitude, and his personality. He was a lot like her, of course, but she had to get used to his voice, taken from a young man she'd known well in DC. When the ladies had felt he was ready to go live, Roishin had opened the door for her.

Now, she strolled into the cave-like space of the tailor's shop, not a care in the world, even as she had eyes all over her head at all times. Jack's smile was large as he walked over to the woman who had asked him to go grab the bolts of fabric.

"Miss Lisa!" Jack strutted over to the woman who ran the shop in an exaggerated way that made the woman laugh. Grinning, Jack eased the bolts off his shoulders and gently leaned them against the wall. "Here you go."

"Thank you, sweetie. I truly appreciate it." The older woman followed Jack's glance then looked back to him. "Go talk to her," she urged, giving him a playful nudge.

Jack gave her a sheepish grin as if "busted" when he hadn't meant to be. The more people that saw interest or interaction between the two, the better. Hands clasped behind his back, Jack meandered his way through the workstations to the one at the very back. The auburn head was bowed as Terryn focused on her work. Her long hair was pulled up into a messy bun.

Ava had to admit, Terryn was a really beautiful young woman. The storms that were her eyes were captivating. She was also incredibly quiet and shy, and it was proving hard to get to know her. She was very much within herself, neither her expression nor body language giving a lot away.

Though Ava understood why, as she was getting an idea of where Terryn had grown up, it made her job harder. She was trying to find an angle that would look natural for the two young people to connect on.

The very stormy eyes Ava had remembered so well glanced up at her from her task. It looked like she was fixing some buttons on a shirt. Her smile was small when she spotted the young man strolling up to her station.

"Hi," Terryn said.

Jack grinned at her. "Hi, yourself." He looked around, noting nobody was paying attention to them. Bending down so his forearms rested on the table where she was working, he met her gaze. "So, how do I go about asking you out?" He was amused at the little blush that colored pale cheeks. "Like, do I need to talk to your dad, or…?"

Terryn looked back down to what she was doing before shrugging a shoulder. "Probably wouldn't hurt." She spared a glance back to him. "Make it more real."

Nodding, Jack said, "I can do that."

"Though," Terryn added, almost as an afterthought. She set the shirt down in her lap as she gave Jack her full attention. "I'm not entirely sure there is any 'asking out' to be done, honestly."

"What do you mean?"

"I don't think dating is necessarily a prelude to a relationship here. From what I've seen, if a guy is interested, well…" Again, she shrugged.

Jack's eyebrows shot up, and he leaned in closer to not be overheard. "Am I supposed to just club you like some goddamn caveman　?" he hissed.

Terryn wasn't successful at hiding her smile but nodded grimly. "Essentially." She tilted her head slightly and looked into Jack's stunned gaze. "You have to figure… *Jack*," she said, seeming to nearly say another name but saved herself at　the last second. "We've all grown up together, overall. So, interest is pretty much a known thing." She shrugged again. "It just kind of becomes an expectation that Person A and Person B will end up together once they come of age."

Jack gave her a lopsided grin. "No Person B for you?"

Terryn shook her head, giving Jack a shy glance. In that moment, Ava was able to see so much sadness in Terryn's eyes. Such a lost soul in so many ways. She wanted to get her out of the tunnels, out of the Shadows, and to a world where she could be herself, whatever and whoever that was. She recognized herself during her years on the earth plane in Terryn. She was dying inside.

It was so easy to see the beautiful person that rested inside those gray eyes, if only given the chance to blossom. Yes, this was a mission for information, but she decided in that moment that it was also a mission to get Terryn the hell out of there, no matter what the bigger picture ended up being.

Making up her mind, Jack leaned forward and left a lingering kiss on full lips, a stunned Terryn looking back at her as she moved away. "Done," Jack said softly. "Claimed."

⚜⚜⚜⚜

"So, you're tellin' me that there's other places out there?"

"Aye, I am."

"No way. That's a lie. Raif says so."

Garratt shrugged and glanced to the man who was helping him cut up the branches that Jack and some of the other guys were gathering. "Who was born here?" he asked reasonably. "Me or Raif?"

Curious on what the other guy—who she thought was named Allistair—would say, Jack listened. Nothing was said, though it was clear the other man was pondering what he'd just been told. Jack was in the middle of sorting the huge armload he'd just brought in. Those that needed to be picked free of little thorny branches were placed in one pile, while those that were ready for chopping were placed in another.

"You got more for us, kid?" Garratt asked, standing at the stump with axe in hand.

"Yes, sirree!" Jack gathered an armload of the "ready for chopping" pile and carried them over to the two sweat-soaked men. He dumped them in the thinning pile they'd been working from.

Garratt studied him, blue eyes sharp and intense. He looked over Jack's face, took in the shaggy, midnight locks that badly needed a trim. He took in the lanky body and curious gaze. For a moment,

Ava was beginning to get very worried. Even so, she took advantage of the close proximity and absorbed and memorized Garratt's energy to show Roishin later, to see if she could make a positive identification of her brother.

"What about you, kid?" Garratt finally said, his gaze meeting Jack's dark eyes. "You think there's more out there?" He shrugged a broad shoulder. "You want to see it?"

Jack ran a hand through his hair. "You know, sometimes I do. Wanna think there's more than this." He indicated the wooded land surrounding them and the tunnel entrance not half a mile away. He grinned sheepishly. "Then other times, I kinda like being a gopher."

Garratt smirked, slapping Jack on the shoulder. "I like you."

Jack grinned big, chest puffed out a bit that an older guy took interest in his thoughts—certainly so Garratt would think so. "What about you?" he asked. "What's out there?"

Garratt looked at him, that intense gaze almost glowing with the promise behind his next words. "Oh, there's a whole world out there, Jack, and I fully intend to show you. All of you."

"That's cool as shit, man," Jack whispered, eyes wide in excitement. "Sometimes it can be so suffocating, you know?" He took his voice low, barely audible.

Garratt nodded, looking around at the other guys helping them. "Yeah, but it doesn't have to be this way." He met Jack's gaze again. "Wouldn't you agree?"

Ava felt that was a completely loaded question if

she'd ever heard one. It was layered and asking many questions within what seemed like a simple pondering posed. "Totally," Jack said sagely.

Garratt grinned, and it wasn't one that made Ava feel particularly good. He slapped Jack playfully on the shoulder. "Naïve kid." With that, he turned his back on him, summarily dismissing him.

Jack swallowed and returned to his task. Ava's heart was racing. She needed to talk to Terryn. They needed to get out of the tunnels and go on a "date," or whatever. She needed to really be able to talk to her to understand the tunnels and the system.

❧❧❧❧❧

That night at dinner, it absolutely killed Ava to be plopped down in the middle of a bunch of men and boys shoveling in food while women and girls served them. It was insane. And, it wasn't even as if these women were servants, like in Roishin's world growing up. These were sisters, wives, daughters, and grandmothers.

Jack kept to himself, eyeing everyone as he ate. No expression on his face, no real interest in any one thing, so it would seem. He did, however, have an eye out for one particular serving wench. Since seeing Terryn in the tailor shop earlier in the day, they hadn't seen nor spoken to each other.

Jack visibly perked up as he stuffed a bite of pork into his mouth when Terryn hurried from the kitchen, a large jug in her hands. He watched as she went from table to table like a little beautiful bee pollinating the flowers as she went. She glanced over and met Jack's gaze. He raised his mug with an expectant look that said, *Anytime, now.*

Terryn gave him a small smile before purposefully

heading to a table in the opposite direction. Jack chuckled, amused as he set his mug down and returned to his food. He glanced to his right when he felt a nudge to his shoulder. A man sat there, perhaps in his forties, his light brown hair smoothed back from his grizzled face.

"Thank you can get yourself a piece of that?" he asked, shoving what was left of his dinner roll into his mouth as he studied Jack.

"What?" Jack asked, using his teeth to tear a piece of meat off the pork chop.

"Terryn," the man clarified, nodding in the general direction where the young redhead was filling mugs. "I know lots of men 'round here been tryin' for years with that one."

"She not interested?" Jack asked, taking a sip from the last bit of ale in his mug. He'd been taking it slow, as Ava wasn't much of a drinker and had little tolerance. The last thing she needed was for an inebriated Jack to do or say something stupid.

He shrugged. "Not real sure. I know her twin has taken down more than one man who's gotten a little too handsy, if you follow."

Jack nodded. "I do." His gaze found Terryn again, now talking to one of the other women serving. It looked like she was receiving instructions of some sort, Terryn's body language stiff, at attention. Her hair was pulled back and covered by what amounted to be a bandana. She looked tired after a long day.

"I know her father a bit," the man continued, garnering Jack's attention again. "If you think you can nab her, kid, you should." The man looked around them to see if anyone was listening. Seeing that nobody was, he looked back to Jack. "Word has it Raif has his eye on her. Already got his two wives knocked up, lookin' like he wants a third."

Ava felt sick at the reminder. "Jeez," Jack said.

The man nodded. "Yup. She's what he likes, young and beautiful. But, whereas the other two got some spunk, Terryn's shy and timid." He met Jack's gaze again. "Not so sure she'd survive it, ya know?"

Jack nodded. There were so many questions he wanted to ask this guy about how things worked, his rights, and all that. But the problem was, Jack would know this already. So, in some ways, Ava had painted herself into a corner by Jack so easily fitting in. There had to be other ways to find out.

Jack and the man he sat next to were pulled out of their conversation when voices began to raise. A couple tables over, Terryn was pinned to the wall by a man easily twice her age. Some of the men at the table next to them were hooting and hollering while others were calling for the man to leave her alone.

Ava groaned inwardly. Jack pushed up from the table, and to her surprise, so did the man he'd been talking to. On a mission—literally—Jack reached the two. Ava's blood was boiling and filled with pure rage, and from the look on Terryn's face when terrified gray eyes swung over to look at her, it was written all over Jack's face.

Knowing there was no other option, Jack grabbed the man by the back of his shirt, yanking him away from the young woman who looked as though she were trying to disappear into the stone wall she was forced up against. The older man sneered down at him, easily three or four inches taller than Jack.

Using what Enori had taught her, Ava focused on her energy, gathering it before she grabbed the front of the man's shirt and, letting that energy go like a slingshot, her punch sent the man flying back several feet and onto his ass. When he landed, he brought up a hand, blood on his fingertips from the corner of his mouth.

"Anyone else?" Jack called out, reaching for Terryn, who immediately moved in against him as his arm wrapped around her waist.

Nobody said a word. In fact, the dining hall was as quiet as a tomb.

Ava could feel Terryn trembling against her, but to her shock, a hand slid into Jack's hair and pulled him down into a kiss. The kiss that morning in the tailor's shop was the first time Ava had kissed anyone, and this was her second. She had no clue what she was doing, but in that moment, she knew Terryn was making a public declaration that they were a couple.

Ava responded as best she could, the two women, doing the best they could under the circumstances. It was sloppy and it was awkward, but it wasn't about love, wasn't even about passion. It was making a point, and it was giving them both cover. After a breathless moment, the kiss came to an end.

Her hand still in Jack's hair, Terryn looked up into Jack's dark eyes. Ava could see the fear in them from the events moments before, but she also saw something else in their stormy depths. Perhaps it was relief. Jack gave her a comforting smile and lightly brushed his fingertips over her cheek. *It's okay, everything will be okay*, it said.

Chapter Sixteen

Terryn's hands were still shaking after she'd left Jack and gone back into the kitchen. She felt like she was near tears but dared not let them fall. Yes, of course she'd known who Jack was and yes, of course she understood their agreement. But, in the dining hall just now, part of her had grabbed him and kissed him just to make it stop.

She'd known young women over her life who had latched on to the first guy who had come a-courtin'. Her mother was an example of that. Regardless of what her life may be with the man, at least it was only that *one* man. Tonight, out there, if Jack hadn't stepped in, it would have been a free-for-all, and Terryn didn't want to think about what could have happened.

For some crazy reason, when a woman hit twenty years old in the tunnels, it was an unwritten rule that it was open season on her, and the hunters came crawling out of the walls. Was it possible to just be happy? She'd love nothing more than to know what that was like. To be happy, and even more than that, to feel safe. Was that possible for a woman?

Her mind went to the night she'd first met Ava, Anise, Enori, and Roishin. After everything had happened and it had just been Roishin and Enori standing out there alone, they'd shared a wonderful hug and a kiss. It wasn't like Raif's two wives, and god only knew if he'd forced them to do that. With Enori and Roishin, it seemed they did that because they *wanted* to. It was out of love.

Did they do the things Raif's wives had done, too? And did so because they were a couple and not in a madman's harem? It wasn't that Terryn thought that's what she wanted. Hell, she had no idea what she wanted, if she wanted anything at all. Well, other than freedom, that is.

Her lips still tingled from when she'd kissed Jack, a.k.a. Ava, a few moments before. But she knew that was simply because she'd never kissed anyone, and in that moment it was the only thing she could do to feel even remotely safe.

She started when she was touched on the arm. Raelene stood next to her, concern on her face. Terryn tried to get her emotions under control but was struggling mightily. "Sorry," she whispered. "Just give me a second, and—"

"No," the blond woman said. She nodded toward the entrance to the kitchen. "Why don't you go with him. Take off a little early."

Terryn was surprised to see Jack standing there. He looked incredibly concerned and, frankly, a bit scared himself. She looked back to her friend. "Are you sure?"

"Absolutely. That was a really frightening situation. We've all been there," she said, indicating the other women in the kitchen. "Go get yourself under control, and we'll see you tomorrow, okay?"

Terryn nodded. "Okay. Thank you." She gave the other woman, just a handful of years older than herself, as much of a smile as she could muster before walking over to the door and Jack. She looked up into his dark gaze, Ava's eyes looking back at her. "Hey."

"Hi," he said. "Are you okay?" He nodded behind her toward the kitchen. "I didn't get you into trouble, did I?"

Terryn shook her head, giving him a weak smile. "No. They told me to leave early, get over this."

Jack nodded. "Can I walk you home? Then I'll know you're okay."

The first genuine smile of the evening graced Terryn's lips, even if it was small. "That's really sweet." She nodded. "Aye."

"Well, hey," Jack said, deepening his voice dramatically as he held his arm out to her. "Gotta protect my lady."

They shared a brief smile before Terryn wrapped her fingers around the bend of Jack's arm. They made their way out of the dining hall, ignoring everyone. She heard a few whistles at the "newly announced couple" but didn't care. She felt so overwhelmed by emotion and fear that she almost felt numb.

"The guy sitting next to me at dinner said you don't date," Jack said conversationally. "That they've tried."

Terryn nodded. "That is true." She blew out a long, tired breath. She felt so tired all the time, soul tired.

"Why?"

Terryn stopped their walking, the two in a tunnel between the community areas and the living areas. She took her hand away from Jack's arm and tucked her hands between her body and the cold stone wall. She looked at Jack, who moved to stand next to her. He crossed his arms over his chest and leaned a shoulder against the stone.

"I don't want to be anyone's property," Terryn said honestly. Shrugging, she continued. "I've never met anyone that I want to be with." She let out another tired sigh as she rested her head back against the stone. "I just wish I could be left alone. You know?"

"I do," Jack said. "I don't have to deal with the way things are here, but I absolutely understand the haven't-met-anybody part."

Terryn glanced over at him. "Really?"

Jack gave her a sad smile. "Yeah."

Turning, Terryn mirrored his position. She studied him for a long moment, again able to see Ava through it. It was so strange, almost like seeing into two different worlds at the same time. She figured it was likely because she knew she was in there, somehow.

"Will you tell me about your world sometime?" she asked softly.

"Of course." Jack grinned and shrugged the shoulder that wasn't pressed to the wall. "I was actually going to ask you if we can leave here at some point. I need to talk to you," He looked around the empty tunnel they occupied. "I can answer all your questions then, too." He smirked. "Don't think it's wise here."

Terryn nodded. "Sure. I'm off day after tomorrow. Will that work?"

Jack nodded. "Absolutely."

Terryn felt so comfortable with this person, and it threw her off. Other than her brother, she didn't feel truly comfortable around anyone. And, even with Laird, she had to be careful. No doubt it was because Jack—well, *Ava*—understood her better than anyone in these tunnels. At least the fact that she had crazy abilities she didn't understand.

Swallowing and feeling a little shy, she glanced up into calm, dark eyes. "Thank you for tonight." Terryn tucked her bottom lip in, again her emotions pricking at the backs of her eyes. "Um…" Her voice broke on that one damn word.

She looked away, as she felt stupid and small, but then gentle hands turned her around and, to her shock, Ava stood before her.

Terryn was gathered into Ava's embrace, warm and comforting. That was it. Terryn broke. She was held tightly, the back of her head cradled against Ava's shoulder. She honestly didn't know why, but Terryn allowed herself to really cry.

As safe as she felt around Jack, somehow with Ava, it was different. No doubt because she was another woman and because she was the *whole* person, but Terryn felt she was able to let go. Ava said nothing, simply held her. She was so soft, so warm, and so incredibly kind and compassionate in that hug.

Terryn had never known affection, other than a quick one-armed hug on occasion from her twin. So, in that moment it was really hard to not just stay there for the sake of feeling another human being.

After a while, she forced herself back under control, the strongest wave of everything washing through and over her. She sniffled as she calmed down, Ava's hand rubbing soothing patterns over her back.

"Are you okay?" she asked softly in Terryn's ear.

Nodding, Terryn made herself let the warm comfort go. She lifted her head and stepped away, using her hands to wipe at her eyes. "Sorry," she murmured.

"Don't you dare be," Ava said. a hand resting on Terryn's shoulder.

Terryn looked at her, taking her in. She shook her head in wonder. "I don't know that I'll ever get used to this." She chuckled, taking in the woman standing before her. She was all woman, curves and all. It was mind-boggling, considering who she'd been mere moments before.

Ava grinned. "Oh, trust me," she said, Jack's lopsided grin on her lips. "I get it. It's a lot of fun passing a mirror."

Terryn burst into laughter, and it felt damn good. The laughter was halted when she heard footfalls coming from farther down the tunnel. She glanced over her shoulder toward the sound of the voices she heard chatting. Turning back, she came face-to-face with Jack.

"I am going to lose my mind before all this is over," she muttered.

Jack grinned and reached out his hand. "Come on."

⁂

Later that night, after being dropped off at home with another hug from Jack, Terryn lay in her sleep nook. She stared up at the ceiling with her hands behind her head. She felt so immensely better about so many things. Part of it was the whole Jack/Ava thing. She trusted Ava, and of course then by proxy, Jack.

Something had occurred to her, though. Ava had no reason to stay once she'd gathered the information she needed. She would leave, thus taking Jack with her. What then? She'd be left in the hunting grounds again—that was what. She hated to allow dark thoughts to crowd in when she'd finally found a sense of peace for the first time in far too long.

And honestly, she was beginning to see Ava as a friend. She trusted her and she liked her. She wondered what she was like to just hang out with, go exploring with. No mask required, just two young women talking and laughing as friends. She'd never experienced that before. Laird had been the only friend she'd ever had. A friend of any real consequence, anyway.

Sure, she had Raelene in the kitchen and some of the women she worked with at the shop, but in the tunnels, the women were mostly worried about survival. Survival came in horrible shades of jealousy to keep a "good man," or face what was left. It came in shades of wanting to keep a good job.

Women were pitted against women. Women didn't

do any job that the men did, only other women. It was ridiculous and so sad, Terryn thought. Honestly, the women should be banding together, not fighting amongst themselves. When she'd seen those four women that night—Roishin, Enori, Anise, and Ava—all working together as one… Wow, that had been eye-opening!

"So, were you going to tell me about him?"

Terryn was pulled from her thoughts by her brother's voice as he entered their bedroom. She turned her head and glanced down at him as he undressed for bed. "What?"

"Jack," he said, looking up to meet her gaze. "Did you have to do that tonight, Terryn? In front of everyone?"

She was stunned as she stared at him, totally left speechless. Finally, she managed to find her voice again. "Do what? As I recall, it was that jerk who started it."

"Make out with him?" he said, ignoring her last words. "Like a goddamn whore."

She rolled to her side and lifted herself to her forearm. "How dare you talk to me like that, Laird," she said in a near whisper, hurt in her tone. "I did *not* make out with him. I wanted it to be known that Jack and I are a couple."

"Since when?" He walked over to the wall, her sleep nook just a couple inches above his head. He rested his hand on the ladder she climbed to get there.

"Since I was threatened to find someone or else," she said, voice growing stronger, angry. "We're going to be twenty soon, Laird. You know what that means."

"What?" he asked, tugging off his shirt and throwing it to the floor.

"It means that you're completely and totally fine and your life doesn't change while *I* am now up for grabs for any asshole who thinks he can get away with it. That's what." She leaned out a bit farther, glaring down at him.

"And, furthermore, where were you? Huh?" she demanded when he didn't answer.

Laird looked away, though not before she saw the guilt in his eyes.

"Maybe if you had been man enough to stand up for me tonight, I wouldn't have had to turn to Jack, Laird." The words were out of her mouth before she could stop them. She wanted to clap her hand over her mouth but somehow managed to restrain herself. No, he needed to hear that.

He glared back up at her. "So, do I have to listen to you two fuck like rabbits in here now?"

She was left nearly breathless at the very words. She swallowed and shook her head. "No, Prince Laird. Your sleep won't be disturbed." With that, she scooted back into her nook and lay down, facing the wall.

⁂

The next morning at breakfast, once again Terryn sat with her family. She was sandwiched between her parents, Laird not even giving her a second glance or a first word. Terryn was busy eating her scrambled eggs when she felt eyes on her. Glancing up, she saw Jack sitting by himself. He sent her a smile when he saw he had her attention. She returned it and waved him over.

He dramatically looked behind him in both directions before looking at her again, eyebrows raised in question and fingers indicating himself. She grinned and nodded. Laird, who was sitting across and to the right of his sister, saw her actions and glanced over his shoulder. Rolling his eyes, he turned back to his food.

Jack gathered his dish and mug and stepped out from the bench seat he'd been sitting on and made his way over to their table. He stood there, looking uncertain.

"Sit down, boy," Ronan said around the mouthful of eggs he'd just shoveled into his mouth. "Need to speak to ya," he added, as if he were the one who had invited him over.

"Sir," Jack said, setting his plate and mug down before stepping over the bench to sit down next to Laird and across from Terryn. The two quickly met gazes before Jack looked to Terryn's father, who sat to Terryn's left. "How are you today, sir?" he asked politely.

Ronan stared at him over the brim of his mug as he took a slow drink of his morning ale. It would be the first of many, many mugs of ale that day, and Terryn was just glad that her father was lucid enough to have this conversation. "You gonna do right by my daughter?" he finally asked.

Jack looked at him then glanced to Terryn, only to look back at Ronan. "Sir?"

"You can move in, boy," the older man grumbled, eyeing Jack as he set his mug down. "I know you ain't got no kin here. But I'm warnin' ya," he said, pointing a finger at the younger man. "You get her knocked up, you stay and be a man about it. Got me?"

Terryn covered her face with her hands, groaning inwardly. She was eternally embarrassed.

"I ain't gonna look after your brats, got me? I done raised my kids," Ronan continued, indicating the twins with a general wave of his hand.

"Um," Jack mumbled, a hand rubbing the back of his neck. Terryn wondered if   the skin was warm to the touch as his face was flushed in embarrassment. "Yes, sir. I take care of my responsibilities."

Terryn had to bite down on her lower lip at that one. She had no idea how Jack was managing to stay so serious and stoic. You'd think the two had been having discussions about this very thing for months now.

Ronan nodded. "All right," he said, sounding placated.

Terryn met Jack's wide gaze, stifling a giggle at the look there. The moment of amusement was interrupted when Laird slammed to his feet. Without a word, he gathered his plate and mug and headed to another table with some of the guys he worked with, including the new guy, Garratt.

"What's with him?" Ronan asked, sparing a glance to his son but not looking at his daughter as he returned his attention to his plate.

"I honestly don't know," Terryn said. "He started acting this way last night."

"Probably jealous," Blair said, her weak voice surprising them all.

Terryn looked over at her. "Jealous? Why?"

"He hasn't found anyone," the feeble woman said, barely picking at her breakfast.

"Are you okay, Mom?" Terryn asked softly, placing her arm around the bird-thin frame of her mother.

"Don't feel good," Blair muttered.

"Help her home," Ronan said, reaching across his daughter to snatch a partial piece of bacon left on Blair's plate.

Without question, Terryn pushed up to her feet, noticing that Jack did, too. He hurried around the table until he could take Blair's other side. He grinned down at her. "Hi there, ma'am," he said sweetly. "Let's get you lying down."

Blair said nothing, the two young people helping her back to the family home. Nothing was said, as it never was. Terryn, her father, and brother knew she was dying, but it was never talked about. She'd been sick off and on most of her children's lives, though with what, Terryn had no idea.

Finally, they reached the home, and Tarryn and Jack got the older woman to her sleep nook. "Want the blanket on you, Mom?" Terryn asked softly. At Blair's nod, Terryn accepted it from Jack, who had pulled it up from where it was shoved at the foot of the nook. Her mother all tucked in, Terryn took a step back, as did Jack. Hands on hips, she glanced over to him, his dark eyes already on her.

With a shrug and shake of her head, Terryn turned and left the bedroom. Jack stepped across the hall, entering the room Terryn shared with Laird. He looked around before looking at Terryn.

"Yours?"

"Yup." Terryn walked over to the wall that held the nooks. She gripped the ladder with her hand. "Mine is up there." She nodded upward.

Jack looked up at it then at her with a raised eyebrow. "Had to be up high, didn't it?"

She grinned. "Penthouse."

He chuckled before growing serious. "I don't want to cause problems for you with your brother, Terryn." He indicated Laird's sleep nook next to where he stood. "If it's an issue—"

"Then he'll have to get over it," she finished. "I'm tired of doing everything he wants, tired of not getting what *I* want."

Terryn didn't even know what she meant by that except that she wanted to help Ava with her mission. She wanted her to have a safe, comfortable place to sleep and wanted to be there for her as Ava *and* Jack had been there for her.

She reached out and lightly tugged on his hand. "Come on. Let's leave and let her sleep."

Chapter Seventeen

It would have been extremely amusing if Roishin didn't have to stay on her toes with these guys. The one who had been wielding the sword, Mikael, stood in the sand, feet spread wide and head back as he groaned almost obscenely. The amount of urine that man was releasing into the sand spoke of someone who had been holding it for some time. All unnecessarily, mind you, as a container had been provided to them in the cave.

The container which she'd made them carry out and dump its contents. It lay on its side in the sand as the other man, Britt, who had received the Enori treatment, walked around. He seemed to be stretching his legs. The two men had already eaten the food Roishin had brought for them that day, a routine she'd done for the five days they'd been in captivity.

Each day, she'd tried to talk to them and each day, they'd refused. Her gaze fell to Mikael when he seemed to finally be finished. "Feel better?" she asked.

"What do you want from us?" Britt asked. Between the two, he seemed to be less of a hothead. She'd actually had a couple of decent conversations with him over the days. Mikael, on the other hand, held his misogynistic views to the point he'd rather die than give in to a woman. So be it.

Roishin met his gaze. "Information," she said simply.

"About what?" he asked, finally seeming to want to know, to make progress.

"Don't talk to her, Britt!"

The man with dark hair glared over at the other man. "Mikael, I want out of here. That ain't gonna happen unless she gets what she wants, so shut up." He turned back to Roishin. "Information about what?"

A valid question. Roishin looked at both men, even if the one with shaggy blond hair refused to look at her. "Do you guys know where we are right now?"

"A godforsaken place in the middle of nowhere," Mikael bit back, glaring at her.

"Right now, yes," she agreed. "This, gentlemen, is called the borderlands. Right now, it may as well be the moon." She indicated the cloudy skies above. "But it wasn't always like this. You see, you call where you live, the Shadows." She nodded. "Good name for it, because it's become a shadow of what it once was."

"That's crap," Mikael exclaimed. "It's always been like this."

"Oh yeah?" she challenged. "Did Raif tell you that? Maybe your parents?" He looked away, so she continued. "The borderlands are part of the Shadows, or better known once upon a time as Bowhar."

"What's Bowhar?" Britt asked.

"It was a huge metropolis, Britt. Filled with people, commerce, and all above ground." She looked to Mikael. "People didn't live underground like rats."

"We live in the tunnels to keep us safe," Britt said, anger in his voice.

"From what?" she asked.

The two men looked at each other, neither seeming to have an answer. Finally, Mikael glared at her. "From evil like you."

"Evil, huh?" she said, crossing her arms over her chest and pushing her weight to one hip in a casual stance. "If I were evil, I would have killed you already rather than taking time out of my day to feed you and take you out to pee, like you were my pet dog."

"You're keeping us locked up," Britt said. "And *that's* why you have to come feed us."

"Aye," she agreed, nodding. "Because you two tried to attack four innocent women." She looked from one to the other. "No questions asked, just attacked. At least I'm feeding your stupid asses. Can you imagine what would have happened to us women had we been captured trying to attack you?" She raised her eyebrows in emphasis.

"You'd get what you deserve!" Mikael growled and began to charge her.

Annoyed, she opened a door and stepped out ten feet to the north. She watched as the man stumbled through where she'd been standing a second before and fell flat on his face in the sand. Even Britt was looking at him like he was an idiot.

"Look," she said, over all of it. "You both have been lied to, *all* of you have been, for generations. And why?" she asked, looking from one to the other. "To keep you down, literally underground. You think you're captive here, Mikael?" The man staggered to his feet, the entire front of his body and face covered in fine sand. "Raif and the men before him are who have truly kept you captive."

"I don't believe you," he roared, spitting sand out of his mouth and brushing it off his face and from his eyelashes.

"I don't care," she countered. "You think you're a big man, Mikael. Why? Because you take your frustrations out on the women or those you perceive as weaker than you because *you* have been all but castrated by Raif and the other leaders." She smirked. "Yet, four women kicked your ass. And today, only one woman did." She held up a finger. "You want to get mad? Then get mad! Get mad at those who have lied to you, kept you living in the dark. You should be living up here." She indicated the barren landscape around them. "In the fresh air and sunlight. And, you can."

She glanced over to Britt, who was chewing on his bottom lip. Clearly he had heard her and was contemplating what she'd said. He sent a side glance her way.

"What do you want us to do?" Britt said, and everything about him changed, from his tone to his stance.

She met his gaze. "Tell me all that you know," she said. "And then fight with us."

⁂

They were back in the cave, sans Mikael. He'd flatly refused to help and said he'd rather take his chances in the borderlands then go back to the cave. Now, Roishin was torn. She knew he'd die out there, as there was no food or water source and no protection from the elements. If it was like any other desert, it got very cold at night.

"He made his choice," Britt said quietly as they stepped inside the cave.

She looked at him. She had the feeling Britt could be a good guy, *wanted* to be a good guy even. "Why is he like that?" she asked. "So angry and stubborn."

Hands on hips, he shrugged, meeting her gaze. The man she was looking at now was more relaxed and almost looked relieved. "What you said is right," he said. "It's miserable down there. Cramped, people on top of people. Pretty barbaric, honestly. Men fighting over women like they were animals." He blew out a breath and ran a hand through his hair, the greasy, shaggy strands flopping back into his eyes.

Immediately, Roishin thought about Terryn and

Ava. "Tell me about Raif."

He leaned against a wall, arms crossed casually over his chest. "He's been the leader now for about six or seven years, I guess. Comes off as a nice guy, helpful, all that, but don't cross him." He eyed her. "He's brutal, Roishin. I'd say one step from crazy."

Roishin had to fight her instincts to head over there right now and yank out the two women immediately. "How'd he come into power?"

"Challenged the last guy to battle. Killed him like that." He snapped his fingers. "He got a lot of the guys, like Mikael, to buy into   it. Promised us we'd become stronger, expand." He shook his head. "All he did was close his grip even tighter on the people. Started collecting wives for himself." He eyed her. "That kid you brought in here that first night, hot little redhead? Word has it he's got a hard on for her."

"Will he force it?" Roishin asked, again thinking of Terryn and Ava down there. She hoped like hell their plan had worked with Jack to at least buy them some time.

"Oh, hell yeah!" He nodded to back up his words.

She wondered, staring off into space as she absently rubbed her chin. "What does he want?"

"Power," Britt said simply. "I think he never had any intention of expanding our community, bringing in any of the others. I think he likes to keep it small and compact."

"Easier to control," she murmured.

"Yup."

Taking a deep breath, she finally forced herself to ask. "And, what of this new guy, Garratt?" She turned to look at him, wanting to read his reaction to the name.

Britt shrugged a shoulder. "He's okay, I guess. Don't know him all that well. Quiet guy. Helpful."

"What are the qualifications for Raif to allow in a

newcomer?"

He smirked. "If you've got a pussy or he feels he can find a use for you."

"So, he felt he could find a use for Garratt, I'm assuming?" she drawled. The guy may *be* a pussy, but he lacked one physically, she thought ruefully.

"Well, yeah. Garratt's a big, strong guy. He's got this almost militant way about him. Raif no doubt thought he could bring him into his personal guard or something," Britt explained.

Roishin nodded. Made sense. The way he described him was totally her brother, and with Terryn's physical description, she was pretty sure it was one and the same. *Damn it.* Finally, she eyed him.

"Britt," she said, walking over to him. "What do you want for yourself?"

He met her gaze, and in the depths of his eyes she saw a man who wanted peace. "I want a family," he admitted. "I wanna be a farmer." He grinned, dimples sinking through the facial hair that grizzled his features. "Pretty simple, really."

She nodded, giving him a smile. "We can make it happen, Britt. If you'll trust me."

He shrugged a shoulder again. "Weirdly, I do. And I ain't got nothin' down there anymore. Folks died when the sickness spread through the tunnels last year. I got no wife, no kids." He shrugged again. "Just me. And," he said, his gaze boring into hers. "There are more of us, you know."

"Meaning? People who want out?"

"Well, yeah, but no, that ain't what I mean."

She looked him in the eye, his gaze unwavering. Reading him loud and clear, she asked, "Do you guys talk about it? Who you are?"

He shook his head. "Hell no. Easiest way to get

yourself killed. Why do you think Mikael and I went after you gals?"

"So," she said. "You go after your own kind, then?"

"Got no choice, Roishin. Me or them," he said softly.

"How many?"

"Dozen or so that I know of." He smirked. "Including that little redhead. I ain't never talked to her about it—or anything else, for that matter. But I sense it, you know? She ain't like me, but she's got something in the blood."

"Do you all communicate with each other?" Roishin asked, stunned at this new information.

"Nah. Can't. Well, the ones who I know and who know me, we got this knock." He turned to the wall and knocked a quick but simple rhythm before turning back to her. "Kinda like, if you recognize this, then you get it. You know?"

Perfect, she thought. She *had* to meet with Ava. "Okay, I'm taking you somewhere where you can get a bath, fresh clothes, a meal, and a bed."

"Oh, thank god," he groaned.

She grinned. With a wave of her hand, she created a door, then grabbed his hand as she stepped through…

…and to the Underground. They were in a dead-end tunnel, out of the way of everyone else. Lit torches sent shadows dancing across the stone walls. He looked around, confusion on his face.

"Wait, I thought you were taking me somewhere else."

She grinned. "I did."

"These are the tunnels," he said.

"Not *your* tunnels." She knocked her knuckles on the stone wall that was the dead end. "Five-foot slab of stone separating your tunnels from what we call the

Underground. Here you'll be safe, and they can work with you, see what you are."

She led him down the tunnel before creating a door to get them quickly to the massive library. She smiled as she pushed through the double doors. She hadn't been there in quite some time. The figure there turned to look at them, an open book in his hands.

"Britt, I'd like to introduce you to a guy we call the Mystic."

⁂

Her brown cloak in place, Roishin used the power of invisibility as she made her way back to the stream. She saw that the funeral pyre they'd built was still there, the flames long gone. It was nothing more than a pile of ash with bone fragments. It was eerie, and she wasn't sure what to do with it all.

Deciding to leave it be, she headed on. Mikael's sword was still stuck in the ground, right where Enori had left it. She thought she should hide it. Things had changed now, what with Mikael wandering in the borderlands and Britt joining their ranks. She yanked it out of the ground with a grunt and dropped it off in the cave before returning.

She looked in the direction of the tunnels. Closing her eyes, she reached out with her senses, feeling for her shadow. She could feel her, though it was almost muffled, for lack of a better way to put it. She knew that was because she was deep in the tunnel system, but she at least knew where to go.

Creating a door, she headed in that direction. Even if she had to hopscotch her way from door to door until she got closer, so be it. She knew she wasn't seen but had to be careful, as the shimmer of each door could be if someone were around and looking at the exact right place at the exact right moment. If they noticed that, they'd notice her.

The beauty of the cloak and the invisibility was playing on the fact that she wasn't being looked for, wasn't doing anything to be noticed or grab attention. Therefore, her energy blended in with everything else. Out of mind, out of sight.

Stepping out of the latest door, she moved away from it and paused. Sounds, and this time it wasn't that of birds or other wildlife. People, men. There was also the telltale sound of a blade chopping through wood: *Thwack! Thwack!* She was in a small wooded area, the tunnels down the way perhaps half a mile or so.

She could feel Terryn much stronger now, though it was still that strange, muffled feeling. She took in the men who were busy chopping wood and chatting amongst themselves. They were trading verbal barbs and jabs, good-natured teasing as men often do. She nearly cried out in relief when she saw Ava—well *Jack*—amongst them. He was loading chopped wood into a wheelbarrow.

Damn, she thought. It was crazy how good his disguise was. If she didn't know the truth and hadn't been there from planning to fruition, she'd never even suspect that underneath that cocky swagger was a lovely and feisty young woman. He was tossing barbs back at the men as good as he was getting.

Roishin watched, so very proud of her young friend and protégé in that moment. As she watched, Jack slowed his pace of pushing the wheelbarrow, dark head lifting, and he looked around. It looked as though he'd heard something. Roishin wondered if Ava sensed her. She moved out from behind the tree she'd been standing by and made her way over to the young man and his wheelbarrow.

Keeping her distance from him, she kept pace. She

was still hidden from anyone else by the trees. Roishin pursed her lips and began a very soft, almost haunting whistle. It wasn't like that of a bird or any other animal. She did it only for a few moments, just long enough to catch Jack's notice, which she did as he looked around again.

When dark eyes swung her way, she pushed the hood of the cloak down. The look of surprise in his eyes was quickly replaced with worry, then relief. He looked away from her.

"Hey, gonna take a piss!" he called out to his workmates.

"Go ahead," one of them called back.

"What are you doing here?" Jack hissed when the two had moved far from the crew.

"I just left Britt in the Underground," she explained. "He was one of the guys who tried to attack us."

Jack nodded. "He going to join us?" At Roishin's nod, Jack grinned. "Nice. The other one?"

"Wandering aimlessly in the borderlands until he dies."

Dark eyes opened wide. "Okay," he drawled.

"Long story," Roishin said, rolling her eyes. "How's it going with Terryn? Have you two made contact?"

Jack smirked and nodded. "Moving into the family home tomorrow."

Roishin's eyes nearly popped out of her head. "Well, that was fast."

Jack quirked an eyebrow, every inch of Ava in that expression. "Okay, *Enori*."

Roishin chuckled.

"Things work a little bit differently down in the tunnels than in real life, Roishin. It's insane."

Roishin nodded. "Exactly what Britt said. Listen, Ava," she said quietly. "It's very dangerous, and I need you to get out as soon as possible."

"I'm not leaving Terryn, Roishin," Jack said, voice quiet but firm. "She's dying down there like I was back in Washington DC."

Roishin nodded. "I agree. And," she added. "Britt said there are more down there. He said there's a dozen or so."

"Really?"

Roishin nodded. She turned to the tree next to them and recreated the knock Britt had done against the wall. She looked into Jack's eyes. "Memorize that. Britt said they use it to communicate, find out if someone is of the blood."

Jack repeated what Roishin had done and looked to her to make sure it was correct. At Roishin's nod, he said, "I think Garratt is trying to recruit."

"So," Roishin said. "You *do* think it's him?"

Jack nodded. "I can't show you here, but when we're in Duras I can."

"Damn it," Roishin whispered, running a hand through her hair. "Recruiting to do what?"

Jack shook his head with a shrug. "Don't totally know, but I think he's trying to sniff out who's unhappy here. I don't know, gut feeling, but I think he's going to try and take control."

Roishin nodded. "Okay." She took Jack into a bone-crushing embrace. "I need to go. You be safe."

"You, too," Ava said.

It made Roishin smile. She was so glad to hear her voice, the much smaller body in her arms as she squeezed one more time. She released her and looked into her face. "Use that knock, find out who is in there."

Ava nodded. "All right."

Roishin gave her a smile and pulled her hood back into place. She was about to leave but stopped at her name.

"Yeah?"

"We've got to see if there's more here, in the Shadows," Ava said.

Roishin gave her a shit-eating grin. "Why else do you think I'm here?"

Chapter Eighteen

She could feel the wind caress her face as she soared. Above was the light of the full moon, below her the tops of the trees as she flew above them at a speed that left them not much more than a silver-tipped blur. Finally, she cleared the trees and a vast, wide-open space spread out before her.

She felt so free. Looking down, she could see her shadow along the moonswept ground and was stunned to see that of a bird, wings spread wide as she coasted along the wind, riding the unseen waves of the skies. Up ahead she saw someone, a lone figure. They wore a cloak, the hood raised into place.

Getting closer, she knew who it was. Roishin. She was making good progress over the barren landscape. In the sky, she smiled and soared along with her, swooping down from time to time. Roishin looked up at her, grinning as she waved to the great black bird that was keeping her company.

Something caught her attention, and she left Roishin and flew up ahead. Ruins. The destruction of houses and buildings was everywhere. Broken timbers, crushed stone and debris. It was raining heavily, the ground growing saturated as she flew along it. There was a structure that was still largely intact, only a single wall missing. She could see the top of it, the roof somehow still there. She felt someone inside.

Swooping down, she flapped her wings as she cruised along just a few feet above the ground, rising above larger piles of rubble before gliding back down. She saw the house, the debris and destroyed stones easily to the waist of a person. Beyond it, in the darkness of the structure, two eyes looked out at her, watched her.

Finding a stone pillar, which once was a support and decorative column for a building, she flapped up to land atop it. Peering down at the house, she saw the eyes were looking up at her. No face, just the eyes and a golden glow within the darkness. Suddenly, the entire area of the ruins began to glow, the source unseen, though she knew it wasn't firelight.

Spooked, she flapped her wings and launched herself off the pillar. She had to tell Roishin.

Elsie shot up in bed, her chest heaving and hair falling into her face like a golden curtain from the sudden movement. She didn't even notice it, her heart racing so fast in her chest that she felt faint. She took several deep breaths as awareness came to her. She brought her hands up and pushed her hair back from her face, the strands tumbling down her naked back.

She was in her bed, the firelight painting everything a golden orange. Glancing to her left, she saw Isla still sound asleep. She lay on her left side, back to Elsie. Elsie considered cuddling up against her, but she didn't want to wake her. Isla had told her that she'd never slept so well as she did now sleeping next to Elsie every night.

And, considering they made love most nights, it sent them both off into calm, peaceful dreams. Or did it? Sitting there for a moment, Elsie saw snippets of her... dream again. Where had she been, and why did she keep going back there?

Not wanting to disrupt Isla's slumber, Elsie decided to get up, as she knew sleep was far from returning. She pushed the covers off her lower body and scooted out of bed as quietly as possible. Feet finding her slippers, they slid inside their warmth, and she stood. She could feel the cool night air on her nakedness, even as the fireplace warmed up the large chamber.

The strange thing was, as she walked over to the table where they ate their meals so often, Elsie felt that the coldness was coming from the inside and had nothing to do with the external night air. She grabbed her mug of watered-down wine she hadn't fully finished at dinner but had asked the servants to leave behind in case she wanted more later.

Her throat was so dry, as though she'd been chewing on dirt. *Or the wind as I flew around as a bird.* It had been so real, though. So terribly real, from the wind blowing over and around her body to the feeling of the cold stone beneath her feet when she landed.

Again, she saw it. The ruins all around her, so much destruction. She took another sip, enjoying the warming effects of the diluted wine within her system.

Closing her eyes, she brought up the hand that wasn't holding the cup and rubbed at them. They burned, both from exhaustion and also from something else. Her entire body felt strange, as though she'd just run to the king's residence and back again—which would take four days on horseback—in an hour.

The strangest part was that it wasn't her body that felt taxed. It wasn't sore muscles or legs or even a kink in her back. It was her mind. Her brain literally hurt, though it wasn't a headache.

She set the cup down on the table and walked to her boudoir and the beautifully intricate piece of furniture that was a jewelry box. It was a gift from the king and queen upon the birth of their granddaughter. Someday, she planned to hand it down to Mariota.

Lifting the top lid, she reached inside and took hold

of the single black feather that had rested upon the back of her chair the morning after the dream of Macha's visit. The dream where her large black raven had perched upon the back of that very same chair. Surely it had been a dream. Perhaps she'd even heard the squawk of a bird that had somehow found its way into her bedchamber and left a feather behind.

Perhaps hearing that while sleeping, her mind had added the featured creature to her dream. Surely. But, as she felt the softness of the black feather as her fingers lightly ran along its length, she didn't feel that was accurate.

"Elsie?"

She looked up to see Isla's silhouette in the dimness of the moonlight coming in through the arrow slit of a window. Elsie just stared at her for a moment, not fully feeling like herself. She felt like she was only partially inside her own body, the rest of her somewhere else, though she had no idea where. It was deeply unsettling and made her feel a bit nauseous.

She set the feather back inside her jewelry box and closed the lid before she walked over to Isla. Standing but a few inches from her now, Elsie could see her face. She looked back at her through sleepy eyes, though they seemed a bit confused and a bit worried. Elsie smiled at that. Her wonderful, beautiful, and deeply loved Isla. Always filled with so many emotions at once and somehow managing to present all of them in her eyes at the same time.

Smiling and feeling herself come a bit more solidly into her own body, Elsie brought her arms up. She snaked them around Isla's neck, her fingers burying themselves in the cool strands of her long hair.

"My sweet, sweet Isla," she whispered. Her smile grew when strong arms wrapped around her, their naked bodies lightly pressed together. "I'm sorry I woke you." She left a soft kiss on full lips. "Had a dream."

"A bad one?" Isla asked softly, her hands roaming up and over Elsie's back.

Elsie shrugged a shoulder. "Strange one. Don't know if 'bad' is accurate, per se, but it wasn't decidedly good, either."

"I'm sorry, my love," Isla murmured.

"Do you believe we can be two places at once?" Elsie asked, shocked that the words had fallen unchecked from her tongue.

Isla cocked her head slightly to the side, studying Elsie's face. She brought up a hand and gently brushed golden strands out of the princess's face. "I remember hearing stories when I was a lass about people who could inhabit other places, or even animals, while still being solidly on the ground."

Elsie was stunned to hear those words from Isla's mouth. "Really?"

Isla nodded. "Aye." She gave her a smile. "Can we continue this conversation in bed? My nipples are about to freeze off."

A burst of laughter escaped Elsie's lips. Grinning, she nodded. "Aye." She cupped Isla's breasts with her hands. "My goodness. You could cut glass." She kissed Isla's lips before taking her by the hand and leading her to the bed. They climbed in and immediately Elsie pulled Isla to her, covering them with heavy blankets. "Better?"

Isla groaned deep in her throat as she snuggled in as close as possible to Elsie. "Mm-hmm."

Elsie smiled, leaving a kiss on her forehead, Isla's head resting upon her shoulder. "I was a bird," she finally said. "I was flying high overhead. I saw Roishin on the ground, no doubt my mind putting her on the quest I know she's on. But I decided to fly ahead to make sure the path was clear." She paused, not entirely sure what to make of the last part of the dream.

Isla's fingers traced random patterns on Elsie's stomach, the touches so gentle. They were as comforting as they were arousing. "Do you feel you were really there?"

Though the question had tumbled from Elsie's lips earlier, she hadn't really thought of that. "I don't know," she said. "It was so real." She could easily remember the feel of the wind and even the cold of the stone beneath her feet as she perched. Then, waking with such a dry mouth. No, she thought. They couldn't be related. "I don't know," she said again.

⁂

Jabari was escorted to the family chambers, and Elsie was very nervous to meet with him. She hoped he could give her some answers but wasn't sure what the questions were. He was dressed similarly to how he'd been the first time she'd seen him. He met her with a deep bow of respect.

"I am honored, milady," he said into the bow.

"Thank you, Jabari. As am I."

He raised himself to his full height but kept his distance, like he was waiting for her invitation to be in her personal space. For some reason, Elsie felt very at ease with this man and knew he was no threat. She looked to the guard who had escorted him in and who stood waiting for orders.

"Please have refreshments sent up," she said to him. With a bow, he left the room. Left alone, she turned to him. "Shall we sit?"

He didn't answer but instead looked deeply into her eyes. She was a bit taken aback at the intensity of that gaze. Elsie was pretty sure he was looking into her soul, and from his next words, she knew that to be true.

"She has blessed you," he said, nodding at his own assessment. He raised a hand, his forefinger pointed at her eyes, though he still kept that distance. "It is all in there."

She met his gaze. "What is?"

He nodded again, almost as if being given a directive or information from a source that only he could hear or understand. "The feather, milady?"

Feeling shy, as she'd brought it out of the jewelry box in her bedchamber and with her just in case, Elsie walked over to the table and picked it up. She held it out, and Jabari looked down at it. His light brown eyes widened a bit and he let out a long, slow, reverent breath. His eyes flicked up to hers.

"May I?"

"Of course."

His hand was so large next to hers, though he used the long fingers to delicately pluck it from her palm. She thought the stark contrast in their skin color was beautiful. He handled it as though he'd just picked up a baby chick that had just hatched. He examined the feather, which he laid across his palm. Nodding again, he stroked it for a moment.

"She has blessed you, Elsie," he said again, though she was surprised to hear her given name upon his lips this time. She didn't correct him. "Macha has blessed you with the wing of the raven." He held up the feather as if to show her what he said was true.

The two paused when there was a knock at the chamber door. "Come in."

One side of the doors opened and two servants appeared. One carried a platter of sliced cheese and smoked ham while the other carried a clay jug of wine and two glasses. Each glass was filled, then the servants left as they'd come, closing the door behind them.

Elsie turned her focus back to him. "What does that mean, Jabari? And, how do you know?"

He held the feather out to her, laid across both palms, as though that were the answer. She took it, looking down at it and trying to see what he'd seen. Her gaze flicked back up to his when he began to speak again.

"Those of the Druid blood all have gifts," he explained, shrugging. "Varying in what and how controlled they are. For some, the blood is thin, diluted. They may have a moment of Second Sight now and then, come at random. Then," he added, his eyes bright. "There are those that, no matter how hot the blood, they are chosen." He smiled. "They are 'made.'"

I made you.

Elsie could hear the words echo in her mind from that dream with the warrior woman. She was suspecting now that had been Macha herself. Needing a moment, she walked to the dining table, the very same one where she'd helped to serve Roishin's family for years.

"Wine?" she asked, grabbing one of the cups and holding it out in offering.

Jabari walked over to her and accepted it with a deep nod of thanks. Elsie took the second and sipped, allowing his words to bounce around in her mind as she stared at the feather she still held. She stared at it for a long time and, to her gasp, she had a quick but vivid flash of the ruins glowing before it was gone.

Putting it down, as she needed a little distance from it, she walked to one of the two chairs before the fire and sat down, Jabari following her lead to sit in the second. He remained quiet, as if understanding that she was trying to wrap her mind around all of it.

Finally, she spoke. "So, what does it mean, then?"

she asked. "That I was blessed with the wing of the raven?"

He studied her for a moment, head slightly cocked to the side. "Last night you fly, no?" His chuckle was deep and rich. "I see it in your eyes."

She smiled as she looked into the crimson depths of her cup. "I have no idea what that was about last night," she admitted. Shaking her head, she looked over at him. "I don't know what to think."

"She has opened your mind," he said, pressing two of his fingers to his temple. "She has connected it to your soul, Elsie. The soul always leaves the body when we slumber. Back home, we go to rest. But you," he said, pointing those two fingers at her. "Your soul now has eyes."

She stared at him, fascinated.

"You have seen a kite, no?" he asked.

When she shook her head, he looked around, as if for inspiration. Popping up from his seat, he hurried to the table, plopping back down in his chair a moment later, sans wine but instead holding a slice of cheese.

"This is the kite, up in the air," he explained, holding the cheese aloft. "The string that tethers the kite to that who holds it," he added, pantomiming, running his fingers down what would be the line of the kite. "Your soul," he said, indicating the cheese. "Your body." He indicated his hand, which was holding the string from the ground.

Her eyes widened and her lips fell open. "Aye," she breathed, beginning to understand.

"But," he continued. "Whereas the kite is moved and directed by the wind…" He bopped the cheese in an erratic way in demonstration before stilling it. "*You* are the wind. Your mind."

All she could do for nearly a full minute was stare between the cheese and his excited face. Finally, she said slowly, "So, I was really out there last night?"

"Yes!"

She had to smile, as he looked like he was about to vibrate out of his seat with a childlike excitement. She outright laughed when he took a bite out of the "kite." She thought for a moment as he finished his cheese.

"Okay, so how do I control the kite?"

"That takes time. Your soul already knows where it wants to go, and it will go, as you saw last night. You will learn to focus your mind, Elsie. Focus your intention. Soon," he said brightly, "it will become second nature to you."

She nodded, understanding that. "I do have a question."

"So do I," he said, a bit shy. "May I get more cheese?"

Elsie laughed and nodded. "In fact." She pushed up from her chair, carried her wine to the table, and sat down. He sat across from her, taking a slice of the cheese and some ham. "When I first saw you," she said, taking her own slice of cheese to nibble on. "You were glowing." She hesitantly met his eyes, afraid he'd be looking at her like she was crazy. "And in my dream—"

"Flight—"

"Flight, last night, I saw a figure. It was hiding, but they, too, were glowing." She paused, still feeling as though she'd lost her mind. She forced herself to say it. "The entire area began to glow. It scared me, so I left."

He eyed her. "What color?"

"Gold."

His smile was large and looked quite pleased. "You, milady, can see the soul of your kind."

She stared at him. "Are you saying I can see the soul of a Druid?"

"That, milady," he said, holding up a piece of smoked ham as if in celebration. "Is exactly what I am saying."

Chapter Nineteen

She was shivering when she came in. It had been a very long day out helping the wood crew. Ava was sore, cold, tired, hungry, and just wanted to cry. Instead, Jack walked on inside the tunnels. He was headed back to the communal bathroom to wash up when he passed by a house, the entrance open.

"Guess you proved me wrong, kid."

Jack slowed and glanced in. He was surprised to see the man from dinner nights before, the one who had jumped in to offer to help when Terryn was attacked. "Hey," he said.

The older man, who had his behind braced against the wall in the small entryway of his home, was leaning over to tug on his boot. He grinned up at Jack. "Got the girl anyway, huh?"

Grinning, Jack rubbed the back of his neck. "Yeah, guess so."

The man grunted as his foot finally slipped in. He stood erect and stomped his foot a few times. "So, guessin' you two will be making things more permanent soon, huh?"

Ava wasn't sure she'd ever get used to how it was done in the tunnels. Forget dating, forget seeing if there's any attraction or chemistry. Nope! Wanna? Sure. Cool. The end. Just nuts! "Yeah," Jack said and chuckled. "Done deal."

The man turned to look at him, finished with his boot. He crossed his arms over his chest and eyed him.

"You ain't got no kin here, do you?"

"Uh, no, sir."

Again, Jack rubbed his neck. Something about the intensity of the way this man, whose name she didn't even know, was looking at Jack was making Ava uneasy. Something inside her told her to do something. The hand that had been on the back of Jack's neck reached out and braced against the doorway.

As casually as he could make it, in case she was wrong, Jack turned his hand and lightly tapped out the opening sequence of the knock Roishin had taught Ava that afternoon. Before he was even done, the man tapped out the last three knocks using the heel of his boot on the stone floor. The two held the other's gaze for a long moment before the older man smiled.

"Knew it," he muttered, almost more to himself. "Dirk." He held out a large, calloused hand.

Jack grinned and took it, returning the firm shake. "Jack. Nice to formally meet you, Dirk."

Dirk nodded. "Listen," he said, looking down the tunnel both ways. When he saw nobody was coming, he looked back at Jack. "I told you I know Terryn's old man. Real asshole. It's just me in here." He hitched a thumb backward into his place. "It's small, but I got two bedrooms and I ain't here all that much. Wife's dead, no children. I want you kids to start out right." He grinned. "Don't care what you do and when you do it. Just be good to your lady, and I'll leave you be."

Jack blinked several times. "Uh…"

Dirk grinned and slapped him on the shoulder. "Come on, I'll show you."

Jack followed him in. Unlike Terryn's family home, there was no front room. The small entryway basically led down a short, narrow hallway with one bedroom to the left and one to the right. Dirk indicated the one to the left.

"Don't use it." He looked at Jack, who peeked his head in. There was only one sleeping nook, though it looked deep enough to accommodate two. It was a very small room, with a little area for storage. "No bathroom here, you'd have to use the communal one. But," he said with a shrug. "More privacy. Less in-laws." He smirked.

Jack laughed outright at that. He turned and headed back toward the entryway. "I need to get to dinner. Haven't eaten all day. Let me talk to Terryn, okay?" He smirked. "I'm moving in tonight with her." He whistled between his teeth. "Just nuts."

Dirk slapped him on the back again as he walked him out. "Well, gotta get it while the gettin's good and before another man steals your thunder."

"Yes, sir." Jack gave him a smile before leaving and heading on to the bathroom to wash up before dinner.

One of the scariest times for Ava was when she had to use the men's community restroom. Most gave her not more than enough attention to nod a greeting before getting on with their own business, but she'd gotten enough side glances to make her nervous.

Jack was a really good-looking young man but not a very big guy comparatively, so she'd been leery of some of the looks. The tunnels were filled with people, and communities of people were filled with both predators and simply men who were attracted to other men. With the amount of testosterone and machismo that flowed through the tunnels, these men had to keep that side of themselves as hidden as if they were of the blood.

It was crazy to her. Doing what Ava did in Duras, missions all through time, she'd seen what progress had been made. Now, in the tunnels, it was a strange mixture of medieval times and 1980s gay bars—men in the bathrooms trying to get an itch scratched that they just weren't allowed to in their normal, daily lives.

Jack decided to pay attention to what he was doing rather than waxing philosophical. He washed his face and finger-combed his hair. Oh, what Ava would do for a full-on hot shower back home! Feeling a bit more human, Jack eyed himself in the mirror, looking at his face this way and that.

Everything was holding up remarkably well, though the woman beneath was finding she was becoming more tired as she held the charade in place for such long periods of time. She wondered if Terryn would be okay if she reverted back to herself to sleep. That seemed to help recharge the battery for the next day's farce. She also tried to come back into herself off and on during the day when an opportunity presented itself.

She joined the crowd headed to the dining hall. Jack's gaze scanned the area for the woman he was looking for. After their very public announcement, as it were, that they were a couple, they'd done their best to keep it going when under the watchful eye of…well, anyone.

Both very busy with their respective jobs—especially with Terryn forced to do double duty with her actual job and seemingly never-ending punishment as a serving wench—the two didn't actually see much of the other during the day.

Jack had made a couple trips to the tailor shop to say hello, but that was about all the time he could muster away from what had become his main job, and that was working with the wood cutting crew. So, times like this, the hugely public events of meals, was their time to make the biggest splash as a new couple.

The dining hall was loud as usual, as everyone got seated or stood in groups chatting and catching up after a long day. Instantly, a smile spread across Jack's lips when he saw Terryn hurrying toward the kitchen, hastily tying the apron she wore at her lower back as she went. He was relieved to see that she was good and looked forward to spending time with her that night and the next day when they were both off.

It was a strange situation, of course, but they were doing the best they could with it. Luckily, they seemed to get along, so that made the very in-your-face instant relationship much easier. It certainly didn't hurt that Terryn was really beautiful, which Ava found confusing. What did it matter?

She saw Dirk sitting at a table with a handful of other men. Jack was waved over, so he headed in that direction. He took the available seat at the end of the bench seat next to Dirk. The other men seated there seemed to range in age from thirty to an old gray-haired man. Though, in the tunnels it was deceiving just how old someone was—a man who looked to be in his eighties could be fifty-two.

Introductions were made, Jack shaking each hand offered. He'd seen most of the men around but didn't really know any of them. The ladies began heading out of the kitchen like a small army, carrying plates of food. Jack absolutely hated it. As hungry as he was, he was tempted to boycott just on principle.

Instead, he was as kind to the women delivering his food as he could be, always sure to thank them and compliment them in some way that was respectful and couldn't be taken out of context by anyone, namely their significant other.

"Thank you so much, ma'am," he said to the older woman who set a loaded plate before him. "Lovely new dress you have on today." He gave her a smile, which grew at the smile his words put upon the woman's lips.

"Thank you, young man," she said, then moved on.

"Some smooth talker, Jack." Dirk chuckled.

"Nah," he said. "I just don't believe women should be treated like second-class citizens is all."

Dirk nodded, taking a bite of the food set before him. "Good lad."

Jack listened to the conversation around him. Most of it was shop talk, all the men at the table the leather workers. Much of their discussion she didn't really want to hear, particularly while eating. She noticed that Terryn was making the rounds with the clay pitcher of ale.

His gaze followed the swift and graceful journey she made around the dining hall. Terryn mostly was like a ghost, grabbing a mug here, reaching over to fill one there, but saying nothing. She didn't smile, didn't initiate interaction. And, curiously, neither did any of the men. They pretty much ignored her presence.

Ava smiled inwardly. It made her feel better, and honestly, like perhaps their ruse was working and Terryn was a bit safer today than she had been even a day before. Jack's head flew up when his name was spoken.

"Huh?"

The man sitting across from him grinned knowingly. "Sorry to pull you down out of them clouds, Jack."

Jack grinned sheepishly. "Yeah, daydreaming."

"Or, night dreaming?" the same man prodded, the one next to him chuckling. The man, who was sitting across from Jack, was named Ray. "I get it, son," he said with a chuckle. "So, I was askin' you if you were gonna be moving to work in the tannery, too." He used his fork to stab a piece of the beef on his plate. "Dirk says you're kinda like us."

"Yeah," the man sitting next to him added. "Good lookin.'"

The table erupted in laughter, including a grin from Jack, who pretended to primp non-existent long hair, which made the table erupt again. He chuckled along with them, Dirk pounding her on the back in good humor. Jack's attention was immediately grabbed when he noticed Terryn headed their way, making a stop at the table over from theirs. They'd be next.

Ava had absolutely no idea why, but her heart did a little flip in her chest that nearly made Jack gasp. She swallowed her reaction down and refocused. Clearing his throat, Jack stuffed a forkful of mashed potatoes into his mouth.

"Well, good eve, pretty lady," Ray greeted kindly when Terryn neared their table. Ray was probably in his forties, maybe fifties, and his smile at the lovely young woman seemed genuine and not lecherous.

Terryn stepped up next to Jack and sent a small smile to the table at large. "Good eve, gentlemen," she said quietly. She smiled down at Jack when he slung an arm around her waist. To Ava's surprise, Terryn leaned down and gave Jack a quick peck on the lips and leaned into him. "Everyone want ale?" she asked.

Ava was delighted to hear the burst of laughter from the woman next to her when a cluster of mugs was held up toward her.

꧁꧂

The two walked hand in hand back from the little corner that Ava had made her own since that first night. All her belongings—a single outfit—were bundled in the blanket Terryn had given her. They were making their way back to Terryn's family home, and their handholding was received with approving looks by those they passed along the way.

"So," Jack said. "We got a very unexpected offer tonight from Dirk." He glanced over at Terryn. When she met his gaze, he continued. "The guy I was sitting next to tonight. His wife died last year whenever that terrible sickness spread through the tunnels. Just him now, and he's got an extra bedroom." Jack shrugged a shoulder. "Figure it may be less stress on your family. But, entirely up to you." He gave her a small smile. "I don't want to take you away from them." *Yet*, Ava thought.

"We'll see," Terryn said, swinging their joined hands gently between them as they walked. "Traditionally, I'd be moving in with you and your family." She spared a glance to Jack. "So, you moving in with us is a bit…unusual."

"Is that why your brother is so upset?"

Terryn shrugged a shoulder. "I think there's a few reasons, honestly. Perhaps that, and I think he's upset that it happened for me first." She sent a smirk in Jack's direction, which was returned. "And," she concluded, growing serious. "I do think there's some twin jealousy in there, too." She let out a heavy, tired-sounding breath. "He's always kind of been the 'man' in my life, as it were."

Jack nodded. "Makes sense." He let out his own heavy sigh. "I'm really sorry I've caused you problems, Terryn."

"Don't be." Terryn stopped their progress. She looked around to make sure nobody was in the tunnel with them, then looked up into Jack's eyes. "Truth is," she said quietly. "I'm not real sure what I'll do when your mission is done and you go."

Absolutely no idea why he did it, as they were entirely alone and there was no need for the show, but Jack lightly trailed his fingertips down a soft cheek briefly before his hand fell away.

"I have no intention of leaving you here when I do," he said. Though the words came from Jack's mouth, Ava meant every one.

Terryn held the dark gaze for a long moment before a small smile graced her lips. Her eyes were guarded, as Jack had become used to. It was hard at times, as Ava was a very open person, thoughts and feelings pretty much telegraphed in her eyes or falling out of her mouth.

But, she thought back to who she was during her years on the earth plane. Terryn reminded her so much of herself during that time: small, closed off, and truly just trying to survive emotionally.

It was very much like Terryn kept herself so walled off in order to not bring any attention to herself. Perhaps if nobody noticed her, they'd leave her alone. Problem was, Terryn was so naturally beautiful, no doubt especially as she'd plowed toward womanhood, there wasn't much she could do to not garner unwanted attention.

Never in her life had Ava felt such a need to protect someone. Once she'd returned to Duras and had detoxed from her years on the earth plane, those closest to her had become Roishin and Enori, both women with their own brand of confidence. It had helped her to find her own voice and know that she'd be heard. And then Livia's wise, quiet, maternal way had warmed her heart, as Ava had no family of her own.

Like Roishin, Ava had been born of one of the many lost earth plane babies, though unlike Roishin, there had been no advance plan for her soul. She just was, which had been one of the reasons she was chosen for the earth plane experiment.

It was clear Terryn had never had that—support, friendship, and protection—even in her own family bubble. Ava longed to bring the other woman into the ring of protection and sisterhood that was her Duras family. With Terryn being Druid, she had no idea how that could happen, but she was determined to find a way.

The two continued on, both lost in their own thoughts. When they reached the family home, all was quiet. Ronan and Laird were nowhere to be seen, but Blair was already asleep. They headed into the bedroom the twins shared, and now, at least for that night, Jack would, too.

Entering the room, Jack peered through the dimness to look at the sleep nook that was Terryn's before looking at the other woman. He grinned. "Um, mind if I get in first? Afraid of heights."

Terryn smiled and shook her head. "I figured you'd want to, honestly." She indicated the room around them. "I usually take my boots off down here, because there's nowhere up there to keep them, then climb up."

Seeing the logic, Jack did just that, Terryn removing hers, as well. They placed them in the corner, then he climbed up the ladder, heart going pitter-patter as Ava was about to have a coronary. But Jack got her there, tossing in his bundle before crawling in after it. He moved as close to the wall as he could. It would be mighty cozy with both of them in there.

Terryn's head appeared and then the rest of her. She spared a glance to Jack before she fully climbed in. She leaned her upper body partially out of the nook as she wrestled with something. Jack was worried she was going to fall out on her head, but a moment later, a heavy piece of fabric was yanked across the opening.

"Laird installed these rods across the top of our nooks a few years back," Terryn explained, her voice heard though she was no longer visible as they were plunged into complete darkness now. "I think it was when he discovered a few things he liked to do." She chuckled. "But I felt too caged in so I stopped using mine."

"Are you okay to use it now?" Jack asked, confused.

Jack was surprised when he felt a hand begin to wander in the darkness. It took a moment, but he realized Terryn was trying to find his head. Once she found it, she cupped one side as she leaned in toward the ear on the other side. As she spoke, her words weren't much more than whispered breath.

"I wasn't sure if you needed to be Ava to sleep," she said. "With you by the wall and the covering, you can have the safety and privacy to do what you need to."

Relieved, Jack changed their position so now he was whispering in Terryn's ear. "Are you okay with me being Ava in here?"

"Of course."

Chapter Twenty

Though Terryn absolutely trusted Jack, liked him even, for some reason it made her feel better that her bedmate would be Ava. That made zero sense, considering they were the same person. But, she reasoned, Ava wasn't a very large woman, so with the two of them instead of Jack's larger persona, they'd fit fairly well, if a bit tight.

"Thank god," Ava's voice murmured, making Terryn smile as she moved away from her to lay down. "Does it hurt?" she whispered. "To change? Do you have enough room?" she asked when she heard Ava readjusting. She smiled. "I'm sorry the accommodations aren't better."

Ava's snort was heard in the darkness. "Well, it wasn't exactly planned for. And," she added. "As for if it hurts to change…"

Ava found Terryn's hand in the darkness and placed it on her hand, which rested on the bed pallet beneath them. It was clearly a woman's hand, smaller and delicate. Terryn gasped as the very solid, warm, and flesh-and-blood hand grew very soft for a moment, then cold, and suddenly her hand was lying atop a larger, man's hand.

"So strange," she whispered. She allowed her fingertips to roam along the back of the hand, with its larger size and somewhat hairy knuckles. Longer, wider fingers. She turned the hand over so it was palm up. Again, she traced her fingertips over the wider expanse, feeling the callouses. A strong hand.

"Magic," Jack whispered. "Or, is it?" Ava asked.

Terryn smiled as the larger hand grew soft, then cold, then was the smaller, more delicate hand of a woman again. Her fingertips trailed down the shorter fingers, smaller, more elegant. They breezed over the softness of her palm and then to the underside of a small wrist. She felt the veins just under the skin, her fingertips easing along them to feel the incredible softness of the underside of the forearm beyond.

The daze she hadn't even realized she was in was broken when light suddenly streamed in around the edges of the makeshift curtain. Laird had entered the room, a lit candle in hand. Terryn yanked her hand away, as if it had been burned by that very candle. She glanced over at Ava and saw that she was indicating Terryn turn to her left side.

Doing as bade, within a moment, Terryn felt a warm body scoot up to brush behind her. An arm eased over her waist and a hand rested against her stomach—Jack's hand. A moment later, the curtain was whipped open, Laird staring up into the nook. Terryn was immensely relieved that Ava had had the foresight to situate them.

"Do you mind?" she asked her brother.

"Is he here?" Laird asked, not bothering to respond to or even consider his twin's irritation.

"Right here," Jack said close to Terryn's ear, his chest pressed more firmly against her back as he leaned slightly over her to be seen. "Long day," he said. "Time to sleep."

"Better be," Laird grumbled, tugging the curtain back into place.

Angry and frankly hurt, Terryn closed her eyes for a moment. Letting out a quiet sigh of resignation, she felt Jack's hand begin to slide away, but she covered it with her own to stop his retreat. She needed the warmth and comfort of another human being in that moment. It was a strange thought, a foreign one.

Jack's hand morphed down to Ava's, which pressed lightly against Terryn's stomach, the heat behind her moving away. Getting the idea, Terryn scooted back deeper into the nook until she felt Ava's body. She felt her breasts pressed against her back and her warmth all along the backside of her body. She needed that so badly, so she allowed herself to sink into it.

"I'm sorry," she whispered into the dimness that was their little world in that moment.

"Don't apologize," Ava whispered so softly into Terryn's ear, she had to focus on what was being said. Obviously, they couldn't let Laird hear the voice of a second woman. "Let's sleep."

Terryn nodded, cradling the hand that had rested on her stomach up under her chin as she closed her eyes.

⁂

Terryn slowly rose into wakefulness. It was complete darkness, which confused her for a moment. Added to that confusion was warmth along her right side and a weight on her shoulder. Blinking a few times, she tried to get her brain to work and figure out what was going on. It was then that she heard the deep, even breathing and felt the soft exhalations across her throat and upper chest.

She remembered the previous night and realized the curtain was still closed and Ava was asleep not only against her, but in her arms. Terryn's right arm was draped over her shoulders, and her left hand was resting on the arm that was stretched across her stomach. Suddenly, there was a little hitch to Ava's breathing then a soft snort as she, too, seemed to be coming to wakefulness.

After a moment, the breathing quieted and the

other woman seemed to be trying to also figure out the where and the why. A small smile brushed Terryn's lips, wondering what must be going through Ava's mind in that moment.

"Um," Ava whispered, head still resting on Terryn's shoulder. "Uh-oh."

Terryn lightly squeezed Ava's shoulder with her hand to let her know she was awake, too, and was quite aware of their position. No doubt Laird was still in his sleep nook, and they couldn't chance him overhearing.

Ava readjusted enough to whisper into Terryn's ear, "Sorry about that."

A little shiver ran through Terryn at the feel of long, dark hair brushing across her cheek and her neck in the process. Why did she have the irrational wish that Ava could settle back down where she'd been and they could just lay there and talk, all warm and comfortable. She was very confused by that sudden and very real wish.

Yes, Ava could easily just morph into Jack and they could do that. But that wasn't what she wanted. Ava did rest her head back down, which made Terryn smile. Neither said another word, just lay there in the early morning darkness. Surely both their internal alarm clocks had awoken them. This would be when they'd normally start stirring for their workday.

Despite her apology, Ava snuggled in even closer, which amused Terryn, who tightened her hold on her. It was just nice to connect for a moment. It was a stressful situation, and no doubt Ava just needed a moment at home base.

"Did you sleep okay?" Terryn whispered, running her fingers through the soft tresses of long, dark hair.

Ava nodded against the shoulder her head rested on. She used a finger to lightly tap Terryn's side, as if to ask, *You?* Terryn nodded as she rested her cheek against Ava's head.

"I did." She smiled. "Surprised, actually. Wasn't sure with it being so tight."

Ava made her giggle as she wiggled her body in as close as humanly possible without lying atop her. Knowing she was teasing, Terryn pushed her off. She grinned at the little laugh she got, almost imperceptible if she wasn't somewhat tangled up with her. After a moment, Ava lifted her head and moved back to Terryn's ear.

Terryn gasped softly as Ava's breast lightly grazed her own as Ava braced the hand that had been resting against Terryn's side on the bedroll next to her, that arm reaching over Terryn's body. She felt a wave of sensation sail through her that almost left her breathless.

"Did you still want to head out today on our day off?" Ava whispered, her words not much more than a breath on the wind, sending yet another wave through Terryn.

For a moment Terryn couldn't speak as she desperately tried to understand what she was feeling. She had the urge to turn her head…just a little bit was all she had to turn it. Before she could tell her body no, her head turned. She felt Ava's warm breath against her face. What had been actually quite comfortable and cozy moments before now felt dense and heavy.

Ava lowered herself to her forearm, her breast now fully resting against Terryn's. The hand that had been on the bedroll moved until it was lightly cupping the side of Terryn's neck. Terryn's heart was racing. She was confused by her body's reaction to this, as she'd had to be close to Jack in ways she never wanted to be close to anyone, and for the better part of a week.

She'd had to hold his hand, she'd had to seek him

out, and she'd had to kiss him. It had all been done in the name of keeping her and Ava safe. But this… This wasn't Jack, and this wasn't in front of an audience of her entire community. It was just the two of them tucked away in the darkness, wrapped in their own combined body heat. There was no need for a show, no need to pretend.

So, why did she want Ava to kiss her so damn bad? She reached up and wrapped her hand around the forearm attached to the hand that rested against her neck. Her thumb lightly caressed the soft skin, almost as if to send the message that it was okay.

Ava shrank away from her when Terryn's father began to cough and hack across the hall, startling them both. Terryn's eyes closed and her heart continued to race, now at the knowledge of what had almost happened. Her hand rested against her upper chest as she tried to get herself to calm down.

"Ready to head out?" Jack asked quietly.

Terryn's eyes squeezed shut for a moment, lamenting the fact that Ava had to go. Finally, she nodded. "Aye."

※ ※ ※ ※

Without a word, the two had gotten up and quietly left the nook and bedroom. Laird was still in his own nook, curtain closed. It made Terryn sad, but at least this situation could be remedied. She wanted to talk to Jack today about taking Dirk up on his offer. She wanted to get away from her family, begin the process of finding her own identity.

The morning was chilly, and Jack was able to layer his clothing between the outfit he'd come wearing, which had long sleeves, and the shirt Terryn had made for Laird, which had short sleeves. She decided her next extra project at work was to make Jack a cloak.

Jack had Terryn's bag slung over his shoulders, inside, her filled water canteen and the food for them both that Terryn had stashed at her workstation for this very outing.

"Definitely going to rain later," Terryn said, glancing up at the heavy, pregnant clouds as they hiked away from the tunnels.

"Yeah," Jack agreed. He reached up an arm, finger pointing to the east. "Look how dark those clouds are that way."

"I think I can get us to the cemetery before it starts," Terryn said, glancing in the direction he pointed to. "I really want to show you and I want to explore."

Jack looked down at her. "Cemetery? As in graves and dead people?"

Terryn smiled and shook her head, her long, auburn hair blowing back from her face in the light breeze. "No, it's part of what was left after the war that supposedly happened." She spared a glance to her companion. "I don't know. I just feel drawn to it."

"I very much want to see it, then," Jack said. Things between them were a bit stilted, and silence stretched out as they continued their walk. Finally, Jack spoke. "I'm really sorry about this morning, Terryn." His voice was laced with what seemed like fear.

Terryn considered the words, trying to formulate her thoughts on the situation that she still didn't fully understand. One thing she *did* know was that there was no blame, and certainly none on the person walking alongside her. Of its own accord, her hand reached out and took Jack's larger one. Instantly, their fingers entwined.

"Ava," she said softly, though Jack was the one currently presenting. She knew it wasn't safe for two women to be walking alone, so Jack's presence was a must. Even so, she knew Ava heard her loud and clear. "A person apologizes when they've done something wrong." She glanced over at Jack, who was looking straight ahead as they walked. "Right?"

Jack's jaw muscles worked, but finally he nodded. "Yes. Right." He met her gaze, the dark eyes, *Ava's* eyes, still troubled.

Terryn smiled and lightly squeezed the hand she held. "You didn't do anything wrong," she finished softly. "There is so much about all this that I admittedly don't understand, including within myself, but I do know that much." She met Jack's gaze. "Okay?"

After a moment, he nodded. "Okay." He held her gaze, and right then something passed between them. They shared a smile, and as if by magic, the air cleared.

"So," Terryn said, feeling lighter, happy. "You said you have some things to tell me." She looked over at him in expectation.

Jack nodded. "I do. Roishin stopped by yesterday to fill me in on what she's learned."

Terryn felt a little thrill pass through her at the mention of the enigmatic brunette's name. Her so-called shadow. It was so strange, but just hearing her name made Terryn feel a yearning to see her, the long-lost sister she'd never known she had. "Okay."

"There are others in the tunnels, Terryn. Others like *us*," he clarified at Terryn's look of confusion.

"Wait, what?"

Jack nodded. "Yup. A dozen or so. Remember Dirk?"

"Aye," Terryn said slowly.

"He's one. I don't know," he added, a look of concentration on his handsome face. "I have a gut feeling some of the guys at dinner with us last night are, too."

Terryn was stunned. She had no idea what to say to that. Finally, she managed, "What does this mean, Jack?"

"Can I tell you about this place?" Jack asked. He glanced to Terryn, who was confused by the seeming non sequitur. "This." Jack indicated all that was around them, the scarred landscape and bruised skies.

"Aye," she said slowly, nervous about what he might tell her.

"You mentioned the war a bit ago. You said that it 'supposedly' happened." He nailed her to the spot with the intensity of Ava's eyes. "It did happen."

"Why?"

"Well, to explain that, I have to tell you what this place was before. You guys call it the Shadows, probably because the real name has been lost over time. This was called Bowhar. It was a beautiful place where humans, Ankou, and Druids all lived out in the open, all together and in peace."

Terryn looked at Jack with wide eyes. "Really?"

Jack nodded. "Yup. And, above ground." He once again indicated everything around them. "Homes, buildings, commerce."

"I've seen pictures of that sort of thing in my books," Terryn said, almost whispering.

Heavy, dark eyebrows fell. "Why do you sound scared to say that?"

"Books are illegal." Terryn swallowed, feeling ashamed. "I found some one day, years ago. I keep them hidden."

Jack stopped their progress with a light tug to the hand he still held within his. She looked up into his face. Bringing up his other hand, Jack gently tucked some auburn strands behind an ear. "Not in Bowhar," he said softly.

She looked into his eyes, feeling herself getting lost in their dark depths. Absently, she reached up and curled her fingers around his, holding them against her chest. She felt that same pull she had that morning, so easily able to see, and more importantly, *feel* Ava inside of the young man standing before her.

Both of their attention was grabbed when a crack of thunder boomed like the pounding of a bass drum in the clouds. Looking up, Terryn realized they were going to get caught out in a very nasty storm if they didn't hurry to the cemetery.

"Come on," she said, tugging on his hand. "If we run, we can make it before we get rained on and find shelter in the ruins!"

Releasing their hands, the two took off. Jack kept pace with her, despite his longer legs. The empty, open landscape was riddled with pockmarks and divots in the ground, which they dodged as the sky began to rumble more aggressively, another boom of thunder rocking the morning.

Terryn felt the first drop of cold rain land on the tip of her nose as they continued to run. A debris field began to appear as they got closer. Chunks of stone and huge boulders split in two. The rain began to spit at them, as if angrily warning them to stay away from such an angry, deeply wounded place.

"Oh, man!" Jack called out as a bolt of lightning lanced through the sky, a moment later sending its thunderous wrath reverberating through the clouds, which had yet to fully begin to weep for what once was.

They zigzagged their way through the ruins, Terryn trying to find the structure that she and Laird had spent the night in on her one and only visit to the cemetery. "There!" she called out, spotting it. "Come on."

Reaching it, Jack shrugged the bag off his shoulders before tossing it inside over the half wall of rubble and debris. "Come here!" he yelled over the angry storm, which had begun to truly unleash. Rain was pouring down in buckets, quickly soaking their hair, skin, and clothing to the bone.

Terryn allowed herself to be picked up bride-style and swung over the barrier until she could slide down to her feet on the other side. She helped steady Jack once he braced his hands on the top of the rubble and threw his legs over. They shared a wide-eyed look before bursting into relieved laughter that they'd made it.

"Come on," he said. "Let's get away from the opening. We're getting rained on."

She nodded in agreement and was about to turn away to follow him deeper inside the stone house when something caught her eye. Peeking out from the open space, she saw the biggest raven she'd ever seen. It was perched atop a stone pillar and looking right at her.

Chapter Twenty-One

Feeling herself shrink down, Ava walked to the back of the structure, looking around to try to determine what it had once been. A small house, perhaps. It reminded her of the little cottage she had in Duras, thought hers with a separate bathroom and bedroom. She walked over to where the bag had landed and picked it up, carrying it to the back wall farthest away from the opening where the wall had collapsed.

Turning, she saw that Terryn was still standing there, looking out. She seemed to be watching something. "What is it?" Ava called out over the rage of the storm.

After a moment, Terryn shook her head and turned away. "That was the biggest raven I have ever seen in my life," she said. "Just sitting out there staring at me. It just flew off." As she walked toward Ava, her eyebrows shot up.

"What?" Ava asked.

"Look at this," Terryn said, bringing up a hand and touching Ava's hair, which fell to her shoulders. "Your hair is completely dry. So is your face and your hands. Yet," she added, looking the other woman over. "Your clothes are soaked."

Ava looked down at herself, noting that, sure enough, the strands of hair that Terryn was running her fingers through were dry as a bone. "Wow," she murmured. She'd never been in this situation before, so she had no idea that would happen. She grinned. "So, I guess Jack protected me from the rain. Best rain slicker ever."

"That is wild," Terryn breathed, even as her own

hair hung in her face in wet, stringy strands that were still dripping.

Ava gasped as the saturated clothing was now soaking into her flesh. "Okay, yeah, that's cold."

Terryn's gaze fell to Ava's chest before it swept back up to her eyes. "Clearly." She grinned.

Ava glared at her. "Whatever," she muttered, amused at Terryn's grin. "Well," she said, looking around at their options. "I guess let's sit and ride this out."

The floor was dirt but at least relatively free of rock and debris in the back portion. She sank to sit on her behind with her back against the wall. Terryn sat down next to her, the women shoulder to shoulder. Terryn reached for the bag Jack had been carrying and unsnapped it, bringing out two apples.

"Here you go," she said, holding out one to Ava.

"Thank you very much." Ava grinned at the woman beside her as she took the fruit, neither of them having eaten before they'd left the tunnels.

It felt so good to be outside, even if they were currently bunked down in a dilapidated old cottage. It felt even better to be outside as herself. She took a bite, as did Terryn. They sat in companionable silence as they ate. The rain was really coming down, lightning lighting up the dreary morning every few minutes followed by an entire percussion section of thunder.

"I love the rain," Ava murmured. "Something about it. Just so…pure, I guess."

Terryn finished chewing her latest bite before she responded. "I can see how you'd feel that way," she said. "But, and this may sound strange to you, the rain here…I don't know." She shrugged, glancing over at Ava. "There's always something so ominous about it. Unnatural."

Ava chewed on that as she chewed her next bite.

"You know," she finally said, swallowing down the food with a drink from the canteen handed to her. "Thank you," she said, passing it back. "I can feel that, too." She glanced over at Terryn. It was *so* amazing to spend time with her as herself, in the light of day. She looked into Terryn's gorgeous eyes, amazed at just how much they matched the angry skies above. She forced herself to look away. "It's like a heaviness, a feeling of expectation. Foreboding."

"Yes!" Terryn agreed, eyes wide. "That's exactly it." She was smiling larger than Ava had ever seen her. "I don't ever get to talk about this stuff, Ava. With anyone." She rested her hand holding what was left of her apple on her thigh, legs stretched out in front of her and crossed at the ankles. "I constantly feel like some giant has all of us, all the Shadows in his hand, and we're waiting for him to decide what to do with all of us. Does he let us continue to play and scurry around like ants in an anthill, or does he finally just squeeze the life out of all of us in one quick go?"

Ava finished her apple, setting the core aside to remember to take back with them. She watched Terryn as she spoke, Again, she felt that heaviness fall upon the shoulders of the small woman. It was the weight of uncertainty and the weight of the unknown.

"There's a hum, Ava," Terryn said softly, almost reverently. "I hear it. I hear it right now and back in the tunnels…you know the dead-end spot where you were staying?" At Ava's nod, she continued. "I hear it there, too." She snorted. "I've even dreamed about it. I *feel* it." She met Ava's gaze again. "Am I crazy?"

Ava shook her head, a soft smile on her lips. "No." She reached over and took the hand that rested casually in Terryn's lap. Their fingers entwined. "You're not crazy, Terryn. You're just waking up."

Terryn looked at her, eyes wide and mouth open.

"That's what he said in the dream," she murmured, almost as if to herself. "I don't know what that means, though."

"It means that you're coming into your own," Ava explained. "It means that beautiful Druid blood that runs through your veins is no longer willing to stay buried in the tunnels. It's coming to the surface, so you better be ready to become the gorgeous butterfly you've always been."

A soft smile graced beautiful, full lips at those softly spoken words. "Should I be scared?"

Ava gave her a lopsided grin as she shook her head. "No." She brought their joined hands up to her lips and left a kiss on Terryn's fingers. "Be proud of who and what you are."

Terryn studied her, her stormy gaze taking in every aspect of Ava's face, her hair, her lips, then coming back to her eyes. "Can I tell you something?"

"Sure you can." Ava's heart began to race at such up close and personal scrutiny from the woman who was making her feel more and more confused by the day, the hour, the minute.

"I think what you can do, your abilities as a chameleon, are so amazing," Terryn said. She smiled. "Watching you with everyone, how they all have absolutely no idea who they're truly talking to." Her smile became a shit-eating grin. "Those big, bad men, no clue they're talking to a feisty and beautiful woman, who they'd never deem worthy to even give an ounce of attention or respect to."

Ava blushed at the compliment, something she'd never really heard before, and certainly not from somebody that mattered. She knew she was good at what she did, and it was a mark of pride for her, but she'd never really been told anything on a personal level about her looks or who she was as a person. Well, that is, except by the men she'd dealt with as a stage actress on the earth plane.

Those men and their thoughts hadn't mattered to her, largely because she knew most of them were simply trying to get her in bed. It was an option she'd never been interested in, and she had never taken any of them—or anyone else—up on it. But, as Terryn sat next to her, their fingers entwined and some quiet truths discussed, she felt everything she'd thought about pretty much anything in that regard changing.

No, it wasn't just the compliment, it was all of it. She'd never felt so close to anyone before, and perhaps it was just the constant danger they had gone through together during Ava's time there as Jack. No doubt it had helped to forge a bond that perhaps wouldn't have formed under other circumstances.

And now, sitting there while the heavens wept outside of their little shelter, they had a moment to breathe. They were away from the tunnels, away from Raif, Garratt, and the rest of it. Was that why she was feeling this? Well, whatever *this* was? She felt an unshakable need to be close to Terryn, to touch her, be part of her personal space.

She'd teased Roishin and Enori mercilessly about how close they were, their immense passion for each other. How, just sitting as a trio having fun or talking details about a mission, it was clear the two were connected. They were always touching in some way, be it a grand gesture or a simple touch in passing.

Yes, the teasing from Ava was all in good fun, but it mostly came from a place of not understanding the point. She always thought she'd feel smothered to be so close to someone, always with them or always touched by them. *Living* with them, sharing a bed with them. Now, as she looked into Terryn's eyes, all her preconceived notions shattered and fell to her feet. She was left feeling confused and a little lost.

"I love watching you as Jack," Terryn continued, pulling Ava from her thoughts. "But I'm so happy today I get Ava."

"Are you saying you don't like Jack?" Ava teased.

Terryn smiled shyly. "No," she murmured, looking down at their hands, which now rested on the ground between them. "I just like Ava more."

"Um," Ava said softly, hoping like hell she wasn't about to get slapped. "I know this is Jack's job, but…"

She released Terryn's hand to bring up her own and cup a soft cheek. She leaned in, hesitating so Terryn could move away if she wanted to. Apparently, she didn't. Terryn's lips were so soft, and it was an entirely different experience to kiss them with Ava's own lips and not through the layers of energy of Jack. It was like receiving a full hug while naked as opposed to through thick layers of clothing.

Terryn must have felt something different, too, because she leaned in in a way she hadn't with Jack. Granted, any kisses she'd shared with him had been with an audience, but somehow Ava didn't think that was what was different. Their lips caressed, two women who had no idea what they were doing learning together.

A hand found its way into Ava's hair as the kiss deepened a bit. At the first tentative touch of Terryn's tongue, Ava sighed as she responded. They were still learning, but the kiss was so beautiful, so unlike anything she'd ever experienced. She fully realized now that the kisses with Jack, not that there had been a ton of them, had all been performative actions to get them through a scene and on to the next one.

But this, *this* was the real Terryn. This was her emotions, her want, and her need. This was her interest, her dedication and commitment to what they were doing and what they were experiencing together. And in that moment, Ava finally understood it, truly got it. This was what giving of yourself meant. It wasn't all about missions or the next disguise. It was about the here and now and truly appreciating it—as yourself.

After several minutes, the kiss came to a natural end, leaving them both breathless. Ava's hand slid from Terryn's cheek to the side of her neck. She looked into Terryn's striking gray eyes and saw a light in them that she hadn't seen there before. It was the sun after the rains in their stormy depths. It was hope.

She smiled and after a moment said, "The rain stopped."

Terryn nodded. "Want to explore?"

Oh, the myriad thoughts that ran through Ava's head at that question. She must not have hidden her thoughts well, because a devilish grin spread across the very lips she'd just been kissing. Terryn gave her a lingering kiss before pushing to her feet and reaching down for Ava's hand to help her to hers.

Remaining as Ava, she grabbed the bag from the ground and held it open for Terryn to drop the water canteen back inside, as well as their apple cores. She shouldered it, and they climbed over the rubble pile, now slippery from the torrential rains that had just blanketed the earth.

Out past the small cottage, Ava turned in a slow circle to get a panoramic view of the entire place. Looking at the piles littering the ground, it seemed it must have been a village. It almost looked like it was the center of town.

"That's where the raven was perched," Terryn said, pointing toward a stone pillar that stood perhaps six feet tall, though it looked as though it was missing the top half, toppled over long ago.

"Looks like this was the support structure to something," Ava said, walking over to it. She placed her hand on the cold, carved stone, looking up at the handful of inches above her head. She looked over at Terryn, who had joined her. "Do birds even fly in rain?"

Terryn chuckled, shaking her head. "I have no idea." She looked around. "You can't even tell what most of this was."

Ava nodded. "I wonder how much of that was from the war and how much has been time."

"What was the war fought over?" Terryn asked, taking Ava's hand as they strolled through the carnage.

"Well," Ava began. "I told you what Bowhar was. You see, this place is a bit of a crossroads between three worlds." She met wide, interested gray eyes. She ticked them off on her fingers. "The earth plane, where Roishin spent most of her childhood and I lived for a handful of very miserable years. Duras, where Roishin, Enori, and I live now, the land of the Ankou. And then, Ryarch," she finished. "Land of the Druid. Anise lives there."

Terryn stared at her. "Really? So, you've been to all three?"

Ava shook her head. "Not Ryarch. That, beautiful lady, is where your kind lives." She playfully bumped her shoulder against Terryn's. "My energy isn't compatible with it."

"So," Terryn drawled. "I couldn't go to Duras then, either?"

Ava shook her head. "Nope. But," she hurried to explain. "That was the beauty of this place." She indicated the destruction all around them. "Everyone could live together in peace. Enlightened humans, and Druids, and Ankou."

Terryn sent her a side glance, a soft smile on her lips. "All together."

"All together," Ava agreed. "But, as I understand it, there was a god out there, a much weaker one. He wanted this for himself."

Terryn rolled her eyes. "Shocking."

Ava smiled. "Exactly. A horrible battle was waged, and honestly, I'm not entirely sure there were any winners, Terryn." She let out a heavy sigh. "This place was destroyed and essentially sealed off to keep that defeated god in here, to contain his chaos."

Terryn was quiet for a long time. Ava could almost hear her brain whirring at a million miles an hour as she considered all she'd been told. "So," she finally said. "We"— she indicated herself and back toward the direction of the tunnels—"are the children of that atrocity?"

Ava nodded. "Yes."

"And," Terryn added, stopping their progress and turning to Ava. "'Enlightened humans,' as you call them, have basically taken it over?"

"Not so 'enlightened' anymore, but I think so, yes. Either that, or at least they have no idea what blood they carry. But, after so many generations, I imagine a lot has been bred out."

"And, they kept *us*," Terryn almost whispered, as if for fear of being overheard. "Down out of fear?"

Ava nodded. "Stands to reason. Especially over time, you don't understand what you're dealing with anymore, so much history lost, so you teach fear to maintain the control over a scattered people." She shrugged, lightly running her fingers along the edges of Terryn's cloak that was draped over her shoulders. "I imagine initially it was about trying to keep people safe, but over time…"

"It became about power." Terryn rested her hands

tentatively on Ava's waist. "Like Raif."

Ava nodded. "Like Raif." She took hold of the cloak she'd just been fingering and used it as leverage to lightly pull Terryn to her.

Their kiss was easy and wonderful, both getting more comfortable with the idea and the close proximity of another person. After the kiss broke, they embraced. It was the most amazing hug to Ava. It involved their full bodies and was the kind you could fall asleep in, so warm and comforting. In Terryn's arms, she felt so much make sense.

"I want Bowhar back," Terryn whispered.

Ava smiled. "That's the plan."

❧❧❧❧

They returned to the tunnels before dark. When they arrived, Ava now back as Jack, it was very quiet. Almost too quiet. Jack glanced to Terryn, who met his gaze before they headed in. The wood chopping crew wasn't outside, though it looked like they had been working. Equipment was left where it was, the axe blade still embedded in the log it had been chopping.

Normally, Jack would have pulled the door open for Terryn to enter first, but this time he slowly entered ahead of her, eyes and ears peeled for anything to indicate what was happening. They made their way down the long tunnel before finally Jack heard it. He slowed them down, a hand on Terryn's arm to stop her as he listened.

Yelling. *Lots* of yelling.

"It's coming from the dining hall," Terryn whispered.

Nodding, Jack got them headed in that direction. When they arrived at the cavernous room, the entire community was there, and it was nearly a free-for-all. It was very clear that there were two sides to what was happening. Garratt and Raif were both being held back by a couple men each.

"You left them to die!" Garratt raged.

"They made their choice!" Raif growled. "Grown men. If they don't return, that's on them!"

Garratt looked at those gathered, many shouting their own opinions. "Look at your leader, everyone," he called out above the ruckus. "This is how much he cares about you. Two men go out to do *his* bidding, and they vanish. They've been gone more than a week, and your leader," he drawled sarcastically, pointing a finger at the seething man held back ten feet from him. "Doesn't give a shit! Not even a goddamn search party. *Nothing*!"

Jack held Terryn to her near the door. Ava had the worst feeling about what was happening and worried she'd have to get them out of there.

"I'm keeping everyone else here safe!" Raif raged, the two men holding on to him even tighter as he tried to make a move toward the other man who dared challenge his authority.

"You never leave a man behind," Garratt exclaimed. "Ever!" He turned to those gathered. "People," he called out. "I served in the military my entire life. *I* know what it means to keep a people safe, and it isn't stuffing them underground."

Ava was pretty sure Raif was about to claw his way through the men holding him. "You're not one of us, Garratt," he yelled. "You haven't been here through it all. Through the sickness of last year that took out a lot of us. *I* was the one who got us through it."

"By keeping everyone here in the tunnels so the sickness could spread like wildfire?" Garratt challenged.

As though a switch had been turned off, it grew quiet as a tomb as the logic Garratt had just posed made its way through the people as swiftly as the sickness had the year before. Garratt clearly took the silence as his opening. He moved away from the men who had been holding him and turned to those watching and listening.

"That man has you all scared to death of your own shadows," he said, voice loud enough to be heard, but calm. It was firm, the voice of a man used to leading troops. "We're all sitting ducks in here, people. What if a fire broke out? Where do we go? Look at your kids," he said, indicating a little girl who clung to her mother. "That girl needs sunlight and fresh air. We all do!"

Voices began to speak out in the crowd, quiet agreement and rumbles of disquiet. Ava felt a cold trickle of dread slowly slide its way down her spine.

Chapter Twenty-Two

Enori glanced over at Roishin, who was about to pace a hole in the rug. "My love," she said softly. When Roishin glanced her way, Enori said, "Stop."

"Sorry." She stopped pacing but resorted to rocking on the balls of her feet.

Amused, Enori walked over to her, snaking her hands up to clasp behind Roishin's neck. "Why are you so nervous, hmm?" She eyed her as her fingers played in short, dark strands. "You are still good with the plan, right?"

"Of course," Roishin said, resting her hands on Enori's hips. "I just don't like surprises."

Enori gave her a sexy little smile. "But I thought you like it when I surprise you."

Roishin leaned in to whisper in her ear. "Waking up with your fingers inside me is a wee different kind of a surprise than this."

Chuckling, Enori left a kiss on her lips before stepping away. "True enough."

Finally, the door to the library opened and a man walked in with Ankou. It was so strange to see the traditional door. Since Roishin had come along, they were all so used to her leaving little rabbit holes all over the place for them to use. But, there was no rabbit hole from where these two had just come. Yet.

She glanced over at Roishin to see if there'd be any sort of recognition on her part, but her partner was simply looking on at the two men.

The newcomer was a very tall, well-built man. He had broad shoulders, big hands, and long legs with thighs like tree trunks, his brown leather pants molded to their shape. The white sleeveless tunic shirt he wore was of the flowing yet somewhat clingy material that showed the outline of a well-developed chest. His shoulders and biceps were sculpted, forearms corded. His body was that of quite the magnificent male specimen.

He was exceedingly handsome and looked to be around thirty. Squared jaw, straight nose, and deep-set dark brown eyes. His dark brown, nearly black hair was long and down, save for the sides which were pulled back into a braid intertwined with leather that carried down the back of his mane.

Enori looked over at Roishin, watching her carefully. She could see those dark green eyes burning as the wheels behind them turned at what she was seeing. The man stepped in, his strides long, black leather boots cupping his calves, the boots reaching to just under his knees. He looked to Enori and gave her a nod of acknowledgement , but it was clear who he was there to see.

Walking over to Roishin, he eyed her like he would a prized stallion. He took his time as he walked around her, taking in her clothing, her short hair, and finally, her face. His dark eyes softened.

"So," he said, voice deep, resonating. "You're Roishin."

Roishin spared a glance to Enori before meeting his penetrating gaze again. Roishin was a tall woman, but this man easily had six inches on her. "I am."

He lowered himself to one knee, dark head bowed. "My princess," he said with deep respect.

"Um," she said, a very confused look sent Enori's way before looking down at him. "Please rise."

He did and stepped up to stand in front of her. He brought up a large hand and lightly cupped her face. The smile across his tanned face was pure love. For Roishin's part, she looked like she wanted to bat his hand away, clearly taken aback by his audacity.

"I have never been more proud to meet someone," he said softly. He smiled, and when he did, Roishin gasped. "You look so much like her," he whispered.

Roishin stared, lips slightly open and tears welling in her eyes. Enori had to fight her own emotion back as she watched this introduction, long overdue.

He hugged her to him, her head tucked under his chin. "I'm your Uncle Ailfred," he murmured into the hug.

Roishin nodded, but Enori could tell she was too overwhelmed to speak. He stroked her back, his large, somewhat brash demeanor totally belying the gentle way he held her. He left a kiss on the top of her head then, with a final squeeze, released her. He smiled down at her, fingers tender as they wiped away her tears.

"I'm sorry," she said with a shy chuckle. "I just know how much Daidí loved you." Her smile was watery. "She still talks about you, to this day." She sniffled and used her sleeve to wipe at her cheeks and eyes. She looked to Enori. "That was not nice!"

Smiling, Enori walked over and gave her a little squeeze before turning to the warrior. "Thank you so much for coming, Ailfred."

"Of course." He placed his hands on narrow hips, grinning at the two women before him. "Anything for the two lovely ladies," he said, all teasing charm. Looking to Ankou, he grew serious. "You said something about an army."

Ankou nodded, walking farther into the room as he'd stood aside, allowing Roishin and her uncle their space and time. "Roishin and her shadow are going to reopen Bowhar," he explained. "There are many, many dead trapped there."

Ailfred studied him, heavy dark brows furrowed in concentration. "All right. So, are you expecting trouble when you open it back up?" He looked from Ankou to the ladies and back.

Ankou nodded, then indicated Roishin and Enori. Roishin, who had gotten herself together, picked up the thread. "Hundreds of years of generations stacked on top of each other, Uncle Ailfred. Living, and dead. Ankou and Druid alike. No trust between any of them, and we don't even have complete numbers as yet."

He nodded. "Humans?"

"I think that's the lion's share of what we're dealing with, but we have an eye in the sky who is giving me daily feedback. She's seeing more and more Druids."

"So," he drawled, powerful arms crossing over his chest. "If you're needing me, I'm guessing you expect trouble." He looked to Ankou.

"Bahutha," Ankou said.

"Ah." Ailfred rubbed at his chin and wandered over to the large stained-glass window, though he didn't seem to be looking at it. "You think some of the dead there will defect to his side?"

"I do." Ankou paused. "It's part of how all this happened."

Ailfred nodded. Finally, he turned to face the room. "Any of the dead who have any self-awareness left"—he looked pointedly at Ankou—"will want nothing to do with you."

"Will you be able to convince any in Yewa to fight? Because only the dead can fight the dead," Enori said. "After all, if Bowhar is reclaimed, it opens it up to us all."

He nodded but shrugged a shoulder. "Aye, but you figure, milady, we all had the option of Duras or Yewa. Those of us who went to Yewa went so we wouldn't have to deal with you living types." He grinned to take the sting out of his words. "So, many likely won't want a thing to do with it. Their fighting days were left behind on the battlefield with their bodies."

"But," Ankou asked. "*You* are willing to do this? To train, to lead."

Ailfred met his gaze and held it. "For you? No. For my niece?" He looked to Roishin, that soft, loving smile returning. "Aye."

⁂

The moonlight shone in and swept through the depths of Roishin's eyes, turning them a dark, luminescent gray. Enori lay on her right side, studying the woman who lay on her left side. The question still hung in the air, and Enori tried to think of the best way to answer it. She gently stroked the naked hip her hand rested on with her thumb beneath the covers, to let Roishin know she was with her.

She'd been incredibly emotional that night after leaving Ankou's and saying goodbye to her uncle. It was a temporary goodbye, but Roishin was so close to Fallon, and she knew how deeply Ailfred's death nearly thirty years ago had shaped a devastated seventeen-year-old sister. Enori wondered if perhaps Roishin felt a bit of guilt that she'd been able to spend time with him and Fallon had not.

"Ailfred is still very angry with Ankou, I think," Enori finally said. "Ailfred and Fallon's brother, Fergus, set him up to be killed. Sent him and some of his men off on a mission that was a lie. It was an assassination mission."

"Why be angry with Ankou for that?" Roishin asked, her fingers trailing over the thigh that was hitched up over her own hip.

Enori loved the soft touches, as comforting as it was arousing.

"I think it is misplaced anger, honestly," Enori said. "A man in his prime cut down by the traitorous act of his own blood."

"Why didn't he come when my parents were here?" Roishin asked, hurt in her voice.

"Nobody has been able to contact him in Yewa, my love."

"Then, how were you able to this time? Did you go there to find him?"

"No. The living cannot go into Yewa." Enori smiled. "Even me. It was Livia." She smirked. "Well, Livia and the help of a feisty little soul hunter."

Roishin smiled. "The little bloodhounds."

"Exactly. If anyone would find him, it would be the two of them. But ultimately, it was Livia that got him to come."

Roishin was quiet for a long moment before she asked, "What did she say? How did she get him to come?"

"You," Enori said simply. She brought her hand up to caress Roishin's face. "He wanted to meet you, the daughter of Fallon." She smiled.

Enori gasped when she was suddenly pushed to her back, Roishin rolling on top of her. Their bodies fit perfectly, Roishin's hips cradled between Enori's thighs. She just looked down at Enori for several moments, her upper body resting on her forearms. Roishin used her fingers to gently brush light blond hair off Enori's forehead.

Her fingertips trailing over the smooth, warm skin of Roishin's back, Enori looked up into her face. It was partially shadowed, but Enori could so easily fill in the blanks of the face she loved so much. She knew this whole situation with Bowhar, and with Ava being on mission there with Terryn, weighed on her greatly.

"What is it, Roishin?"

"I want to marry you," Roishin murmured.

"Oh, I see," Enori said, fingers running up Roishin's back to her shoulders, enjoying the softness. "You live with me for more than two years and *now* you want to, huh?"

Roishin grinned. "Well, you know," she said, using Enori's teasing tone. "Had to make sure, and all." She lowered her head and placed a soft kiss on Enori's lips. "I know it may seem silly, considering it's quite clear we'll be together forever, but…" She shrugged a shoulder, the fingers of one hand lightly tracing over Enori's features, her fingers receiving a kiss when they passed over Enori's lips. "I really want you to be my wife, Enori."

Enori felt those words to her soul, and for a moment, she couldn't respond. So, she urged Roishin's head down and initiated a slow, sensual kiss. So often words weren't her first go-to, but her body was. When the words just weren't strong enough, she preferred to *show* Roishin how she felt.

She knew Roishin knew this, so wasn't entirely surprised when she adjusted her hips for a better connection. This made them both moan softly into the kiss, which continued as they began to slowly move together, hips lazily thrusting and counterthrusting as Enori said everything in her kiss that she was still a bit too overwhelmed to say verbally.

It didn't take long before they were breathing too hard to kiss, but Roishin didn't move away, staying in Enori's personal space. Their movements stayed slow, a gentle rocking. Enori looked up into Roishin's eyes, able to see eternity there. She knew in that moment that not only did she want to become Roishin's wife and for Roishin to become *her* wife, but there was something else she wanted, too.

Her eyes squeezed shut and her neck and back arched as her release washed over her with startling intensity and speed. Her cry was loud, her fingers claw-like as they grasped the backsides of Roishin's shoulders. Her body was still pulsing when Roishin's loud gasp and growl in her throat alerted her own release.

Enori held the woman atop her tightly as Roishin buried her face in Enori's neck, her quick, whimpering breaths heating her skin. Stroking soft hair and the smooth skin of Roishin's back, Enori kissed the side of a dark head.

"Yes," she whispered. "With all my heart, yes, Roishin."

⚜ ⚜ ⚜ ⚜

On the grounds of their property, Enori wore a simple white summer dress, her feet bare on the emerald-green grass. Livia, who stood up for her, had surprised her with a ring of white flowers, which she wore like a small crown. Roishin, ever attached to her flowing cotton pants and white tunic shirt, held her hands as they stood across from each other. Ailfred stood up for his niece.

Ankou, in the blue cloak of the Order, officiated. Even as he began to speak, Enori couldn't take her eyes off the deep green of Roishin's eyes, made even more so by the green of the grass at their feet and trees that surrounded them in the spacious front yard of their home.

"It is my privilege today," Ankou began. "As head of this Order and a loving father, both by blood," he said, glancing to Roishin. "And by heart." He smiled at Enori.

"Two precious souls, created from one. A bond like no other that will stand the test of time. One of the greatest joys of my existence has been to see the two of you, my two daughters, come together, the two halves brought back as a whole."

Enori heard the words and felt the love coming off Roishin in waves. They'd decided to do this simple yet profound ceremony in Duras with the two that could not go to the earth plane. When they could, they would do this again with the rest of those they loved.

"Roishin, speak your heart to Enori," he said.

Roishin looked down at their joined hands for a moment before clearing her throat and looking back into Enori's eyes.

"Since I was four years old," she began. "When I first met you, I knew I loved you." Her smile was radiant. "In the forest that day, me crying over a rabbit I'd accidentally mortally wounded. Your kindness, your compassion, the way you guided me one step closer to myself…" She slowly shook her head as if in wonder, her eyes never leaving Enori's. "You became my angel that day. And now, all these years later, you still are and will forever be." She smiled. "I adore you. I respect you. I love you so much it hurts." She lifted their hands and kissed Enori's fingers.

Enori's heart was pounding, her chest so filled with love and gratitude that she truly feared it might explode.

"Enori," Ankou said. "Please speak your heart to Roishin."

"My pleasure," Enori said softly, Roishin meeting her soft smile with one of her own. "My mortal life began with pain, fear, and loneliness. I wandered, looking for anyone safe, a safe harbor for a broken soul."

She rubbed her thumbs gently over the backs of Roishin's hands, needing a moment. Taking a deep breath, she continued.

"The day a Druid and an Ankou found me on the Breton waterfront, saved me. I thought it was the best day of my life. And then, when Ankou made me his daughter, I thought *that* was the best day of my life. And," she continued, a little smirk curling her lips. "When he assigned me to a very spunky little girl, I wondered if I was being punished."

"Ha!" Roishin exclaimed with a loud laugh, followed by laughter from those gathered.

"Aye," Ailfred muttered. "You're Fallon's kid, all right."

Enori smiled, loving the joy she saw in Roishin's eyes. "But," she continued, growing serious again. "It was the day that I realized that I loved you, Roishin, and that you loved me in return. *That* was the best day of my life." She blinked a few times when she felt emotion trying to rise. When she felt she could speak without crying, she concluded with, "This broken soul is broken no more."

Roishin blinked several times as tears welled in her eyes at those softly spoken words. *I love you*, she mouthed, Enori responding in kind.

Ankou brought up his hands, a thick gold band held in his fingers. "I had this forged by Kazia," he explained. "From one piece of gold, one band." He smiled, pulling his hands apart, fingers of both holding a thinner gold band. "Then I had it split into two." He handed the one in his left hand to Enori, the one in his right to Roishin. "One becomes two, once more."

Both Enori and Roishin's fingers had been measured, so she knew the bands would fit. She was so deeply moved by what Ankou had done. And she was moved   by what, yet again, Kazia had made for her. She held the simple yet beautiful band in her fingers, which would be slid upon

Roishin's finger, as Roishin held hers.

"Roishin," Ankou said.

Roishin held Enori's band in the fingers of one hand while she took Enori's left hand with her free hand. She looked to Ankou.

"Say these words," he said. "This ring symbolizes my love, my commitment, and my soul connected to yours for all time."

"This ring," Roishin said. "Symbolizes my love, my commitment, and my soul connected to yours for all time." Her smile was nearly blinding as she slid the ring onto Enori's finger. She bent her head down and left a kiss upon the ring once in place.

"Enori," Ankou urged. "This ring symbolizes my love, my commitment, and my soul connected to yours for all time."

"With all my heart," Enori began softly, looking into Roishin's eyes. "This ring symbolizes my love, my commitment, and my soul connected to yours for all time." She slid the ring into place.

"With my blessing," Ankou said. "You are now and forever recognized as joined. You may kiss your wife."

Enori wrapped her arms around Roishin's neck as their lips met, Roishin holding her tight. She dimly heard applause and cheers as, indeed, that broken soul became whole.

Chapter Twenty-Three

Terryn had the most awful feeling begin to niggle at her gut as she and Jack stood there watching and listening. It was very clear that Garratt was pushing for a leader change, and like a seasoned politician, he was pitching his case that he was the man for the job. She couldn't take her eyes off him, but she couldn't figure out why.

As he extolled the virtues of what *he'd* do if *he* were in charge, Garratt turned his head, and his blue eyes met Terryn's across the expanse of the entire community. As he continued to talk to the masses, he was looking at her. His blue eyes that she wasn't able to necessarily see so clearly across the expanse, but *feel.*

A black swirl, like smoke rising from the campfire. Round and round until it began to straighten out, like an uncurling snake. Floating, all movement stopped until it surged at her, twin glowing eyes of icy white boring into her very soul.

Terryn gasped loudly, staggering backward until she backed into something. Steadying hands rested on her shoulders. Whirling, she found herself looking into the deep-set, concerned eyes of Dirk. He met her gaze then looked to Jack.

"We need to talk," he said quietly. "You need to gather your things and come to my place." With those cryptic words, he turned and left the dining hall.

Terryn, still deeply shaken from the vision a moment ago, looked to Jack. He smiled down at her reassuringly and grabbed her hand. Without a word, the two left and hurried through the tunnels to Terryn's family home. Neither her father nor Laird were home, which wasn't a huge surprise. Blair, however, was in bed.

"Terryn," she croaked, her voice weak.

Terryn glanced to her parents' bedroom before looking to Jack. "Gather everything from my sleep nook," she said softly. Jack nodded and hurried off to do her bidding as Terryn went into the dim room where her mother lay tucked into her own sleep nook, which honestly, looked more like her open coffin.

"Hey, Mom," Terryn said, walking over to her.

Blair looked over at her one and only daughter, her eyes sunken back into her head and deeply shadowed. She was skeletal and looked like she was ready to die. Her arm flopped out from the carved space, hand offered to Terryn. Surprised, the younger woman took it in her own hand.

"Don't let them find you," Blair whispered.

Terryn stared at her, eyebrows falling. "Who?"

Blair just stared up at her, her gaze scanning Terryn's face as if memorizing it. "Don't let them know," she whispered.

Terryn was beginning to think her mother was just talking nonsense in the haze of her illness until she said something else.

"Follow the raven, Terryn," she said. "She'll lead you home."

"Mom, what do you mean—"

"I need to sleep now," Blair said, giving Terryn's hand a faint squeeze before she pulled her arm back in and settled in for sleep.

A baffled Terryn left the room and headed to her

own. Jack was nearly finished gathering her things from the sleep nook. He'd stuffed as much as he could in the bag he'd carried all day, the rest laid out on the floor for the two to carry.

"Everything okay?" he asked.

"I'll tell you when we're situated." Terryn herself was quite *unsettled* by what she'd been told and wanted to bounce it off Ava later.

Jack nodded, squatting to roll up the bedroll. "Did you tell her you're leaving?"

Terryn moved out of Jack's way and bundled her clothing into her blanket. "She told *me* to leave," she said quietly. She met Jack's surprised gaze then, as if unspoken, the two quickened their efforts to get out of there.

Both with arms full, they headed out. Terryn was all eyes as she had an incredibly nervous and disquieted feeling in her gut. No doubt it was simply because things were not as copesetic as usual. Love it or hate it, things were usually fairly predictable. With what had happened that night, she felt things were anything but.

She was grateful that Dirk lived somewhat out of the way and that none of the main corridors had to be traversed to get there. Terryn didn't feel like she'd feel anything near okay until they were there. She could see in his eyes not an hour before that he felt it, too. Something was wrong. Just up ahead, she was relieved to see Dirk lean out of his doorway. She could see the equal relief on his face when he saw them coming.

He ushered them into the room they'd be using, then said, "You get unpacked, then come to my room." With that, he left them be, sliding a wool blanket across the doorway on a rod, much like that over the sleeping nooks in Terryn's old room.

She looked to Jack, who was just standing there

staring at the blanket, looking as surprised at the consideration as Terryn was. They met gazes for a moment before the spell was broken and they unloaded their wares. This sleep nook wasn't high above the floor and easy to climb into with a little lift onto tippy-toes.

Terryn smiled, thinking Ava would be thrilled, as she had said she wasn't huge on heights. In the dimness, they got everything situated. "I should have brought candles with me," she said.

"Um, Terryn" Jack drawled, almost a whisper. "You're kinda a living candle."

Terryn stopped, confused by the comment initially but then blushed deeply. "Um, right." A very quiet chuckle from Ava and a quick kiss as a bonus before they continued their work. A handful of minutes later, Terryn asked, "Ready?"

Seeming to understand what was being asked, Jack responded. "Everything is put away."

Terryn smirked at the response, then pulled the blanket curtain open. She was surprised, and a bit nervous, when she heard other voices coming from across the hall in Dirk's room. She really, really hoped they hadn't jumped from the pan into the fire and had gotten themselves trapped.

Her concern grew when she glanced to the entryway of the home to see a man leaning against the stone wall just inside. He glanced over at her, face relatively expressionless. It looked like he was on guard duty or something. She glanced back to Jack to see that he, too, had noticed the man. Their gazes met before they headed to Dirk's room.

Dirk and two other men sat on wooden chairs. There was one empty one left. Terryn recognized the other two from the table in the dining hall that night but didn't know their names. One was the man who had been sitting across from Jack and had seemed nice enough. The other man was actually young like they were, his bright red hair flopping in his face, which was a smattering of freckles.

"Come on in, you two," Dirk said. "Only got the one chair." He began to stand.

"No," Jack said. "I'll stand." He lightly touched Terryn's back to offer her the chair.

She sat, though she felt on edge. She was glad when Jack stood close to her, his hand resting on the back of her chair, which caused it to rest against her upper back. She leaned back against it, appreciative of the connection.

"Now," Dirk said, looking at the newcomers. "I got Stanly watching the door to make sure we won't have no trouble so we can talk open and honest."

Jack moved his hand and placed it outright on Terryn's shoulder, which made her feel so much better. She honestly had no idea what Dirk had to say. He still had the deep concern etched into his features that he'd had in the dining hall, but she felt that she and Jack were truly cornered if this didn't go their way.

"So," Dirk continued. "I think we got us a real problem with this Garratt fella. Something about him ain't right." He looked to Jack and Terryn. "We all feel it. And," he added, his gaze boring into Terryn's. "I know you saw it tonight. Didn't you?"

Clearing her throat, Terryn took a deep breath and decided to share what she'd seen, and not just tonight. "A couple weeks ago, my brother and I went out exploring. We came across wreckage of some sort and a dead man in a stream a few miles away from here." She looked up at Jack and nodded. "Same stream." Looking back to the men, she continued. "Further upstream I came across some blood on the shore. No body, nothing there, just blood soaked into the sand. I knew it wasn't from the dead man. But when I really studied it—" Her voice cut off as she was forced to swallow again, emotion rising from just how shaken she'd been that day and tonight, as well.

"It's okay, Terryn," Dirk said, leaning over and lightly patting her knee. Jack began to gently massage the muscle that connected her neck to her shoulder.

Taking another deep breath, Terryn continued. "I saw something. It was this…this *smoke*, I guess. Or a mist. It was black and it had these eyes that glowed white. It lunged at me, then the vision disappeared. Scared me to death. Well, tonight," she added, looking at all three men who were looking intently back at her. "When I was looking at Garratt up there talking, I saw it again."

The men all exchanged looks with each other, a silent communication seeming to happen between the three. Finally, the ginger grinned. "You two owe me a mug of ale."

"Damn it," the one who had been sitting across from Jack at dinner that night groused. He looked to Terryn. "Moe, here," he said, backhanding the redhead kid on the arm, "said you was Druid. We were just sure you was Ankou," he added, indicating himself and Dirk.

"Takes one to know one," Moe said softly, crossing his arms with a look of satisfaction on his face. "Right, Terryn?"

She felt downright emotional, relief washing through her like the unleashed dam of honesty that was before her. All she could do for a moment was nod. "Aye," she finally said, Moe grinning at her.

He reached across the space, holding his hand out to her, which she took. His hand was so warm as it engulfed hers. "We have to stick together," he said softly, with a smile. He met her gaze, and in their blue depths, she recognized the kindred spirit for what it was.

Nodding, she returned his smile. "Aye. We do."

"He'd gone dormant for about what," Dirk said, looking to the other two as Moe released Terryn's hand and sat back in his chair. "Ten years, maybe, Ray?"

"If that," Moe said.

"Who?" Jack asked.

"What your lady saw," the man named Ray added. "These dumb bastards think it's folks like us that are the boogeyman out there, when it's been him this entire time."

"You mean, Bahutha, don't you?" Jack asked, voice quiet.

Ray looked up at him with raised eyebrows. "You all know about him on the outside?"

"Outside?" Terryn asked.

Ray's gaze drifted up to Jack. "She knows about you," he said. "Don't she, Jack?"

Terryn dragged her gaze from him and looked up at Jack, who was staring at Ray, uncertainty in his dark eyes. Swallowing, Jack looked decidedly uncomfortable.

Ray and Dirk exchanged another glance before, to Terryn's absolute astonishment, both men vanished, in their places two very different people appeared. Dirk became a woman in her thirties, maybe, if not a bit younger. Her jet-black hair was cropped very short, perhaps just long enough to run fingers through. Her eyes were an icy blue and her skin was pale.

In a way, she reminded Terryn of the dark-haired version of the woman called Enori. She had that same aloof, almost ethereal quality to her. But, whereas Enori's beauty almost gave her an angelic, soft quality, this woman seemed the opposite side of that stunning coin. Her gaze was intense, not much more than blue-tinged chips of ice that could freeze anyone to the spot. She exuded a presence of power that was almost frightening.

The man who had been Ray was still a man, though no longer tall and gangly but tall and thick, arms large, and shoulders and chest broad. He looked to be in his late forties, early fifties. His long, dark hair was pulled back into a single, thick braid that went down his back. His skin tone was not as dark as Anise's had been, but darker than those around him. His features were strong, dark brown eyes set beneath heavy eyebrows.

"We are the Ancients," the woman said, her tone firm and accented. "Big Bear and I have been here since the war." She indicated the man sitting on the other side of Moe, who remained Moe but didn't look fazed in the least by this startling revelation.

Terryn's mouth fell open and her eyes grew huge. It didn't matter that she'd seen Ava transform a half dozen times now, to see these people do it right in front of her, with the ease and grace as Ava did, was stunning. She also heard Jack gasp above her.

"Who are you?" Jack whispered.

"I am Senara," the woman said. She pushed to her feet, Dirk's clothing hanging off her frame. She wasn't as tall as Roishin but stood taller than Ava and Terryn's more diminutive height. She walked over to Jack, those eyes, which were almost luminescent, looking straight into his. Terryn watched with fascination. "And, you are?"

Terryn stood and moved out of their way, watching with great interest. Jack morphed into her true form, Ava looking into the woman's eyes. It was so wild for Terryn to see the woman with others, as it had been such a closely guarded secret between them.

"I'm Ava."

The slightest smile quirked Senara's full lips. "You are from Duras?"

Ava nodded. "That I am."

The smile grew. "Then, you know Enori." A statement.

Ava's own smile was instant. "Absolutely."

Senara's eyes closed and her hands came together before her mouth, almost as if in prayer. After a moment, she dropped her hands and asked, "How did you get in here?" She shook her head. "Has been locked all these years."

Ava reached for Terryn, gently pulling her to her side. "Roishin, Ankou's daughter and, ironically, Enori's partner. She is Terryn's shadow."

Senara looked to Terryn, eyes wide. "It worked," she whispered. She turned to look at the other two men, who had also stood. She turned to look at Terryn, bringing up her hands and cupping her face. "You," she said softly. "You have been the key."

Terryn had no idea what to say, as she had no idea what this woman was talking about. A glance to Ava showed her a look of pride and admiration. She also seemed to somewhat understand what Senara was talking about, based on her expression. Looking back to the woman before her, Terryn swallowed.

"I don't understand," she said. "I know what a shadow is, she explained that to me, but…"

"Your shadow," Big Bear explained. "Is of Ankou blood. You, Druid. It was an Ankou and a Druid who locked Bowhar down to contain Bahutha."

"Ankou and Macha," Senara supplied.

Big Bear smiled, and though genuine, it did little to soften such bold features. "Together, you and your combined energy with your shadow unlocked the door." He turned to Ava. "Is the shadow here, too?"

Ava shook her head. "No. Roishin has been here, though."

"We need to light the fires," Moe said.

Terryn looked to him. "Light the fires?"

"You need to get her here," Big Bear said to Terryn.

"Tomorrow," Senara said. She glanced at all present. "It is late. Tomorrow, we go home." Looking back to Terryn, she again cupped her face, the intensity in her eyes softening. "Rest tonight, little one."

As soon as her hand fell away, Senara vanished, leaving Dirk behind. Big Bear followed suit, though Ava remained. Terryn felt like she was in the craziest dream of her life. She looked to Ava to see if everything had really happened.

"Come on," Ava said, reaching for Terryn's hand. "Let's go to bed."

In the other room and with the curtain closed behind them, Terryn stood there, hands to her mouth. Her brain was so overwhelmed with everything that happened within the last hour. Finally, she dropped her hands and looked at Ava, who stood nearby but was touching her. She seemed to be waiting for Terryn to let her know what she needed.

"Did you know?" Terryn finally asked.

"About them?" Ava asked, indicating Dirk's bedroom. At Terryn's nod, she shook her head. "I had no idea. Honestly, I'm as stunned as you are."

"What are the Ancients?" Terryn asked.

She had no idea what to do. Should she take off her boots and climb into bed? She was so exhausted, but everything felt like it had changed. That day, she'd come to feel so close to Ava, finally getting to spend time with *her* and not Jack. And their wonderful kiss and the few they'd shared while on their little adventure.

But now, after the revelations of moments before, she felt like such an inexperienced child next to all of them, including Ava. Did she see her that way? Now that she was with her kind again, did she still want to be close to Terryn? Still want to touch her and kiss her? Did she still feel connected to her?

Perhaps sensing her sudden fears, Ava walked over to Terryn and took her in her arms. She just held her, their bodies pressed together. Eyes squeezing shut, Terryn held on, needing so badly to feel grounded. She felt like everything was about to change so drastically, and she had not one iota of an idea of what it all meant.

"I feel so lost," she admitted into the hug.

Ava ran her fingers through long, auburn hair. "I know," she murmured. "Everything is going to dramatically change, Terryn. But," she added, pulling away just enough to look into Terryn's face. "I'll be with you."

"Promise me," Terryn whispered. "Promise you won't leave me."

Ava's smile was so beautiful as she cupped Terryn's face. "I promise," she said with a kiss.

Chapter Twenty-Four

Ava rose into wakefulness in the pitch darkness that was their sleeping nook. For the second morning in a row, she was cuddled up to Terryn. She wanted to groan in embarrassment, as clearly she had sought out the other woman in her sleep yet again. She was worried she'd become addicted to her, in all honesty.

She lay there still for a moment, allowing herself to just revel in the closeness. She closed her eyes again and inhaled the scent of Terryn's neck, which her face was partially buried in. Their bodies were as close as they could be while remaining two separate individuals. How on earth did she become so needy of this woman, who was a veritable stranger just over a week before?

Though she knew there was a lot she needed to learn about the woman, she knew that she knew her soul, and the need growing for it scared her. She smiled when she felt fingers begin to run through her hair.

"Are you okay?" Terryn murmured, her voice such a comfort in the darkness.

Ava nodded. "I am." She didn't bother to keep quiet or change into Jack. Luckily, their host knew who she was. Such a relief, as short-lived as it may be, as they'd have to leave the house eventually.

"You know," Terryn said, resting her head against Ava's. "In the two nights you've been with me, I've slept better than I ever have. What am I going to do when you go?"

"I already told you," Ava said, sliding her hand from

where it rested on Terryn's stomach over to her side to cuddle in even closer. "I'm not leaving you here."

"Where will we go after this?" Terryn murmured, her fingers beginning to trail along Ava's forearm. It was sending wonderful sensations up Ava's arm and down through her body.

"I don't know," Ava answered honestly. "I can't take you to Duras with me, but I imagine the Druids will want you to go to Ryarch."

"The homeland of the Druids, right?"

"Mm-hmm." Ava was drawn to the warmth of Terryn's neck again.

She liked the little sigh she got when she left a small kiss there. No idea what possessed her, but she did it again. The roaming fingers on her arm slowed into more of a caress. Her own hand roamed down along Terryn's side to her hip, where it stopped and quickly began to move upward again as her lips left another kiss, this one lingering a bit.

Terryn's fingers stopped combing through her hair and buried themselves in it instead. Her head turned in the darkness until their lips met. Ava pushed herself up to a forearm as their kiss deepened. It was incredible how things had changed in the span of one day. This time the morning before, she'd woken up mortified, no idea how to get herself out of the bind her unconscious body had put her in.

Now, her tongue gently stroked Terryn's in their kiss, both of them learning more about the beautiful act. Each kiss had gotten better than the last since their first several nights ago in the dining hall when Terryn had all but plundered her mouth in desperation after the attack. Now, it was so sensuous, like a dance of lips and tongue.

Ava realized her hand had moved up dangerously

close to the side of Terryn's left breast, and it sent a thrill through her that nearly made her gasp. Terryn sighed into the kiss, her back arching a bit as if her body was sending an invitation for touch that Ava wasn't even sure Terryn was fully cognizant of.

Taking a chance, Ava slid her hand up a bit more, her thumb coming into contact with the soft roundness of the side of the breast. Again, Terryn arched her back, making it very clear what she wanted. Ava's hand slid up and over the soft firmness to fully cup her through the material of her shirt.

Terryn gasped, their kiss pausing as they both took in what was happening. The first time for one to be touched so intimately, the first time the other to touch someone so intimately. Ava lifted her lips from Terryn's as her hand lightly squeezed the breast in her hand, the hardening nipple poking against her palm.

Never had she even imagined or dreamed she'd touch another woman like this, let alone initiate such a touch. She could almost hear Terryn's thundering heartbeat in the darkness as Ava lightly brushed her palm back and forth over the nipple before she took it between thumb and forefinger. She lightly tugged at it, Terryn grabbing the back of her head and tugging her down into an all-consuming kiss.

The kiss only lasted a brief moment before voices could be heard out in the tunnel beyond Dirk's house. Panicked voices, and one was headed toward the small house.

"Dirk!" a man's voice exclaimed. Ava thought it sounded like Ray. "Wake up!" The words were followed by the slap of a hand to stone. "Wake up!"

Ava moved away from Terryn, who sat up. They both sat there frozen for a moment before Terryn threw the blanket off her and climbed out of the sleeping nook. Ava followed suit, searching for her boots. She tugged them on before changing into Jack. Her heart was still racing from earlier activities, and she was quite uncomfortable in her underwear, but they needed to get moving.

"Ready?" Terryn asked.

"Go ahead," Jack said, Terryn shoving the blanket curtain aside.

The two nearly ran into Dirk as he hurried from his own room. He held a lit candle in his hands, the concern written all over his features. He nodded at the two, and all three hurried from the house with Ray in the lead.

"Where're the others?" Dirk asked the man in front.

"Figured we pick them up on the way," Ray said.

As they made their way toward the more populated part of the tunnels, the cries and yells got louder. Ava's blood went cold when she realized what was happening. "Oh my god," Jack whispered. "They're rounding them up."

"You killed him!" a woman screamed.

Jack nearly ran Terryn over when she stopped in the middle of the main tunnel they were running down. In an offshoot tunnel, Ava recognized Raif's wives standing out in the corridor. The brunette was covered in blood, though she didn't look to be injured. One of the men that Ava recognized as becoming a very close friend of Garratt's in the last week grabbed the brunette and pulled her away from the pregnant blond woman, who she had seemed to be trying to protect.

"No!" the brunette screamed. "Rhea! Don't hurt her, she's pregnant! No!"

Another of the men, who had clearly become one of Garratt's goons, grabbed the blonde by the hair with one hand, the other hand holding up a knife that already literally dripped with blood. He leveled the blade to her very swollen belly, intent clear.

"No," Jack hissed, covering Terryn's mouth with his hand as she began to scream when realization hit her. He literally picked her up to get them away from there. There was no way in hell Ava wanted Terryn to have that horrendous image in her mind.

Once she knew Terryn would move on her own, Jack grabbed her hand and yanked her behind him, forcing her to run or be dragged behind him. The other two men were already well down the tunnel, the small bit of light from Dirk's candle barely a glow in the darkness. None of the morning crew had lit torches yet. And frankly, Ava wasn't so sure they ever would again.

"Light it!" Jack called out.

"I can't!" Terryn exclaimed, her voice shaky with fear.

"Yes, you can, Terryn. You can! You have to!"

Jack was nearly pulled off his feet when Terryn stopped them. She was trembling as suddenly a stream of fire erupted from her hands to arch along the rounded ceiling. She cried out in surprise, and Jack's eyes nearly popped out of his head. Finally, she got it down to a dull roar, her hand effectively becoming a torch.

"Holy…" Shaking himself out of it, Jack grabbed her other hand and off they went again.

It took two turns in the system to finally catch up with the two men. "This way," Dirk said, taking a sharp left down a narrow tunnel Ava had never been down before.

The tunnel was incredibly narrow, and all three men's shoulders brushed against the stone on either side. The yelling and carnage grew fainter, and Ava had to wonder where the hell they were being led to. Finally, they ended up in an open cavern.

"What is this?" Terryn asked.

"It's the tannery," Ray explained.

As Terryn moved her hand, the light of the flame hit upon every kind of sharp scraping, cutting, ripping, and poking tool imaginable. Jack was wide-eyed and Ava was disgusted. "Why did you bring us here?" Jack asked.

"There's a door back here," Dirk explained.

"Oh my god!" Terryn screamed.

Jack whirled to see what was wrong. On the sturdy metal hooks pounded into the stone that were used to dry a hide, they saw Moe hanging there, the hooks protruding through his chest. Hooded blue eyes stared sightlessly into eternity.

Jack grabbed Terryn and turned her away from it and into his neck. "It's okay." *Christ!*

"The door's locked," Ray said from deeper in the room. "The fucking door is *locked.*"

Terryn pulled away from Jack slowly, as if in a daze. She looked up into his eyes for a long moment, as if she didn't know him. Her gray eyes glowed with the fire that was wrapped around her hand.

"What is it?" Jack asked.

"She said I could call for her," Terryn said softly.

"Who?"

"Roishin."

Jack ran his hand through his hair as he blew out a relieved breath. "Yes." He turned to the other two men who had walked over to them. "Where do we need to go from here?" he asked them.

"We need to go light the fires," Dirk said, his voice melting into the smoky timbre that was Senara as she emerged, Ray also losing his veneer.

"Where at?" Ava asked, Jack pushed away.

"The ruins," Terryn said, her voice that same, dreamy tone. "We have to get out of here."

"I don't think so."

All four turned to see Garratt and four of his men standing in the entryway to the tannery. Ava stared at him. He no longer looked like the man she'd first seen more than a week ago. Yes, same basic features, but everything about him had become more intense, almost animalistic. His eyes were no longer blue but pure black, irises and all. Even his stance, shoulders a bit hunched, looked as though he were constantly ready to pounce.

"What have you done, Garratt?" Ava asked. "Why are you killing these people?"

He looked at her, a little smirk on his lips. "Because it's easier to control the dead than it is the living. They're either so pissed off and volatile with each other that they leave me the fuck alone, or they're so devastated at what happened, they don't care. Either way, their bullshit helps keep the living scared shitless."

Ava felt a cold sweat begin to gather under her arms. "Is that your intent with us?" she asked, not really interested in the answer.

"Nope," he said. "I plan to use you three bitches to breed with. Make more little magic babies." He tilted his head toward the man standing next to him. "Ever fucked an immortal before, Eddie?" he asked, a grin on his face. "That cunt." He pointed at Senara. "I remember you. You and that Enori bitch." His grin was pure hatred. "I'd love nothing more than to fuck you until you scream." His jaw clenched. "And Brielle."

"You will never get the chance, Bahutha," Senara said calmly.

His grin widened. "It's nice to see your lips wrapped around my name. Know what else I wanna see them wrapped around?"

One of the men gasped. "Where'd she come from?"

Ava didn't even have to look, as she saw it written all over Garratt's face. His rage erupted from him as he looked past the four standing before him. His face twisted from the handsome if not grizzled face of Garratt to what almost looked like the head of a snake made of smoke before the human face returned.

"Go!" Terryn yelled to the three others as she turned back to Garratt and his men.

Ava heard the others run to the back of the cavern. A quick glance showed Roishin standing next to the door, waving them all through. For a moment their gazes met before Roishin looked past the two women to her brother… well, what was left of his humanity, anyway.

Terryn slashed her arm through the air in an arc, the fire that danced around her hand spraying forth as if from a flamethrower. The five men tried to duck away from the fiery wrath, but it was too late. All of them ignited upon contact.

She turned to Ava. "Go," she insisted, pushing on her. "Go!"

Ava turned to run to the door, only Roishin waiting now. Realizing Terryn wasn't with her, she turned to watch. The Druid walked over to Moe's body. She was chanting as she lit his body aflame, sending him to their land of the dead with dignity.

With that, she clapped her hands together, the fire vanishing without so much as a wisp of smoke. Absolute determination on her face, Terryn hurried over to them. She took Ava's hand, the two running through the door…

…and to the middle of the ruins. The other two already waited for them, Roishin stepping through last. Ava looked around to find them exactly where they'd been the day before. She couldn't help but look over at their crumbling cottage and smile. Her attention was taken from it and to Roishin, who reached her hand out to Terryn, who took it.

The two walked to the centermost part of the village, avoiding the rubble as they went. Ava stood back with Big Bear and Senara. Roishin stopped their progress and turned to face Terryn. They stood not a foot apart. Left hand clasped left hand, right hand clasped right hand, their arms forming an X.

Eyes closed, they both began to softly chant, murmured words just barely audible. Two separate chants, two separate languages, spoken in unison. Ava wanted to ask what they were doing but didn't dare speak.

Suddenly, all around them, *whoosh!* One after the other after the other, fires burst to life. Ava's mouth was hanging open as she turned to see them all spark to life around the little destroyed village. There was no source—not a torch or a candle or even a stick of wood. The flames just…were.

Her gaze turned back to Roishin and Terryn as their chanting grew louder, both their heads fallen back, faces raised, and eyes closed as their mouths worked continuously.

It was then that Ava realized that she heard others chanting, too. She looked to Senara and Big Bear, neither saying a word but both looking around, too. Ghostly hooded figures began to crawl out of the piles of rubble, becoming more solid as they climbed. One, two, five, twenty, thirty-five, fifty.

They gathered around the fires, arms raised to the heavens and long sleeves of their robes falling to reveal their hands and arms. Their voices grew louder and louder until it was an entire symphony of voices, all chanting together, female and male, all as one. Tears were in Ava's eyes as she watched and listened.

A loud crack rent the air. Looking around to try to find the source, Ava's eyes found the skies above. The heavy, steel-gray skies were beginning to literally crack. Jagged lines trailed across the undersides of heavy, pregnant clouds.

As the chanting continued, growing to a deafening cacophony, a piece of the sky began to fall. But, before it could hit the ground, it exploded into birds of every size, shape, and color. The winged creatures sang their song of freedom as they soared high overhead, including a huge black raven.

Another massive piece of the sky fell from its moorings, slowly plummeting to the earth. Upon landing, a mass of horses thundered from the dust, beautiful manes flowing as they galloped and pranced.

On and on it went. A herd of reindeer galloping. Majestic elephants with trunks raised high trumpeting, with running chickens and colorful peacocks dodging the huge, lumbering creatures. It was every animal known to man.

Finally, what was left of the sky shattered like glass, the pieces blowing away on the warm winds that began to sweep the land.

Huge swaths of sunlight poured in, as if someone had dumped an endless container of water. The light traveled along the gray, broken, and pockmarked landscape, pouring color wherever it went: blue sky, dark soil, endless colors of wildflower blossoms. Green wild grasses spread across the ground as if a massive rolled carpet had been kicked to unfurl.

Endless gallons of water began to shoot out of the ground like a geyser, melting the parched earth as lakes and waterways began to form, waves pounding the rock debris apart until it sank beneath the surface.

It was so sudden that it was truly deafening as the chanting stopped all at once. The scattered fires slowly burned themselves down until they vanished. Ava looked to Senara to see that silent tears trailed down her cheeks as she, too, was taking it all in. Their gazes met for a moment before Ava turned to see Roishin and Terryn sharing a tight hug.

The ruins still existed, but now wildflowers, moss, and animals wandered the decrepit structures. They, after all, could be rebuilt. The two pulled out of their hug, and Terryn looked over to Ava, meeting her gaze and holding it as she turned away from her shadow. She walked over to the woman who waited for her.

"Hey," Terryn said, something in her eyes that Ava had never seen there before. A woman reborn, a woman found.

She smiled. "Hi."

Terryn snaked her arms up around Ava's neck, giving her the most beautiful smile as she cocked her head slightly to the side and studied Ava's face. "I think we're starting to get Bowhar back."

Ava grinned. "I think you might be right." Her eyes closed as their lips met.

Epilogue

Her wings flapped as she soared overhead. Like little ants, people began to appear from the deep recesses of the Shadows, looks of wonder and confusion on their faces as they looked around, watching life springing up all around them.

Kids ran and danced, falling to their hands and knees on this new thing called grass. Adults looked at each other, mystified.

She flew on, wings beating against the air as she reached the ruins. She watched as all the robed figures converged on the four women and one man at the center. It was joyous, apparently so much so that two of the women were kissing. She continued on.

People ran from an entrance that seemed to appear like magic from a mountainside. These people were not joyous and happy, but frantic. Smoke billowed out after them. They scattered like cockroaches in every direction. When it seemed there was no more left to escape, one man did. As soon as he got past the huge open door, he fell to his hands and knees.

She swooped lower until she landed on the back of the axe head that was embedded in an upturned log. She turned her head this way and that to get a better look at this man. His clothing had all but been burned off his body. What was left of his hair was still smoking. He fell to his side and finally to his back.

He was coughing violently and lay there for a moment, his body badly burned, one hand not much more than a stump of charred flesh. As she watched, something began to happen to this man. Oh so slowly, the singed skin began to heal, his face the very picture of agony. His back arched, and a long stream of black mist oozed from his mouth.

This black mist began to dance over his body, swirling under a leg and over his chest, then around his head and then slowly over his chest again. The healing began to happen faster. The charred skin took a familiar shape and form. The black turned to an ugly red then to a pink color, and finally that of normal flesh.

The man's face relaxed, becoming more recognizable as first a human, then a man, his eyes closed. The mist slowly swirled around him then up into the air before it arched gracefully back down toward him in a long, thin stream. It eased slowly back into his mouth, disappearing inside him.

A moment later, the man's eyes opened, and they glowed white.

With a gasp, Elsie's own eyes opened. She stared blankly at the underside of the canopy above her. She took several deep breaths, her being easing back into place. Finally, she let out a long, slow breath before speaking.

"It begins."

Continued in Book 6—*She Who Would Be Queen*

About the Author

Kim has spent her life in Colorado and can't imagine living anywhere else. She's been writing since she was 9 and stumbled into her first book being published in her mid-20s. She's worked in the film industry as a writer, director and producer, but now enjoys the quiet, happy life of a professional author. She can be reached on Facebook and on her website at, www.kimpritekel.com

If you liked this book...

Share a review with your friends or post a review on your favorite site like Amazon, Goodreads, Barnes and Noble, or anywhere you purchased the book. Or perhaps share a posting on your social media sites and help spread
the word.

Join the Sapphire Newsletter and keep up with all your favorite authors.

Did we mention you get a free book for joining our team?

sign-up at - www.sapphirebooks.com

Check out Kim's other books.

1049 Club - ISBN - 978-1-939062-97-0

Almost two hundred souls, one plane, six survivors, endless heartbreak.
When flight 1049, headed from Buffalo, NY to Italy falls from the sky, a firestorm of drama, pain, angst and sorrow ensues. Can an author, a business owner, a teenager, good ol' boy, veterinarian and ruthless lawyer survive? Better yet, can those left behind?
1049 Club is a story of survival, love, deep regret and miracles. Can the living make peace with the presumed dead? Can the presumed dead make peace with the lives and loves they thought they had before?

Blinded – ISBN – 978-1-943353-53-8

After a horrible explosion sends local television news reporter, Burton Blinde reeling both physically and emotionally, she walks away from her life and the dream job she was about to start at a major news network.

For six long years she hides out in a small mountain town, working at the local library, though is haunted by the life she had, including mysterious messages and gifts she was receiving before her life was turned upside down, a veritable bread crumb trail leading to the unknown.
Unable to resist, Burton begins to follow the clues, which will lead her into the darkest places of human nature that she may not be able to return from.

Damaged - ISBN - 978-1-939062-45-1

Family. A group of people you are related to by blood or love.

Nora Schaeffer has come home to her family after twenty years working around the world as a photographer for National Geographic. She's welcomed into the open arms of her father and siblings.

Family. A group of people who support you, lift you up when you fall.

Shannon, the youngest of the four Schaeffer siblings, has vanished, leaving her five-year-old daughter, Bella, terrified and alone. To help find Shannon, Nora has no choice but to turn to the dark-haired specter who has haunted her for twenty years. Along the way, she finds her own long-dead heart and uncovers chilling family secrets beyond imagination.

Family. A group of people who will stick together to hide the rotten soul at its core at any cost.

Who will live? Who will die? Who will be the most damaged? And who will learn to love again?

The Gift - ISBN - 978-1-948232-47-0

The dead do speak. You just have to listen. Homicide Detective Catania "Nia" d'Giovanni is the only daughter in a large Italian family of six children. The backbone—a position not applied for nor wanted—she continues to create new glue to hold the dysfunctional group together. For Nia, family time feels more like herding cats than spending time with her brothers and feisty, aging parents.

Her heart has always been in her career with the Pueblo Police Department, especially since it will never be okay with her very Catholic mother to openly give her heart to any woman, until she meets a secretive waitress who has her at, Can I take your order?

And then it begins...

Three murders that are so gruesome, so horrible, they rock the small town to its core. Nia and her partner Oscar are left to piece together a deadly puzzle to find the key to unlock the monster they hunt.

Or, are they the hunted?

As they dissect the murder scenes where not one shred of evidence is left behind, more bodies begin to show up, each cleaner than the last, the shadowy specter that is the killer vanishing without a trace, making the woman Nia loves disappear right along with it.

When there is no evidence to follow, Nia must trust her instincts...or, is she being guided?

The Plan – ISBN – 978-1-948232-43-2

As the dark days of the Dust Bowl came to an end, the midsection of the United States tried to rebuild and revitalize. In the small, dusty farming town of, Brooke View, Colorado, teenager, Eleanor Landry and her mother were dealing with her father, a self-appointment fire and brimstone preacher to his congregation of two. A plan to survive.

As the dark era of the robber baron comes to an end, giants of industry and innovation emerged with fabulous fortunes manifested in the mansions that dotted the landscape across the country. Lysette Landon, the teen daughter of the wealthiest family in Brooke View, was everything a good, proper girl of privilege should be. Only problem was, she wasn't dreaming of finding a young man to raise a family with. A plan to be free.

One look, one touch, all plans are off.

Secrets deeper and darker than the grave would bring Eleanor and Lysette together, their families connected by a web of lies and broken promises. A plan to escape.

Be careful because, life has other plans...

The Traveler Book One: The Hunted - ISBN - 978-1-948232-91-3

A story so epic one book can't contain it. BOOK ONE:

1977: In the era between flower power and the yuppie, Sonia Lucas is a young wife and mother, just starting out in life. Without warning, a strange presence and dark force enters her life, clouds building...

1917: ...and a storm brewing as the world reeled from the horrific events of World War I just before it was ravaged by a Spanish flu epidemic that would kill millions. Sephora Lloyd is a 16 year old girl lost in the responsibilities of an adult world helping to support herself and her mother. A beautiful young nun-in-training enters her life, bringing love and hope with her. That is, until a force bigger than either of them threatens everything Sephora holds dear.

Four women - three deaths - two words - one house
THE HUNTED

The Traveler Book Two: The Hunter - ISBN - 978-1-948232-93-7

A story so epic one book can't contain it. BOOK TWO:

1890: In the dying days of the Old West, Sally Little runs her booming brothel with the passion and tenacity the business of sex requires. Savvy and indulgent, there's one itch Sally can't let herself scratch. Afraid of hurting the woman she loves, she instead unleashes...

Present Day: ...her renovation crew and fixer upper TV show on a dilapidated mansion that has known nothing but death since a murder there in 1977. Samantha Leyton sees ratings gold in bringing the sagging old house to life, but instead she discovers only she has the power to unlock the mystery that hunted four women across time, leaving death and destruction in its wake. Can she release her sisters who came before her and finally be granted the gift of love that is stronger than any evil?

Four women - Three deaths - two words - one house
THE HUNTER

Finding Faith (Wynter Series Book 1) - ISBN - 978-1-952270-16-1

Faith Fitzgerald thought that if she got an education and became a high-powered attorney in Manhattan, maybe—just maybe—she'd gain the attention and respect of her absentee father. Considering he was the only parent she had left after her mother's suicide when Faith was just a child, she thought that's what it would take.

She was wrong.

What she dreamed would be glamorous and satisfying turned out to be grueling and thankless. Since she wasn't willing to play the game between the sheets, she was forced to stay in the cubicle jungle doing all the heavy lifting while the men got the credit and the rewards.

Deciding she is done, Faith packs up and, with the flip of the bird to the rearview mirror, leaves New York and heads home to Colorado. She has nothing there: no job, nowhere to live, no relationship with her father. Truth is, she barely has a relationship with herself.

On the drive home, she finds herself in Wynter, a tiny mountain town at the foot of the Rockies. Looking more like it belongs in a made-for-TV Christmas movie than on the map, Faith is utterly enchanted. When she tries her luck and buys a raffle ticket at Pop's, Wynter's charming café, her prize is far more than meets the eye—or the heart.

Enter Wyatt, a feisty, sexy southerner and waitress at Pop's, who just happens to be married to a local sheriff's deputy. All is not as it appears with the All-American boy and his Georgia peach.

A colorful cast of unforgettable and charming characters will teach the jaded attorney that sometimes to find yourself all you have to do is go back to the basics...and have a little Faith.

Taking Liberty (Wynter Series Book 2) - ISBN- 978-1-952270-24-6

A victim of a massive corporate downsize, Liberty Faulkner suddenly finds herself without a job, without a home, and without a plan. Though certainly not part of her vision, Libby decides that the familiar is the safest path back to her life goals. In this case, the devil she knows is home: the tiny mountain town of Wynter, Colorado, a close-knit place where everybody knows everybody and everybody's business. Seems like the perfect place for the twenty-five-year-old to start over and figure out who she is without being noticed...not.

Sergeant Grace Montez escaped her dead-end job and toxic relationship in New Mexico and moved to Wynter to help build their police department from scratch. Now an established figurehead in the community, she's got her professional life dialed in and even mentors new recruits on the force. After a challenging childhood and lifetime of abandonment and disappointment, Grace hasn't been interested in another relationship— especially because no one has caught her eye since a certain quirky college student who used to make her caramel macchiato at the local coffee shop moved away three years ago.

Now that quirky college student has returned as the beautiful, mature woman Libby has become. Can Grace keep her distance, or will she finally take liberties with what is being offered?

Justice Won (Wynter Series Book 3) - ISBN - 978-1-952270-36-9

In 1890, seventeen-year-old Justice Kilkoyne and her mother, Ninny, are one bad decision away from living on the streets of Azrael, Pennsylvania. Ninny's propensity for the bottle has left Justice to play the adult, her androgynous good looks helping her pass as a young man to gain employment and keep them—if just barely—above water.

Determined to find a better life for them, Justice saves every penny to get them on a train headed west to the sunshine of California. Before they can leave, the bigotry of one shopkeeper sends Justice on the run, chased by the police for a crime she didn't commit and straight into the unwitting arms of a stunning young prostitute, who, after an unexpected connection, becomes Justice's Angel.

The day arrives to leave Pennsylvania for good. As Justice and Ninny get settled, they're surprised by the appearance of Angel, also wanting to start anew. When the trip is violently interrupted in Colorado, Angel just may be lost to Justice forever.

Can Justice find a new life when she makes her way to the fledgling mining town of Wynter, Colorado? Can her heart ever be whole again?

Curtain Call - ISBN - 978-1-952270-42-0

What do you do when you come from a long line of dancers that spans the globe and generations, yet you can't tell your right foot from your left? You fall in love with a dancer, of course!

Gray Rickman is an awkward seventeen-year-old when she first sets eyes on Christian Scott at the dance studio/theater Gray's parents own and run in Denver, Colorado.

Though only a handful of years older than Gray, Christian carries herself with poise and wisdom far beyond her years. A woman of few words, she speaks volumes with her body.

Before Gray even really knows what her type is, Christian stars in endless daydreams and even fulfills a couple of her fantasies before vanishing out of thin air, leaving Gray in an empty bed with nothing but bittersweet memories and broken dreams.

With no choice but to move on, Gray attempts love, even moving with her college girlfriend to New York City to pursue a career in journalism. But her standard has been set, the bar way too high for any other woman to reach or clear. It's an unexpected encounter in an obvious place when Gray sets eyes on her dancer again.

Will the bright lights of Broadway illuminate the way back to the woman of her dreams? Or will they blind her to any other possibility of happiness?

Break a leg, Gray. The Great White Way calls.

Encore Performance - ISBN - 978-1-952270-52-9

Grey Rickman, a journalist for The New York Times, is offered the opportunity of a lifetime and a huge boost to her career—ghostwriting a memoir for one of the world's most beloved actors. She is deeply in love with her girlfriend, dancer Christian Scott, and her world couldn't be better.

Christian, though proud of Grey and all that she's accomplished, is facing her own career dilemma. All she's ever wanted to do is perform and create, her body her kinetic canvas. But, in one of the few industries where youth matters above all else, her time is coming to make decisions that no woman in her mid-thirties should have to make: is it time to retire?

As the career of one begins to explode into the stratosphere and the other's implodes after a career-ending injury that makes any retirement discussion irrelevant, Grey and Christian begin to drift apart. Changing priorities and newly built walls lead to fears and accusations, further tearing at the fabric of the love they've worked years to create.

Will cooler heads prevail to warm up the hearts of the deeply passionate couple in time to create a new dream for their second act?

Swann Song - ISBN - 978-1-952270-63-5

Christine Swann is a world-famous singer/songwriter and lesbian icon, known for her edgy style and heart-pounding songs. Gorgeous, rich and miserable. Her music has always been her life, her escape from an unimaginable childhood, and choices no thirteen-year-old should have to make.

Now, pushing thirty, she wants out. From all of it.

Willow Bowman lives in the farmhouse her beloved grandmother left her, with her husband. A pediatric nurse and small-town girl, she relishes in the safety of her marriage that keeps difficult questions at bay and keeps her life quiet and peaceful, because that makes sense to her.

Until one night when Willow is driving home and is about to cross the old, rickety Dittman Bridge not far from the farmhouse, and she sees a figure jump off into the cold waters below.

The moment she jumps in and pulls the woman dressed in leather pants out, both their lives change forever.

Keeping Hope (Wynter Series Book 4) - ISBN - 978-1-952270-78-9

Twenty-four-year-old Hope DeSilva has been released from a three-year stint in a Georgia prison. After returning to her family property in a tiny Georgia town, she decides she's had enough of the poverty, violence, and progound family dysfunction. It's time to get out on her own. She buys a $400 car and heads to find work out west.

After the car breaks down in Colorado, she's given a ride into a mountain town called Wynter where she runs into brash, aggressive police officer Samantha Gains, who has not one ounce of patience or sympathy for a felon in her black-and-white world of right or wrong, good or bad.

But, running from her own family trauma and inexplicably bewitched by the young newcomer Hope, Samantha begins to realize that maybe her strict worldview isn't as simple as it seems. When a freak accident brings the two women together, it will take both of them letting go of their pasts to truly move on.

Take another trip to Wynter and revisit old friends as they work their magic to help Hope and Samantha find their footing—and ultimately bring them home.